Dacia Wolf

& the Phouka's Curse

A modern magical fairytale

Dacia Wolf

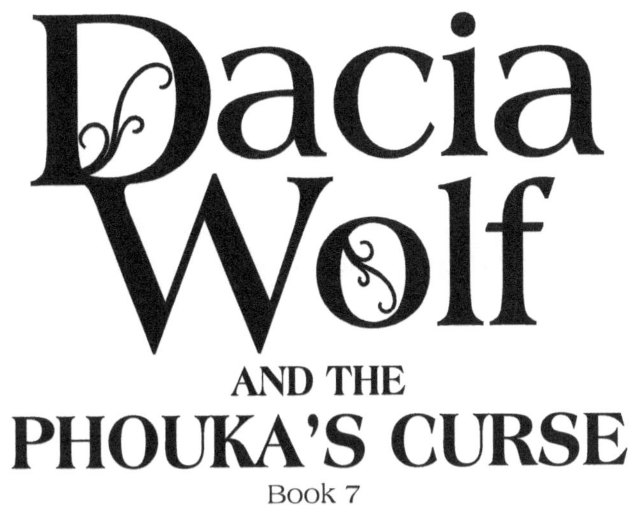

AND THE
PHOUKA'S CURSE

Book 7

Visit Mandi Oyster online at
www.MandiOyster.com

Facebook: https://www.facebook.com/MandiOysterAuthor
Instagram: https://www.instagram.com/MandiOyster/

This book is dedicated to Dana & Mariruth,
girls' nights, and friendship
that withstands the tests of time.
I love you, both!

Fairies vs. Faeries

In my previous books, there were fairies.
Fairies are kind and pure spirits.
They can be mischievous but are not dangerous.
They helped to heal Dacia and remove
the demon taint from within her.

In this book, there are faeries.
Faeries are mischievous, malicious,
and sometimes evil creatures.
They see humans as little more than
bugs or playthings due to their short lives.

Chapter 1

Bringing Down The Wards

Liam stood in front of me, wearing his standard uniform. T-shirt, cargo pants, combat boots. All in black. To any students who walked by my open door, he looked like a normal guy, but I saw him for what he was.

An angel.

Well … half.

Tan and cream wings pushed through the slits he'd cut in his shirt, folding against his back. Their tips dragged over the carpet. They were magnificent. Stunning. Awe-inspiring.

My magic cloaked them from everyone else. I wished I didn't have to. I was convinced that if people saw them, their beauty would help heal the wounds of the world. But, I also knew they would likely cause panic and fear. So, I stood behind him, hiding the wings that were impossible for him to conceal on his own.

He dipped his finger into an open wound on his forearm and smeared his blood over the angelic symbols that surrounded the door. He had already tried altering the glyphs and washing them off, but after nearly two weeks, Mavros still couldn't enter either apartment.

My demon guardian stood across the hallway, leaning against the wall, watching Liam through half-lidded eyes. His hands were tucked into the pockets of his fitted black jeans. One foot was crossed over the other. He looked like he didn't have a care in the world, but I knew the truth of it.

I shot him a sympathetic smile, and his lip curled in response.

"Have you figured anything out?"

I jumped when Liam's voice punctured the silence. Without meaning to, my gaze automatically slid to my arm. Kieran's tree was covered by the sleeve of my Phlox Phoenixes hoodie, but that didn't stop me from picturing the mighty oak, its leaves rustling in a breeze that nobody could feel. I uncurled my fist and stared at the roots that extended to the tips of my fingers. "No." The word was filled with all of the anguish and desperation that had set up a permanent residence inside of me.

"I've been thinking about it." He turned, and his steel eyes pierced mine. "You can't let even one leaf fall." There was an urgency in his tone that I wasn't used to hearing there. "Faeries are tricky … manipulative. If only one ever falls, it's still the last."

The truth in his words made my insides feel like they were crumbling, but I stood tall and, not trusting my voice, nodded at him. Why hadn't I realized that? Why hadn't I even considered it?

My breath caught in my throat as I jerked my sleeve up. The tree had grown until the top of it touched the inside of my elbow. The twisted, gnarly branches looked like a one-hundred-year-old oak, but it was only a few weeks old. The leaves were the green of a warm, spring day after a nourishing rain.

"What am I going to do?" I looked from Liam to Mavros. "How do I stop it?"

Flames flickered through Mavros' eyes before they turned back to their normal obsidian color. "I could take you to another realm, but Kieran's magic might be able to reach you there."

Something told me that wasn't the solution. How could it be when Faerie was already a separate realm? I turned toward Liam, but he just shook his head. I knew neither of them had any ideas. None of my friends did. We had all discussed it a thousand or more times since Kieran had pressed the acorn into my palm.

"You wanna try to walk through?" Liam stepped away from the door and stretched his back. When he caught me watching, he tipped his head to the side. "The wings are giving me more of a workout than my shoulders are used to."

I remembered Liam's defined muscles and the way he moved when he trained me in Krav Maga. "Really?"

"Yeah." He reached up and massaged the back of his neck. "It's getting easier, though."

Mavros inched closer. Hope softened his features until he scrubbed his hands down his face. When he looked at us again, all traces of optimism had been wiped away. He twisted his lips into a smirk and nodded at Liam. "When are you going to use them as more than just decorations?"

"I don't know." Liam shrugged, and some of the color drained from his face. "I thought maybe this weekend we could all go flying. One of you can catch me if I can't figure it out."

"Angel-boy's afraid of flying."

Mavros' mocking chuckle made Liam stand a little taller and hold his chin a little higher. Even though he was shorter than Mavros, he seemed to look down at him. "Watch it, demon, or you'll never step foot in here again."

"Oh, don't ruffle your feathers." A smile danced in Mavros' eyes. "I'm motivating you." He took a deep breath before gingerly placing his foot over the threshold.

Black smoke drifted off of his boot, and he jerked back with a hiss.

I darted around Liam, but he grabbed hold of my arm before I stepped into the hall. I didn't know what my guards were afraid of. The danger was on my arm, not waiting for me outside of my apartment.

"I'll be fine. The pain's gone already." Mavros positioned himself so that if Liam let go of me I still wouldn't be able to leave the room. He held his elbow in one hand while tapping his finger on his chin. "It looks like flying isn't the only thing you suck at, angel-boy."

Instead of responding to Mavros' snide remark, Liam stared at the symbols framing the door and shook his head.

"There is no way these were put up in one day. They're the strongest I've ever seen."

I had watched Troy draw glyphs before. I remembered him chanting while he painted his blood over the ground outside of my cell. When he had finished, he'd looked at me through brown, hate-filled eyes and told me that the cage was my new home. I had thought I would be able to escape if Mavros' blood burned away Troy's wards, but now I doubted it. "Wouldn't someone have noticed them appearing?" My eyebrows lifted, and I pursed my lips. "Predators tend to smell fresh blood."

"True." Liam rubbed his jaw, and the familiar sound of his beard scratching against the calluses on his palms filled the apartment. "He may have been able to cover it somehow." He ran his fingers over the symbols that he hadn't altered. "Troy was always the best at setting wards."

"They'll figure it out, Dacia," Mavros said in the soft voice that he reserved only for me.

I looked over my shoulder at Cody's bedroom door. "I hope so."

For nearly two weeks, Cody had taken to sleeping in his room so Malcolm could hold my dreams at bay. I hated not waking up in his arms every morning, but more than that, I hated what me sleeping in another man's embrace was doing to him.

Dark circles ringed his eyes, and the happiness had fled from them. He tried not to let me see his anguish, but there was no hiding it.

Liam strode into the kitchen and pulled out one of the chairs. He sat down with his arms folded over the back and stared at the brown tiles. "I'm going to have to talk to Troy." He let out a deep breath, and pain flickered across his face.

Once, Liam had respected Troy. He had trained under him and thought of him as a hero, but those feelings died when Troy captured and tortured Liam, Olivia, and Diana—maybe even sooner, maybe when he'd imprisoned and tormented me.

"I'm sorry." I kept my voice soft, not wanting to startle him while he was lost in his memories.

His gaze lifted toward mine, and he blinked, clearing whatever he was imagining. "I don't have any other ideas. Diana, Olivia, and Vicki don't know what to do." He rubbed his hands over his face. "I'm just …"

I knelt next to him and patted his knee. "Believe me. I understand."

"Yeah."

Malcolm, Cash, and Seth returned from hunting before I needed to leave for class. I didn't know if Jax was still with them or not. Over the last couple of weeks, I had almost asked multiple times, but if he didn't want his presence known, I didn't want to bring it up.

Turning away from the dragons, I glanced at Cody's door again, wondering if he was still sleeping or if he was avoiding me.

While I stared at the wooden barrier between us, a hand clamped down on my shoulder, and I looked up into Malcolm's bronze eyes. "Jealousy is a poison." He squeezed my arm, then let go of me. "Unfortunately, even though he knows I am only protecting you, the seed of doubt has been planted and will continue to grow."

I dropped my chin to my chest. "What are you guys afraid of?"

His dark eyebrows pinched together, and he cocked his head.

"In my dreams." I dragged my hand through my hair before quickly pulling it away. I didn't want Kieran's tree anywhere near my face, but years of instincts were hard to override. "He's already cursed me. What more can he do?"

Malcolm jerked back, almost as if I'd slapped him, then seemed to freeze in that position. "Don't—" he swallowed hard "—don't ever ask if worse things can happen." Turning me toward him, he gripped my shoulders and held my gaze. "The universe has a way of showing you that things can always get worse." He slid his hand down my arm to the oak tree. "Among other things, he could pluck a leaf off of the tree and let it fall."

"Okay." Liam's earlier warning slammed into me, knocking the air from my lungs. I struggled to catch my breath before saying, "Fine." I turned around and took an off-balance step toward Cody's door. I threw my arm out to steady myself before striding the rest of the way to it. Not wanting to wake him if he was sleeping, I rapped my knuckles softly against the wood.

"Yeah."

I pushed the door open, peeking in. Cody's denim and tan comforter was pulled up. He was better at making his bed than I was, not a wrinkle marred its surface. He sat at his desk, dressed in blue jeans and a navy long-sleeved t-shirt that would make his eyes sparkle if his emotionless mask wasn't firmly in place. His arms were folded over his chest. Everything about his posture was closed off and uninviting.

Seeing him like this broke my heart, but I tried not to let it show. I stood in the doorway, wondering if I should go to him. Not wanting to make things any harder on him, I decided to stay put. "I'm … uh …" It shouldn't have been this hard to talk to Cody. He had been a part of my life since second grade. He had always been the first person to stand up for me, to tell me things would be okay, but without him, they wouldn't be. They couldn't be okay if he wasn't there.

"Class?" His voice was distant.

When he made no move to come toward me, I swallowed hard and nodded.

He swiveled his chair so that he was facing away from me. "Have fun."

My throat tightened until a painful lump formed in it. I stumbled backward, and Malcolm grabbed hold of me, gently guiding me away.

Everything moved in slow motion. There seemed to be a disconnection between my mind and my body.

Cash grabbed my coat from beside the door, held it open, and waited patiently while I slid my arms into the sleeves. Then he zipped it like I was a little kid. He pulled my hood up and wrapped my scarf so that it covered my mouth and nose. When he finished, he pressed his hand to the middle of my back and led me through the living room.

On the way out the door, he grabbed my backpack and flung it over his shoulder. Mavros joined our group and led us down the five flights of stairs and outside.

The cold air hit me in the face, a sharp slap that snapped me back to myself with a gasp. Tears stung my eyes, silently trickling down my cheeks. I hoped that none of my guards noticed, but it wasn't likely.

Mavros held the door to Stellaria Hall open. When I walked past him, he lifted his hand toward my face but let it drop without touching me. People strode past us in the halls and on the stairs, but they were just a blur through my tears, objects to avoid. My guards led me to our normal seats in the back row of the classroom. Cash started to unzip my coat, but I pushed his hands away, slowly going through the motions. I slumped down in my chair, leaned my head against the hard plastic, and stared at the ceiling.

Tears rolled along my cheeks and into my ears. There had to be something I could do, some way for me to show Cody what he meant to me. Somehow, I needed to spend some time alone with him or at least some time where it felt like we were alone. I needed him to understand that, more than anything, he was what I wanted.

Before I could mention it to Malcolm, Dr. Yarrow called the class to attention. I fought through the entire period to keep my focus on her and not on my problems. They would still be there, waiting for me when her lecture was over.

Malcolm opened the apartment door and froze. A low, rumbling growl filled the hallway. Other students stopped and turned toward us. Their faces were ashen.

"Does someone have a dog?" I asked loud enough for my voice to carry to them.

Cash moved me to the side, stepping in front of me. "Must." When he looked over Malcolm's shoulder, the growl that thundered from deep inside of him was feral.

"That must be one big dog." I heard one of the other students say as they turned and hustled down the hall.

I placed my hand on Cash's arm and lifted onto my tiptoes to see around him.

Unbidden, magic rose up inside of me. I could almost feel the serpent writhing under my skin. Hatred and fear battled each other to be my dominant emotion.

I wanted to back up, to look away, but I couldn't move. Shock held me in place.

Chapter 2

"Take her across the hall." The words came from Malus Tribulus. The only part of Malcolm left was the body, and it looked like he was struggling to hold onto that.

The last thing we needed was a fully formed dragon standing in the hall, so I backed away, never pulling my gaze from Troy's.

Cash pressed on Malcolm's chest, shoving him through the door before slamming it shut. I slumped down onto the couch, dragging a shaking hand through my hair. "Why?" I looked from Cash to Seth to Malcolm. "Why is he here?"

"I would venture to guess that he is taking down the wards." Seth's voice was calm, relaxing. His eyes were human. His dragon nowhere to be seen.

I tilted my head toward my right shoulder. "Why?"

"I don't know how much you could see from behind Malcolm and Cash." He pointed at the couch, a request to sit next to me. I nodded, then waited for him to get comfortable before he continued. "His left arm was cut open, and he had blood on the index and middle fingers of his right hand."

I closed my eyes and took a deep breath, releasing it slowly. "How could Liam bring him here without warning us?"

I stared through the walls into my apartment. An inferno raged inside of me as soon as I saw Troy. All the anger, fear, and hatred that I had felt for him came rushing back all at once. When I'd let him live, I thought I had let go of all of those emotions, but I'd never expected to see him again.

My hands trembled. I clenched and unclenched my fists, but the shaking only worsened. I remembered his body pressed against mine while he chained me to the cage, my fear when he pulled his knife out and waved it in front of my face, the coppery, warm taste of his blood sliding down my throat, the feel of it spilling over my chin and onto my neck. I remembered him slamming my head against the bars, holding me down on the cot, threatening me. Every moment that I'd spent in Troy's presence, every word he had ever said to me, everything. I remembered it all, and all the emotions that I thought I had tamped down rose to the surface.

I leaned forward, clutching the hair on the sides of my head, and focused on my breathing. Malcolm and Cash needed me to get myself under control. The room was too small for them to be trapped in here with my terror.

Staring into my apartment, I watched him, hoping I would see some remorse or a redeeming quality that could take the edge off of my hatred.

The orange uniform he was wearing didn't cling to his body the way his t-shirts had. It was loose and untucked. Dark hair covered his head, hiding the top of his tattoo. He dipped his fingers into the gash that ran from his elbow almost to his wrist and chanted while he wiped his blood over the glyphs.

Liam stood behind him. His fists were clenched at his sides. The veins in his arms popped up, ready to burst through his skin. Several other Nephilim were in the room. They stood at attention, completely focused on Troy. Their eyes followed every move he made.

Cody, Samantha, Dan, and Russ stepped between me and Troy. It took me a second to realize they were in the hall and not in the room with us.

I imagined Cody opening the door and Troy grabbing ahold of him, creating a portal, and disappearing before anyone could stop him. Panic made my heart race and the breath catch in my throat. I shot up off the couch, and Seth grabbed my hand. "Russ, in here," I shouted before my friends stepped anywhere near Troy.

Russ stood in front of my apartment door, blocking the others from entering, and pointed toward our guardians' room. As I watched them, I realized that Mavros wasn't standing in the hallway. I had always assumed he'd waited there for me, but maybe he just showed up when I needed him.

Cash opened the door and ushered my friends through it.

Samantha cocked her head to the side, seemingly taking us all in, then said, "So, what's going on?"

"Troy." It was all I could say. I shouldn't have been afraid of him anymore. I had defeated him. He'd given up before making me kill him. As long as I had my magic, he was no match for me. Yet, fear had all of my senses on high alert. I jammed my hands into my armpits to hide their trembling from my friends.

Seth, the only one of my guards that didn't seem to be affected by Troy's presence, answered, "It appears that he's taking down the wards."

Cody turned his head as if he could see through the walls, too. When he looked at me again, his emotionless mask was gone. His expression shifted between sympathy and outrage as he made his way to the couch. He sat down next to me and pulled me against his side. "I'm sorry."

"It's not your fault," I mumbled.

He shook his head. "For everything." Swallowing hard, he added, "The way I acted."

"Will he actually do it?" Dan sat in one of the armchairs, and Samantha joined him. "Or will he make things worse?"

Another wave of terror crashed over me, and Seth grabbed hold of my hand, sending energy into me. Like his voice, it was soft, soothing. It didn't overwhelm me.

He nodded at Dan. "Liam and several others are monitoring everything. I believe he will remove the wards."

I stared through the walls again, watching Troy. He moved from the door to the kitchen window. Then he went into each of our bedrooms. When he finished, a Nephilim with short, black hair pulled Troy's hands behind his back and slapped cuffs on his wrists.

Liam opened the door. The bottom of his wings brushed over the brown carpet. He needed magic to conceal them, but I couldn't bring myself to let Troy see me. Liam glanced down the hallway, and when he found it empty, the tension in his shoulders released.

Mavros appeared in front of him, and Liam backed away, swinging his arm wide in an invitation to enter. Mavros' hesitation was clear. He didn't trust Troy any more than I did. He slowly reached his hand up, holding it just outside the door. Then he inched it forward until it was clear that he'd breached the barrier.

He tucked his hands into his jacket pockets and strode inside like he owned the apartment.

"He took them down." The relief that pulsed through me left my limbs shaky. I slumped back against Cody, realizing Malcolm wouldn't have to hold me at night to keep my dreams away.

Samantha stood and slung her backpack over her shoulder. "That's great. I need to get lunch before my next class."

"Wait." Malcolm's voice was closer to his own than it had been, but there was still a rumble in it that wasn't usually there.

I returned my attention to my apartment. Troy narrowed his eyes at Mavros and backed into the guard behind him. His lip curled up on one side, but Mavros paid no attention to him. Instead, he held his hand out to Liam, who didn't hesitate to shake it. Troy's lip curled in revulsion as he watched the interaction.

Guards stood on either side of Troy, each holding one of his arms, and led him toward the door. Mavros stayed planted right where he was, forcing one of the Nephilim to step in front of Troy and one behind him. Troy pulled his body as far from Mavros as he could, but his shoulder still brushed against Mavros' on his way past. A look of hatred and disgust flashed across Troy's features before he stepped into the hallway.

Malcolm reached for my hand, pulling me behind him. Cash, Russ, and Seth stood next to him. A solid wall of dragon blocking me and my friends from Troy.

Liam opened the door and stepped inside quickly. No doubt he was concerned about being seen with his wings. The other Nephilim followed him in, dragging Troy along with them.

Troy smirked at my guards. "What is it you expect me to do?" Two weeks in prison obviously hadn't had the same effect on him that one week had had on me. He was still arrogant.

The dragons didn't say anything. They just moved as one, keeping their bodies between us and him, making it so my friends and I could leave without any possible contact with Troy.

"Go." Cody pressed on the middle of my back.

I shook my head and moved to the side. "After you guys."

They practically sprinted across the hall, and Cody held the door open for me. As soon as I stepped into our living room, I relaxed. Mavros was there, and Troy had never tried anything with Mavros around.

Malcolm walked in and strode straight for the kitchen window. He opened it as far as it would go. I tipped my head toward my shoulder and pinched my eyebrows together.

"The room reeks of his blood." His fangs extended over his bottom lip. "I want his stench out of here."

"Do you want me to open the windows in my room?" I hung my coat up on the hook by the door and set my backpack on the floor beneath it.

He dipped his chin toward his chest, a subtle movement that I barely noticed. "If you want me to watch over you while you sleep."

"I'll be with her." Mavros leaned against the refrigerator with his hands crossed over his chest and wagged his eyebrows at me. "We don't need a babysitter."

Cash strode across the room and stood between them. "Not now."

"Anybody else hungry?" Samantha clapped her hands together. Her voice was too cheerful, but if anybody else noticed, they didn't say a thing.

Cody looked at Mavros, Malcolm, and Cash, then at me. He closed his eyes, breathed in deeply, then let it out before saying, "Always."

When Graphic Design ended, I took my time stuffing my things into my backpack. Malcolm, Cash, and Seth watched me, but I pretended not to notice.

"Ready?" Cash asked and hefted my bag onto his shoulder.

I zipped my coat and nodded. In the hallway, I stopped at the drinking fountain and gulped water down, drinking even though I wasn't thirsty.

We stepped out into the sunlight, and I walked to a bench by the door. Lifting my foot onto it, I re-laced one winter boot, then the other. The ties on them were for decoration. They zipped on the side, but even though it was a long walk back to the apartment, I wanted to slow it even further.

I slipped my sunglasses on and closed my eyes. Immediately wishing I hadn't, I snapped them open. Troy's cruel face had filled my mind. I didn't want to see him again. Ever. The fear that he would be in the dragons' apartment removing wards when we got back made me drag my feet. My stomach turned at the idea of seeing him once more.

Malcolm walked next to me. He slid his hand through mine and squeezed. "Do you want to go somewhere else for a while?" His voice was soft, understanding.

I pulled my lip into my mouth, chewing on it. "He won't still be there, will he?"

"We'll keep you safe."

I nodded, trying to hold my tears back. "I know. I ... I don't wanna see him."

"You won't." His energy trickled into me, but it wasn't refreshing like normal. It was dark and angry.

I sucked it in, hoping it would take away the helplessness that I had felt ever since seeing Troy.

Cash opened the door to the apartment building, looked down the hallway and up the stairs, then nodded at Malcolm. Malcolm pulled me against him and teleported to my room.

The window was still open, and cold air blew the curtains back. I held onto Malcolm, shivering against him, not quite ready to face what might be out there.

"Stay here." He pulled away from me and walked out the door. A minute later, he came back into my room. "They're gone."

I walked out into the living room, took my coat off, and hung it on the hook by the door. Adrenaline had kept me going since seeing Troy this morning, but now my legs shook. Deciding I needed to sit before I collapsed, I turned around and noticed Liam. He sat at the table. His arms were folded over the back of the chair. The bottom of his wings pooled on the floor. His eyes were closed, and tension lined his features. He reached his hand over his shoulder, and when his fingers brushed against his feathers, his head sagged.

"I'm sorry." His wings were beautiful, but until two weeks ago, they hadn't been a part of him. For fear of being seen, he couldn't leave this room without me or one of the dragons. We hoped that somewhere inside of him he had the power to hide them on his own, but so far, it hadn't surfaced.

"Don't be." He looked up at me. There was no ill will in his steel eyes. "They'll be a blessing once I get this figured out."

Samantha opened the door to her bedroom and peeked out at us. She lifted her lips in a timid smile.

"Hey, Sam." I took a couple steps toward her confused by her hesitancy. We were all friends, and after all that we had been through, I couldn't figure out why she would act so shy. "What's up?"

"Kieran is a faerie, right?" She looked down at the floor in front of her feet. Her focus drew my attention to the penguins ice-skating on her socks.

"Yeah."

"So"—she twisted her bracelet around her wrist, pulling it first one way, then the other—"do you think there might be something in a book that could help you figure out how to beat him?" She finally glanced up at me. "Maybe some of the stories are true."

Seth sat on the couch and stretched his legs out in front of him. "Many of the tales are based in truth. However, nobody has bested Kieran."

"No." She came into the room. "But maybe another faerie has done something like this."

"It's worth a shot." I looked down at my arm. My sleeve was pulled over the tree, but I could see the roots and part of the trunk on my hand. "I have no idea how to stop it."

She shot me a smile that let me know how much she wanted to help. "I'll start researching."

While Samantha and Dan went to the library to check out as many books as they could, I grabbed my laptop and searched faerie curses. A ton of books popped onto the screen. Fantasy novels with heroines holding swords. Gorgeous elves. Blood red capes draped over the shoulders of beautiful girls.

I skimmed past them. The next bunch of results was for role-playing games. After I passed them, I found a few posts that looked promising and started jotting down some notes.

My pen hovered above my paper, and I looked up at Liam. "Are faeries really dumb enough to be confused by people wearing their clothes inside out?"

He grinned at me—it wasn't like one of Dan's smiles, the kind that could melt a glacier, but it was sweet—and nodded. "Believe it or not, they are."

"Wow." I shook my head. "It's amazing that something could be that devious and that stupid at the same time." I jotted down a list of things that deterred faeries: Rowan, holly, salt, iron, St. John's wort, church bells, and four-leaf clovers. Then I kept looking, hoping to find something that would help me beat Kieran.

I stared at the computer screen until the door creaked. Jerking my head around, I watched Cody stroll into the room with Russ.

"Homework?" He set his bag down and strode over.

"I'm learning everything I can about faeries." I pushed the screen down.

He pulled out a chair, sat next to me, and nodded at Liam. "Think it'll be that easy?"

"No." I snorted, then covered my mouth. "I don't think I'll find anything to help with the curse, but I might find something to hold him off until I can figure it out."

"Where're your guards?"

Liam nodded toward the door. "Cash and Seth are across the hall, Malcolm's hunting, and I have no idea where Mavros is."

"Really?" My head tilted toward my shoulder without me consciously thinking about the movement. "He wasn't in the hall when Troy was taking down the wards either."

Cody grabbed the lid from my Dr. Pepper and spun it, making it dance across the table. "Wonder where he goes."

"That's really none of your business." Mavros' silky-smooth voice startled me. "Now, is it?"

I turned to see him leaning against the fridge. His hands were tucked into his pockets, and a mischievous light sparkled in his eyes. "You're not stealing left shoes, are you?"

"No." He smiled at me but didn't elaborate at all before he disappeared again.

Chapter 3

Learning To Fly

Friday morning, I woke up wrapped in Cody's arms with Malcolm and Mavros watching us. I barely noticed my guards, though. Cody's sapphire eyes sparkled like the sun reflecting off a mountain lake. It had been too long since I had seen him this happy.

"Morning." He traced his finger along my face and down my arm. "How'd ya sleep?"

I savored the feel of his featherlight touch. I'd missed it. "Mmm … good."

"Me, too." He pulled me closer to him, and Malcolm growled.

I snuggled against Cody, not willing to let go of him yet. "Go away then."

"I'm going hunting." Malcolm's aura disappeared a split second later.

Mavros kicked his feet up onto the comforter. I glanced at him just as he folded his hands behind his head. "I'm good."

"Leave." My voice was hard enough that I didn't expect him to argue, but just in case, I added, "Don't make me use your name."

He pulled his feet off the mattress slowly, then sauntered past the bed. "Your wish … my command."

As soon as the door clicked closed, I turned back to Cody. The sparkle in his eyes was gone.

"Doesn't matter. In here, out there, he's watching." He flopped onto his back, and I laid my head on his bare chest.

Absentmindedly drawing circles on his abs, I said, "I'm sorry. Hopefully, someday things will be different."

"Won't." He flattened my hand with his.

"Probably not." My stomach dropped. "Maybe we'll be able to get used to this."

Mavros went to class with me. He sat next to me and made sure I was protected. He walked me back to my apartment, then disappeared as soon as I was safely inside. Right before I went to bed, he materialized in the living room.

I cocked my head. "Where've you been?"

"Don't worry about it." He pressed his hand to the small of my back and guided me into my room. "I haven't been causing any trouble."

Saturday morning, as soon as I opened my eyes, Mavros said, "I'll be here if you need me."

Before I had a chance to respond, black vapor rose from him, and he was gone.

"Where's he go?" Cody's voice startled me.

I sat on the edge of my bed and stared at the last place I'd seen Mavros, wondering if he was lying on a beach somewhere, his olive skin glistening in the sunlight. Shaking that image out of my head, I said, "I have no idea."

"He hasn't said anything to us." Cash's voice drew my attention to him. He folded his arms over his chest and leaned back until his shoulder thunked against the wall. I wasn't sure when he came into my room, but it seemed pretty clear that he wasn't planning on leaving anytime soon.

Realizing Cody and I weren't about to be alone, I got up and grabbed my clothes. I set them down on top of my dresser and chewed on my lip, dreading asking the question that burned in my throat but needing to anyway. "Should I be concerned?"

"No." Liam stood in my doorway. "I can still barely sense any evil in him. I don't think you need to worry."

A tidal wave of relief surged through me. Its force nearly dropped me to my knees.

"No matter what the demon is doing"—Malcolm's voice carried through the room with the force of a hurricane—"you need to train."

My shoulders slumped, but the comment wasn't unexpected. I needed to regain my stamina. Being captured by Troy and having my powers bound had set me back further than we had initially thought. "Sure. Fine." I picked up my clothes and headed toward the bathroom.

When I stepped back into my room, Cody was the only one still there. He had made my bed and sat on the edge of it, watching me. I plopped down next to him and slid my hand over his. "I guess I'm training today. What are you going to do?"

"Spar with Drew." He shrugged. "If he's up for it."

His response threw me off. I didn't know he talked to Drew anymore. They had been roommates our freshman year, but I hadn't seen much of him since. "Really, Drew?"

"Knows Krav Maga."

"Oh." My throat tightened. I remembered the bruises that had covered Cody after practicing with my guardians and my reaction to them. "Be careful, okay?"

He tucked a strand of hair behind my ear, letting his fingers linger. "You, too."

As soon as I walked out of my room, Malcolm said, "Ready?"

"Sure."

Cash, Seth, and Malcolm stepped toward me, but Liam stayed in the kitchen, sitting backward in one of the wooden chairs. He looked miserable. His wings drooped, and his lips were pulled down in a frown that seemed to encompass his entire being.

I remembered how when he came to my house, he had wanted to do something. He was the kind of guy that needed a purpose. "Are we going to take Liam flying?"

Liam's eyes widened until the whites could be seen all around his irises. "I, uh—" he cleared his throat and rubbed his hand over his head "—I don't know if I'm ready for that."

"Hmph. I'm not sure that matters." I tapped my chin gently and looked up at the ceiling. "No … I can't recall ever being able to say that."

I strode toward him and held my hand out. He slid his fingers into mine much slower than he normally would. As soon as he did, the dragons joined us. My body stretched and pulled, and then I was falling. The ground was thousands of feet below us. As soon as the cold air touched my skin, wings burst from my shoulders. My body grew, transforming into the massive dragon that was my alternate form.

Liam toppled through the sky, tumbling end over end.

I dove to get beneath him, positioning myself to catch him if necessary. The scent of his panic made my thoughts shift.

Prey. The thought went through my mind before I could stop it.

Instead of wanting to help him, I wanted to hunt him. Backing away from him, I pressed my eyes closed and fought the dragon's instincts, reminding myself over and over again that Liam was my friend and not a meal.

"Steady yourself," Malcolm roared.

Liam jostled a little more before finally stabilizing his body in a belly-to-earth freefall position.

"Now, spread your wings."

They snapped open as soon as Malcolm gave the command. Liam's scent changed. The panic turned into excitement.

My desire to attack him lessened. I flew closer but not near enough that I would hurt him if I lost control.

The air currents tossed him around until he learned to move with them. Once he got the hang of soaring, he flapped his wings and surged forward. His laughter filled the sky, bouncing off the mountain peaks and echoing back to us.

The sound was so infectious that I couldn't help but join in. In this form, the laughter rumbled out of me like a distant thunderstorm.

He flew straight through a fluffy cloud. When he burst out of the other side, he shook, and water splashed against my blue scales.

"Let's see what you've got." Malcolm ascended, and Liam grinned like the Cheshire Cat as he followed.

When Malcolm folded his wings back and dove, Liam did the same, whooping as he plummeted to the ground far below us.

He spread his wings just above the tops of the trees, and the scent wafting off of him changed again to joy.

The five of us flew together, each of us challenging Liam to perform different aerial maneuvers. He did one after the other, gaining more confidence with every flap of his wings.

Cash led us to a clearing, transforming into a human as soon as he landed. The wind lifted his purple-streaked black hair, blowing it across his face, but he never took his gaze off of me.

I landed next but didn't change back. It was too cold up here, and Mavros wasn't with us to give me his coat.

Liam circled, and I remembered the first time that I flew as a dragon. The uncertainty of landing, the fear of crashing into the ground or making a fool of myself in front of Malus Tribulus.

He soared toward the clearing, lowering himself until his feet touched the ground. Then he ran across the snow, slowing his momentum while he folded his wings in. As soon as they closed against his back, they disappeared.

He stumbled forward, catching himself on a lodgepole pine. "What the hell?" He reached over his shoulder, feeling for the appendages that were no longer there. "I finally use them, and they disappear?" He slumped forward. The sense of loss that he was feeling drifted through the air to me.

My stomach rumbled, and I stepped toward him. Unconsciously, I lowered my body, readying myself to strike.

"Dacia." Malcolm's voice was a warning.

I lifted my head and shook it, pulling my focus off of Liam. I'd never had this problem when flying with the others. Dragons and demons didn't smell like food.

Seth tipped his head to the side, and not for the first time, I was reminded of a bird. "I believe they will respond when you need them." He pressed his hand against Liam's back and led him away from the trees. When they were standing at the precipice, Seth said, "Maybe they needed to be used before concealing themselves. Magic works differently for each of us."

"Maybe." Liam rolled his shoulders. "It's so weird not the feel them. I was finally getting used to their weight."

"That's the way of things." Seth's voice was soft, soothing. Listening to him talk, it was hard to believe anything could be wrong with the world. Everything seemed so peaceful right up until Seth shoved Liam over the cliff.

ഇ30ഗ

ഇ30ഗ

Chapter 4

One Down, One To Go

Fire burned inside me, scorching my throat as it made its way to my mouth. A minute ago, I'd wanted to munch on Liam, and now the urge to kill Seth was nearly overwhelming. I lunged toward him, but my attack fell short. The human side of my brain recognized I might be able to save Liam if I hurried.

I turned and ran toward the edge of the mountain, ready to dive off. I skidded to a halt when I saw Liam. Wings extended from his shoulders. Tan and cream feathers caught the wind. He threw his head back and laughed. "Glad you were right."

"Me, too." Seth grinned at him. "I would hate to see you splattered all over the pristine snow down there."

Liam flew over the clearing, landing away from the cliff's edge, and folded his wings in. Once again, they disappeared.

Malcolm shot him a smile that showed his fangs. "Looks like self-defense training resumes tomorrow."

Working on Krav Maga meant spending more time with Cody, but it also meant my guardians thought I would need to use it. It meant there were more threats out there like Troy.

As soon as I thought his name, Troy's tattooed face flashed through my mind followed by images of Sebastian and Micah. I pictured Sebastian sitting on my cot in the dark cell. His hand was pressed against my mouth and his cognac eyes stared into mine as he tried to determine if my magic had returned. I remembered Micah leering at me while I washed with the cold water from a bucket at my feet. His arms were folded over his chest, and his toothpick hung out of his mouth.

They were still out there, along with others who saw me as a threat. There was always a chance that they would come for me.

"Okay." I morphed into my body. "So, what's on my plate today?"

By the time we returned from training, my legs felt like rubber. I wobbled with each step I took across the hall to my apartment. Malcolm had pushed my pace to what it had been in the caves before I had faced Argentum. Every last drop of magic had been drained from my body, and none of the dragons seemed inclined to replenish it.

We walked in, and Liam headed straight for an armchair. He leaned back and stretched his legs out in front of him, letting loose a deep, drawn-out sigh. "You've no idea how good this feels."

Cody and Dan watched him from the couch, their video game forgotten. Samantha looked up from her spot at the table. Her homework was spread over the surface. They stared at him with their heads tilted and their eyebrows pinched together. Dan was the first to find his voice. "What happened to your wings?"

"They gone?" Cody asked.

Liam folded his hands behind his head. "Only until I need them."

"How do you know they'll be there when you need them?" Samantha rested her elbows on the table and held her head in her hands.

Seth walked behind Liam and patted his shoulder. "Because I pushed him off a mountain to find out."

Samantha's hand flew to her mouth, covering her gasp.

"Take it you learned to fly."

I couldn't quite make out the look on Cody's face when he made the comment, but the first thing that came to mind was envy. It had to be hard for my friends to see the dragons, the Nephilim, Mavros, and me do so many things that they could only dream of.

"Yeah—" a wide smile covered Liam's face "—I did. It was amazing."

"So, one problem down." Samantha walked into the living room and plopped down next to Dan. "Any ideas on the other one?" She pointed to where she'd been sitting. "I haven't found anything yet."

I looked at the table, seeing now that the books scattered over it were all about faeries. "Living in Faerie can't be that bad." I pressed my arm against my side, resisting the urge to look at the tree. "Can it?"

The air smells different. Earthy. The sky is cobalt blue, and the trees surrounding me look superimposed against it.

Never in my life have I heard so many animals singing, chirping, and chattering at once. I stand in the clearing and feel the peace of this place settle deep inside of me.

"It's amazing here, isn't it?" Kieran's voice is so soft that I almost don't recognize it.

I turn toward him. Pointed ears peek up through his shaggy hair. Even though he still looks human, there's something different about him here, something off. His features seem sharper, more angular. His eyes are brighter, and his skin has a slight green tint to it, like the first leaves after a long winter.

He reaches down and plucks a purple flower unlike any I have seen before. Then he steps closer to me and slips it into my hair. He smells like spring: rain and plants and rebirth.

I find myself unintentionally leaning toward him, longing for the cold, harsh winter to end.

"Would it be so bad—" he grins, showing unnaturally pointed teeth "—to stay here with me?" He snatches my hand and starts dancing me around the clearing.

It takes a couple of minutes for my mind to catch up with what my body is doing. I pull my hand out of his grip. "No!" I will my feet to quit moving, but like a spasming muscle, I seem to have no control over them.

Kieran glances from my face to my feet and claps his hands. "Oh, what fun we will have, you and I."

I jerked awake, snapping my eyes open and shaking Cody's arm off of my shoulders.

"You okay?" He looked down at me. His expression was hard to make out in the dark, but the sound of his voice made it clear that he was worried.

Rubbing my hands down my face, I looked around the room. Samantha and Dan were snuggled together on the other side of the couch. Liam stretched out in one armchair, and Seth sat in the other. The movie I had been watching still flashed on the screen.

"I dozed off—" I twirled the bottom of my braid around my finger "—and ended up in Faerie."

The words barely had time to escape from my mouth before Mavros was standing in front of me. A muscle in his jaw ticked, and flames flickered in his eyes. "I leave you alone for a few hours and you can't stay awake?"

Somebody paused the movie.

"First, you left me alone all day." I stood up and jabbed my finger at him. "You won't even tell me where you're going. You just leave. Then the dragons trained me to exhaustion." I lifted my hand to the top of my head before remembering my hair was braided. "So, excuse me for falling asleep."

He reached toward my face, but I pulled away. "Done?"

I pinched my eyes shut and breathed in deeply. "Yeah." I felt a tug on my hair and snapped my eyes open.

Mavros held a purple flower between his fingers. "Did you want this?" Before I could say anything, he crushed the bloom, grabbed my arm, and shoved my sleeve up. With a feather-light touch, he trailed his finger over the tree.

Goosebumps rose on my flesh, but I tried to ignore the sensation, focusing on Kieran's curse instead. It didn't look any different. The tree hadn't grown for a few days. The leaves still rustled in a breeze that no one but me could feel. He brushed his thumb along the trunk before pulling the sleeve back down.

"If any of you—" Mavros flicked his gaze over everyone in the room before continuing "—sees her napping, wake her up immediately."

"Yes, sir." Liam sat up straight and saluted, always a soldier.

Mavros nodded, then turned his focus on Seth. "If you do that to her again, I'll end all of you."

Seth's features morphed. Blue scales lined his face, and smoke rolled out of his nostrils. The voice that responded wasn't his usual soft, soothing one. It was a low growl that raised the hairs on my arms and sent shivers racing down my spine. "You can try, demon."

Mavros shot him a lopsided grin, the kind that starts bar fights, and turned toward me. He lifted my hands in his. "I can't be here all of the time. *You* have to take care of yourself."

"Why?" I pulled back, but Mavros clutched my fingers tighter, refusing to let go. "Why can't you be here?"

He shook his head. "I'm trying to find a way to end your curse."

Chapter 5

No Rest For The Wicked

I slowly peeled my eyelids open. I wasn't ready for morning, but I knew Malcolm wouldn't want to hear any excuses. He wanted me to train with Liam. He wanted to make sure that I could protect myself without my magic if it ever came to that again.

Rubbing my face, I tried to scrub away the fogginess that lingered. Mavros had woken me several times through the night when Kieran's magic pressed against his. Somehow, the phouka was testing Mavros' power to hold my dreams at bay.

Cody's hand trailed along my spine. "Everything okay?"

"Sure." I shrugged and tried to remember the last time everything in my life had been okay. I couldn't help but wonder if it would ever be that way again.

I felt him sit up behind me. "Sunday's a day of rest."

A startled laugh snuck out of me at the same time that Malcolm said, "Sunday's a day that she could learn something that might save her life."

"No rest for the wicked." Mavros chuckled as he strode toward me. When he stood in front of me, he gently lifted my chin so that I gazed into his obsidian eyes. "Don't overdo it. Don't fall asleep without me around."

I nodded. "I'll do my best." As soon as I responded, he disappeared.

"Fifteen minutes," Malcolm said as he strode out the door.

I threw my legs over the edge of the bed, but Cody caught me by the waist. His lips pressed against the back of my neck and shivers raced through my body. My eyes fluttered shut, and I leaned into his embrace.

Cody's kisses trailed up to my ear. "Fifteen minutes alone?" His words were barely a breath, but I imagined Malcolm and whichever other dragons were in the apartment heard them.

Fifteen minutes alone with Cody. The last time that had happened, I had fallen asleep and realized I had not only killed Argentum but that I drank his blood and savored it.

As much as I wanted to be alone with him, there were reasons I couldn't be. "Someday." The pain and regret in my voice startled me.

"Someday." He rested his chin on my shoulder. "Do you think someday will ever come?"

Invisible fingers seemed to caress my arm. A chill spread from the roots of the mighty oak all the way up to its crown. I stared at it, praying that whatever had just happened wouldn't knock loose a leaf. I waited for one to drop from the tree. When none fell, I let out a deep breath. "Not if I don't figure this out."

Before I had my leggings and rashguard on, Malcolm was knocking on the door. "Time's up."

"Well, you're going to have to wait." I tugged my shirt on, then pulled my hair out of the collar and started braiding it. Hearing his growl, I added, "I'm almost ready."

Malcolm transported Cody, Liam, Cash, Seth, and me to a clearing I had never seen before. Snow swathed the tops of the mountains, but here in the valley, spring had arrived. Indian paintbrushes, elephant heads, columbines, and blanket flowers covered the ground.

I closed my eyes and inhaled deeply. Realization jolted me out of my reverie. "This … this can't be." I staggered back a couple of steps. "Spring doesn't come in January." I looked at my guardians, waiting for them to explain this to me, but they all seemed to be frozen.

"Ah, right you are." Kieran appeared in front of me, and the flower-covered vale was replaced by one blanketed in snow. "Wasn't my version far superior to this?" He waved his hand through the air.

I folded my arms over my chest, trying to conserve the warmth that had flowed through me. "Winter is just as beautiful." I pulled my bottom lip into my mouth with my teeth. "Spring will be here soon enough."

"How I would love to lie as humans do." Striding toward me, his eyes seemed to light up. "You do it so easily, so convincingly, even if it's just to fool yourself and no one else."

I planted my feet and bent my knees slightly, ready to defend myself against him. "I'm not lying. Winter *is* beautiful. It's cold and harsh, but it's also beautiful."

"Fine." He tossed his hands up in a gesture of surrender. "In Faerie, you won't have to worry about cold, harsh beauty if you don't want to." The snow disappeared, and the valley filled with blooms once again. He plucked a yellow flower and twirled its stem between his fingers. "You could if you wanted to, though. Spring is but a blink away from Winter." Covered by a heavy layer of frost, the flower in his hand wilted.

"What's that supposed to mean?" Confusion relaxed my stance. "Doesn't winter just come at the end of fall?"

He shook his head while saying, "No, no, no." As if he had been standing still for too long, he bounded around me like a two-year-old with a sugar rush. "Not where I reside. Winter is a realm. You would be in Spring with me. There is an abundance of flowers, regrowth, and birth. The world is fresh and new. The mornings are cool, and the days are perfect." His eyes had a faraway look to them. "You won't ever miss the other seasons." He stopped in front of me and reached for my hand, but I snatched it back, keeping him from touching me. Anger flashed across his face so quickly that I wondered if it had really been there or if I had just imagined it. "We'll have so much fun together."

"I would miss the other seasons." I stepped back, putting myself out of his reach. "I would miss my friends and family. Why can't you just visit me here? Couldn't we have fun here?"

"Here?" His face scrunched up like he'd taken a drink of curdled milk.

"Yes." I glanced over my shoulder at my companions. They hadn't moved at all since we'd arrived. *Malcolm, wake up.* "Here. This is where I live."

He brushed his hair out of his eyes, but it flopped right back down. "This place wreaks of iron and death. Can't you smell the fear … the unhappiness … the grief?"

"So, everyone in Faerie is happy?" *Cash? Seth?* Whatever spell Kieran had my friends under seemed impossible to break through. My gaze darted to my guards and then back to Kieran. I didn't trust him at all, but I was torn between seeing what was going on with my friends and not letting him out of my sight.

"Well, no"—his eyebrows pinched together—"but the air isn't saturated with their despair." He stepped closer to me, and I moved back again.

Mavros, if you can hear me, I need you now.

"In Faerie, there is no iron to sicken me."

I expected a black mist to float through the air and slowly coalesce into Mavros, but there was nothing of him. No voice in my head. No sensation that he was nearby. Nothing.

"Eating the food in Faerie is like a small taste of Heaven." He licked his lips, and his tongue was too long, too different to pass as human. "Once you take a bite, you will never want to eat anything from this world ever again."

Chaódis Skotádi, please come to me!

Kieran held his hand out, wiggling his fingers, expecting me to take it. "Come with me now. Let's not wait for the game to end. I know you will love it there. You will never want for anything. You will never have to save the world again."

I stretched my hand toward him. Faerie called to me. The promise of the peaceful life I could find there was enticing. I took a step forward, and excitement sparked in Kieran's eyes, making them shine as brightly as the noonday sun.

Behind Kieran, smoke drifted on a breeze. A hand reached through the haze and grabbed ahold of Kieran's collar. He stumbled off-balance, falling into a fully formed Mavros.

I shook my head, and whatever enchantment Kieran had placed me under disappeared. The idea of being trapped in Faerie was no longer alluring.

Mavros narrowed his eyes at Kieran. "What are you doing here, phouka?"

"Nothing you haven't tried, demon." Kieran pulled away from Mavros and tugged the sleeves of his green shirt down to his wrists. Then he brushed dust off of his khakis. "The difference is, I'll win. I always do."

Flames flickered in Mavros' eyes. "Not this time." He waved his hand at the dragons, and his fingers were tipped with sharp claws. "She's ours. Let her go before we kill you."

Kieran tossed his head back and laughed into the sky. The sound made me think of the whinny of a horse. When he looked at Mavros again, his black hair flopped down into his face. He brushed it back, revealing yellow eyes alight with mischief. "Oh, I knew I would have fun with you." He slapped Mavros on the shoulder. "The game's begun. You know you can't interfere unless you want Hell to rain down."

"What?" My mouth fell open, and my chest tightened. Kieran's words ran through my head, chasing after each other until all I could hear was a repeated chorus of, *You know you can't interfere. You know you can't interfere. You know you can't interfere.* I slapped my hands over my ears. "What do you mean?"

Kieran's sunny eyes sparkled. "Darlin', do you think I'd play a game that I can't win?"

Mavros lifted his lip in a snarl, but it was too late. Kieran was gone.

One of the dragons roared. The sound filled the snow-covered valley, echoing off the mountains. I was terrified it would cause an avalanche, but I kept my gaze pinned on Mavros. "What did he mean?"

"He means he's protected." Mavros' claws morphed back into human-looking fingernails. The fire in his eyes died, replaced by their normal obsidian depths. "The phouka is the queen's pet. His mischief brings her great joy."

"The Queen?" I swallowed over the ball of fear that had bubbled up in my throat. I'd read too many books about the Seelie and Unseelie Queens to think this could be a good thing. "Like in the stories?"

Mavros shrugged. "I've never read the stories, but I imagine she's probably worse."

The snow crunched behind me. "Upsetting the dragons, the demon prince, and some of the Nephilim will bring the faeries immense pleasure for centuries." Seth's voice held a sharper edge than I was used to hearing in it.

"So, what does it mean that he's protected." The words shook as they tumbled out of my mouth. I needed the answer, but I didn't want it.

Mavros stretched his hand out but let it fall between us. "It means you've got to figure this out." He looked over my shoulder at someone. "Keep her safe," he said before he disappeared.

I stared at the spot he'd vacated. They all knew something that they weren't telling me, but now wasn't the time to get into it. I could sense Malcolm's dragon, closer to the surface than was advisable for training in Krav Maga. "Seth, can you take Cody back? I think we should fly or run or just about anything but fight."

He nodded, making the blue spikes of his hair bounce. "Wise decision for a young pup."

"So, what's it going to be?" I asked as I turned around.

Malcolm's black tongue darted out between inhuman fangs. "Fly."

Knowing I had to keep my emotions under control, I lifted my lips in an imitation of a smile and waved at Cody. "See you later."

"Yeah." His mask was firmly in place. "Be careful."

I pushed off the ground. It had been a long time since I'd flown as a human, but like riding a bike, it came back to me without any conscious thought. When I was above the tree-tops, I transformed. Massive wings sprouted from my shoulder blades. My body lengthened, and a long tail whipped through the air behind me.

Liam, Cash, and Malcolm surrounded me as we soared far above the clouds. Malcolm and Cash were too riled for games or fun, so we flew hard and fast until my wings ached and Liam fell too far behind to protect me.

Knowing they would follow, I aimed for a rocky cliff high above the valley. The snow had been blown from the edge, leaving a brown and gray patch open. My legs wobbled when my feet touched the ground, but I managed to remain upright. Liam wasn't as lucky. He dropped to his hands and knees, panting.

"If you can't keep up"—Malcolm's growled words were hard to make out—"go back to the apartment."

Liam pressed his hands down against the barren earth and pushed himself into a standing position. His wings disappeared, and he rolled his shoulders. "Easy there. This was only the second time I've flown. I'm better on my feet."

No weakness. Cash's voice in my head startled me. *None.* He transformed, and I followed suit, taking off at a jog before Malcolm prompted me to. Cash matched his pace to mine and nodded at me. The movement was so subtle that I doubted the others noticed.

As we ran, I covered my hands, face, and neck in scales to help ward off the cold. I juggled fireballs and made a gust of wind push us farther up the mountain.

Malcolm followed behind me, and with the way Kieran's presence had affected him, I wondered if he felt like he was chasing after his prey.

Our footsteps pounded against the snow-covered ground, and wind howled through the trees, bending them at precarious angles. The sun rose high in the sky, occasionally hidden by fluffy, white clouds.

And, still, we ran on.

I used my magic in little ways, hoping not to deplete it too quickly, hoping not to show any weakness.

You're doing great, Dacia. Cash watched me without making it obvious. *His dragon is retreating.*

I tried to smile at him, but it seemed like too much energy would go into that motion.

And, still, we ran on.

Climbing the mountain, my pace slowed. My breath heaved out of my lungs. With each stride, I realized I couldn't feel my legs anymore. The dragon scales faded, and the cold hit me. Steam rose from my exposed skin, and I shivered.

"Stop." Malcolm slapped his hand down on my shoulder.

As soon as I quit moving, my legs gave out.

Malcolm knelt beside me, and his energy flowed through my body, rejuvenating it as it went. "Forgive me."

My breath burst out of my lungs in quick puffs that made it impossible to respond, so I set my hand on top of his, gently squeezing his fingers.

Liam plopped down next to me. His face was bright red, and sweat made his black t-shirt cling to his muscled chest. For the last few weeks, he hadn't been working out as much as he was used to. The wings had been too much of a hindrance. "I'm done for." He paused to suck in a deep breath. "How 'bout you?"

"I'm all right now." I grabbed his hand and transferred some of Malcolm's energy into him. When his breathing evened out, I let go. "Now—" I raked my fingers through my hair, hoping what I was about to ask wouldn't rile Malcolm up again "—how can I break whatever spell Kieran had on you?"

Malcolm's grip on my shoulder tightened before he jerked away and stomped off. His low growl rumbled through me, lifting the hairs on my neck.

Cash's amethyst eyes never left Malcolm. "Kieran's power can be drawn from all of Faerie. That is why we cannot break free from his hold."

"You must be the one to break it." Malcolm's voice carried over from where he stood looking down on the world. "Alone, we cannot." He turned and strode toward me. His fangs bit into his bottom lip. "Together, we could, but Kieran was right. Hell would rain down upon Earth. The queen would let loose all her beasts if we stood together against him."

Chapter 6

On My Own

$\mathscr{B}$efore we left the mountains, Cash and Malcolm made sure that I had energy enough not to fall asleep as soon as I sat down. Once I did, Malcolm teleported all of us back to their apartment. He pulled his hand out from under mine as soon as we arrived. I looked up at his face, wondering if he was okay. His eyes were bronze with a thin pupil slicing through them.

I set my hand on his forearm, stopping him from opening the door. "We're all okay."

He dipped his chin toward his chest. "For now."

"You should hunt." I turned my attention to Cash, wondering what condition he was in. His eyes looked human, but his posture was rigid. "You should, too."

"Call the demon back." Malcolm opened the door and led us across the hall to my apartment.

As soon as the door opened, I saw Samantha and Dan dancing in the kitchen. Dan swung Samantha out from him, and she threw her head back and laughed.

I rubbed at the sudden burning sensation in my chest, hating that I was jealous of them. I should have been happy to see them enjoying themselves. Instead, all I could do was wonder if I would ever be that carefree again.

Dan spun her toward me, and she stopped. Flour coated the front of her slate-colored shirt. "Hey, Dacia." She grinned. "We're making dinner. Are you going to be here?"

"She'll be here," Malcolm said before I even had a chance to unclamp my jaw. "She's not going anywhere tonight—" he squeezed my shoulder, making sure he had my attention "—right?"

The burning in my chest disappeared, replaced by a dull ache that spread through my body and left me feeling empty. "Yeah, I'll be here."

"I won't let her out of my sight." A silken voice filled the room.

Turning my head, I saw Mavros sitting in the chair with one leg thrown over the arm of it. My eyebrows pinched together as I looked at him. I hadn't called him yet. I didn't know how he knew we needed him here. Shaking my head, I decided just to accept it for what it was. Somehow, he knew, and that was all that mattered. "You will." I walked to my room. "I need a shower."

I jumped when I opened my door. Cody sat on my bed reading. He slipped his bookmark into place and looked up at me. "Okay?"

"Yeah." I wanted to sit next to him and lay my head on his shoulder, but I was sweaty, dirty, and gross. "It was tense, but it's okay now."

"What the hell happened anyway?" He pulled his hand down his face. "I couldn't move, couldn't hear or talk, but saw you with him. It was—" he waved his hand through the air like he was searching for the right thing to say "—foggy."

I walked to my dresser and pulled out clothes. "I'm on my own again. Kieran has the power of Faerie behind him, and nobody can help me."

"I'm sorry." He stood up and wrapped his arms around me. "Any ideas."

I held onto him and tried to let everything but his embrace disappear. "None." I stepped back, wiping under my eyes. "Do you know what they made for supper?"

"No idea." He brushed my hair back, tucking it behind my ear. "Had a lot of fun doing it, though."

"Yeah." I stared at the door. "They were dancing when I came in." I gave Cody a quick peck on the cheek. "I need to get cleaned up."

By the time I finished my shower, the smell of something cooking filled the apartment. It was a familiar scent, but I couldn't quite place it. I got dressed in a pair of leggings and one of Cody's hoodies, then walked into my room, drying my hair off as I went.

"Lasagna." Cody watched me from my bed. He was stretched out on top of my pink and purple comforter with his ankles crossed and his hands behind his head.

"Really?" I inhaled deeply. Now that I knew what it was, it smelled like lasagna, but that didn't make sense. Samantha's shirt had been dusted with flour. I shook my head and rubbed the towel over my hair one more time before tossing it onto the floor. "Malcolm and Cash are hunting. I need to go out soon or Mavros will come in."

Cody squeezed his eyes shut and breathed in deeply. Then he stood and took the two steps necessary for him to stand in front of me. "Too bad." He wrapped one hand around my waist and slid the other into my hair. "Been waiting too long to be alone." He tipped my head back, and his lips crashed down on mine.

I stumbled back slightly, but he held me tighter, pulling me against his body. He slipped his hand under my shirt, splaying his fingers out over my back.

I held onto his arms and pressed up onto my tiptoes. A surge of heat flared through me, making a tingling sensation erupt in the pit of my stomach.

The kiss was wild and hungry.

It was longing and need.

Fear and desperation.

All of the feelings Cody had bottled up inside of him bubbled up like a pop that had been shaken before being opened. They exploded out of him in the way his mouth moved against mine.

He skimmed his hands down my body and lifted me. I wrapped my legs around his waist, clinging to him like a lifeline. His lips slid from mine, kissing a path from my mouth to my ear and then down my neck to my shoulder.

I leaned my head back and moaned. All thoughts of Kieran and Mavros fled from my mind. There was nothing in this moment besides Cody and me. Nothing but passion and desire.

He carried me the two steps to the bed and gently laid me on it, slowly kissing his way back to my mouth.

My fingers twined in his hair and dug into his back, pulling him down so that there was no space between us. Our hearts pounded in time with each other as if we were one.

All of my senses were focused solely on Cody. His wintry scent drowned out the smell of dinner cooking. Our soft moans and harsh breathing were the only sounds I heard. His lips and body pressed against mine. The rough hairs on his face scratching my skin were all I felt. His mouth was all I tasted. When I opened my eyes, he was all I saw.

He leaned back, and a ragged breath shuddered through him. I tried to tug him down again, but he shook his head and stared at the door. "Yeah?" His husky voice sent a burst of heat flaring through me.

"Supper's ready," Samantha answered.

Cody rolled off of me, and a chill spread through my body. "We'll be out in a minute." I propped myself up on my elbows and breathed in deeply through my nose, hoping to settle my racing heart.

"Figured it was Mavros," Cody said as he combed his fingers through his hair.

A chuckle from the desk chair startled me. I jerked my head in that direction.

Mavros plopped his feet on the bed and leaned back with his hands behind his head. "Since when do I knock?" He sucked in a deep breath, and his eyelids fluttered. "Good thing the dragons left. You smell good enough to eat." He stood and pointed at the door. "Shall we?"

"In a minute." I grabbed my wet towel off of the floor and carried it into the bathroom. My bright eyes reflected back at me while I tugged a brush through my tangled curls. The gold flecks looked like miniature firestorms in my otherwise green and black irises. They seemed to dance like flickering flames. My lips were swollen, and my face was flushed.

I splashed some cold water over my burning skin, doubting it would help, then walked into the kitchen. Cody, Liam, and Mavros were already seated at the table. Liam must have brought a couple of their chairs over when he finished with his shower. Samantha was setting the last plate on its placemat, and Dan followed behind her with a tray of garlic bread.

"Okay, guys," he said as he set it down, "I've never made this before. Mom talked us through it. If you don't like it—" he flashed one of his award-winning smiles at everyone "—pretend like you do."

I squeezed in between Cody and Mavros. "It smells delicious."

"Not as good as you." Mavros leaned close to me and inhaled deeply. Crimson flames ignited on my cheeks, and he pulled away. "I didn't realize it could get better."

I smacked his arm. "Shut up and eat." I sprinkled Parmesan on my lasagna and took a bite. The sauce burned the roof of my mouth and tongue. I waved my hand in front of my face. Then took a drink of water. Smiling, I said, "This is delicious, guys. You're the new cooks forever."

"Thanks." A rosy glow covered Samantha's cheeks.

"Nah." Dan covered his mouth with his hand, hiding the bite he'd just taken. "You and Cody can cook tomorrow."

Samantha slumped forward slightly. "We should've seen if Cassandra and Bryce wanted to come over. There's plenty of food."

"Next time," Cody said before shoveling his mouth full.

Dan waited until he'd scraped the last bite off his plate before turning to Mavros. "Where've you been hiding lately? We hardly see you."

"Out." Mavros' eyes were narrowed, and his posture was closed off.

I swallowed the food that was in my mouth before saying, "For whatever reason, he doesn't want to tell."

"Is there a she-devil in your life?" Cody snickered.

Mavros raised his eyebrows and looked me up and down. "I don't know that I'd call her that." He brushed my hair back behind my ear, and a jolt of desire that wasn't my own flared inside of me.

Cody's fork clanked against his plate. The mirth was gone from his eyes. They looked like a dark, ominous sea.

"Lighten up, lover boy." Mavros let his hand linger for a moment before pulling it away. "You started it." Mischief danced across his face. He grabbed ahold of my wrist and pushed my sleeve up, exposing the mighty oak. He brushed his fingers from my elbow to my wrist, a soft, barely-there touch.

The urge to hide the tree made me reach across my plate for it, but I stopped and clenched my hand into a tight fist. Looking at it, a weight settled in my stomach. I didn't want to be reminded of Kieran or his curse. I didn't want anyone else to see it.

"This"—Mavros kept running his fingers along my skin— "didn't just grow on your arm."

I jerked away and yanked my sleeve down. "What do you mean?"

My friends had stopped eating. Everyone's focus was on Mavros and me.

"I've been searching for the actual tree." He picked up his glass and took a long drink. "If I can find it, you might have a chance to beat him, but … you'll never be able to if I don't. You can't just stop the leaves falling there." His gaze darted to my arm, and I wondered if he could see the curse through my sleeve. "You have to stop it on the real tree in Faerie."

I didn't know what to say. It had never occurred to me that the oak might exist in reality. I opened my mouth, but no words came out, so I snapped it closed.

Liam picked up his fork and pointed it at Mavros before scooping another bite onto it. "How do you expect to find it?"

"I have no idea." Leaning back, he seemed to deflate. The ever-present cockiness disappeared, and he looked more vul-nerable than I'd ever seen him. Dropping his chin toward his chest, he fiddled with his napkin. "I have a couple of cats helping, but now that I need to stay by Dacia's side, it won't be very easy."

"Cats?" Samantha's head tilted to the side.

He smiled at her and transformed back into the Mavros we were all used to seeing. "Not your average cats. Faerie cats."

An image flashed through my mind of cats with butterfly-like wings. I shook my head, doubting they would be either cute or cuddly. "Kieran said he's from Spring. Does that mean anything to you?"

"That's mostly where I've been looking."

I slipped my hand into my hoodie's pocket to keep my gaze from darting to the curse. "I could help you."

"No." Mavros' eyes widened, and flames swirled in them. He tossed his napkin onto the table. "What are you thinking?" Pushing his chair back, he paced between the refrigerator and oven. The movement reminded me of his panther. I could almost see the giant cat stalking me. "You cannot go traipsing around Faerie until the tree has been found. If Kieran finds you there, he'll make it drop its leaves."

Chapter 7

Training Day

*M*avros stared at me from the end of the bed. In the darkness, his eyes shone like a house cat's. A yellow, green glow that seemed to penetrate deep inside of me. Some nights, it was easy enough to sleep while my guardians watched, but tonight, there was too much information running through my head. An endless loop of questions with no answers.

Cody's breathing had evened out within minutes of coming to bed. The arm that he had draped over me no longer pulled me against his body. It was relaxed.

Looking from me to Cody, Mavros quietly got up and padded over to my side of the bed. "You've got to sleep, Dacia," he whispered. "Malcolm wants you to train with Liam tomorrow after classes since it didn't work out today."

"I know." I yawned, and Mavros mimicked the action. "There's just too much to think about."

He walked back to the desk and leaned against it instead of sitting. "Yeah." His muscles were tense, but I doubted he'd tell me what was bothering him. I watched him until my eyes grew too heavy to keep open.

Millions of stars fill the night sky. The Milky Way cuts a path through the darkness. The snow sparkles in the dim lighting, and my breath frosts the air. I shiver, and a coat is placed around my shoulders. I jump to the side and throw my elbow back.

"Easy." Mavros chuckles. "I didn't mean to startle you."

I send a burst of heat through my body and down to my bare feet. "Why are we here?"

His obsidian gaze travels over me before locking onto my eyes, and he rubs his chin like he's thinking of the perfect response. Lifting one shoulder, he shoots me a crooked smile. "I like seeing you in my jacket. It gives me hope." He stares up at the sky, and I get the impression that he's weighing his options, trying to decide if he should tell me what's really on his mind. "But that's not why." Shoving his hands into his pockets, he says, "I want to let Kieran get through to you."

My eyebrows pinch together. "Through to me. What do you mean?"

"In your dreams. I want him to show you where the tree is. It may be our best bet at finding it."

I slip my arms into the sleeves of his coat, relishing the lingering warmth from Mavros' body. "Why are you telling me this here? Why not tell me at dinner? Why'd you get mad at me for offering to help?"

The tendons in his neck bulge, and he clutches his hands at his sides. "I don't want you there in real life, only in your dreams." He takes a deep breath and closes his eyes for a few seconds. When he opens them again, his rage is gone. "The dragons don't agree. They don't want Kieran near you in your dreams or reality." He leans back against a lodgepole pine, and snow dusts his shoulders. "They're afraid that he will somehow make a leaf fall, but Dacia, we need to find that tree before he decides he's tired of playing."

Even though I could feel his gaze on me, I didn't spare a glance in Mavros' direction when I woke up. I kissed Cody on the cheek, rolled out of bed, grabbed my clothes, and stumbled into the bathroom. Staring into the mirror at my once green eyes, I focused on the black and gold flecks in them, wondering what would happen if I opened myself up to Kieran. Would I change again? How much more would it take until I no longer recognized myself?

I shook my head. It didn't matter. Whether I opened myself up to Kieran now or later, eventually, I would have to face him, and if it changed me, I would somehow learn to cope with it.

Turning away from the mirror, I took Mavros' coat off. No matter how many times I woke up with one of them on, I would never understand how that magic worked.

After getting ready, I walked through my room without checking to see if Mavros was still sitting there. I didn't want to talk about Kieran. I didn't want to hear that I needed to let him invade my dreams. Maybe part of it was because I knew that when it came down to it, I didn't have a say in the matter. If Mavros wanted to let Kieran into my dreams, he could, and there was nothing I could do to keep him out.

The only light in the apartment came from the kitchen. Cody stood in front of the stove in just his shorts. "Hey." He shot me a quick smile before turning back around. With a flick of his wrist, the eggs in the pan flipped into the air and landed perfectly. Even with my magic, I doubted I would ever be able to master that skill. "Want some?"

"Sure." I grabbed a glass from the cabinet and filled it with milk before mixing chocolate into it.

The toaster oven dinged. Cody slid the eggs onto a plate, picked up a knife, buttered the bread, and then handed the food to me. "What's bugging you?" he asked as he cracked more eggs into the skillet.

"I don't have any control over my life."

He looked at me with one eyebrow raised. "You think any of us do?"

I stopped with my toast hovering in the air in front of me and just stared at him. He was right. You could have everything planned out, everything lined up perfectly, and then it could be tossed to the side like garbage because something unexpected happened.

My parents hadn't planned on having a daughter with powers like mine. They hadn't planned on losing their son. They hadn't planned on having their house and all their possessions burn to the ground, and yet, it had happened. None of it had been in their control, and if they could've set the course, they never would have chosen that one. Instead, they took what was given to them and tried to make the best of it.

Cody, Samantha, and Dan had been kidnapped and tortured because of befriending me. Cassandra had been controlled by a demon before even meeting me. I had crushed Bryce's hand, and still, they chose to be my friends.

The prophecy had made me the one who had to face Nefarious, but it had also made Sarah the one who had to train me. It had dictated and controlled her life. She could've chosen to ignore her grandfather when he told her about it, but then when Nefarious returned to Earth, she would've had to live with the consequences of her decision.

Maybe none of us had a whole lot of say in the direction our lives went.

I could have chosen to join Draconian, to be his protégée. A lot of things would have turned out differently, but as his underling, I wouldn't have had a say in my future.

If I had chosen to be with Mavros, I would have stood by his side while he wreaked havoc. I wouldn't have been able to choose to stop him.

"Okay," I finally said, "touché." I took a bite of my breakfast and watched him finish cooking, then sit next to me.

His leg pressed against mine. "You might have fewer choices." He put his eggs between his toast, picked up his sandwich, and took a bite. "What's this about anyway?"

I glanced at the armchair, wondering if Jax was sitting in it, and lifted my shoulder like it was nothing. *Mavros wants me to let Kieran into my dreams.* Cody opened his mouth like he was going to say something, so I quickly added, *He doesn't want the dragons to know.* "Sometimes, I just wish I didn't have to deal with all of this."

"Yeah." His shoulders sagged. "Wish you didn't, too."

I angled myself into my seat so that Mavros was out of my line of sight. Sooner or later, I would have to talk to him, but I wasn't ready yet.

Malcolm sat on the other side of me, and Seth and Cash were in front of us. Their muscles were taut. Normally, I would have wondered who or what was after me but not this time. This time, I was positive that my emotions were the reason behind their tension.

When Professor Natterjack excused the class, Malcolm leaned around me. "What did you do to her, demon?"

Mavros' chair scraped against the tiled floor. I could feel the loss of his warmth on my back as soon as he stood. "I guess I said something I shouldn't have." Regret tinged his voice.

"It's nothing," I said as I slid my arms into my coat. "Just a difference of opinions."

Malcolm stood and held his hand out for me. "We'll train until lunchtime, then again after your next class."

"Okay." I shoved my things into my backpack and pulled the strap over my shoulder. "I'd like to spend some time researching faeries tonight, too."

He nodded his agreement before leading me out of the room.

Liam and Russ were with Cody, so I expected training to be flying and pushing my powers to their limits. I was quite surprised when Malcolm teleported us. We didn't fall through the sky. We landed on the ground. The air was hot and dry. There was no green, just rocky, barren earth.

I took my coat and sweatshirt off and tossed them on a boulder next to my bag. "What now?" I asked.

"Fight." The word was little more than a growl. "Do whatever you need to."

I stretched my arms and rolled my neck. Then I turned away from Malcolm and faced the others. Jax stood next to Mavros, Cash, and Seth. "Well, that answers that," I mumbled to myself as I looked into Jax's lilac eyes.

Mavros and Cash both charged at the same time. I lifted my hands and sent a strong burst of wind at each of them. They staggered back, and an arm wrapped around my neck.

Six seconds.

That was how long Liam had told me I had to get free from a chokehold.

Liam's warning played through my head on repeat while I tried to use what he had shown me, but my attacker just laughed.

Jax.

My time was running out. Giving up on Krav Maga, I teleported high into the washed-out sky. Wings exploded from my back, knocking him loose.

I flapped them, slowing my plummet, and realized I wasn't a dragon. I glanced over my shoulder and saw pristine, white feathers.

Folding my wings against my back, I teleported to the ground. I didn't look at Malcolm. I didn't need to. I knew he would not approve. I knew what he thought about my angel wings. I knew his dragon would be even more agitated now.

Seth ran at me. I lowered myself into a defensive position, held my hands out in front of me, and blasted him with fireballs. Several struck him in the chest, burning his shirt away.

He grinned at me and ducked under my hands. Grabbing me around the waist, he flipped me over his shoulder.

I thought about cold and snow until my body was a solid block of ice.

Seth tightened his grip on me, and a pained moan slipped out of him. Scales covered his body, shimmering in the bright sunlight. Frost formed on them. Tiny crystals spread over him, but the cold no longer bothered him.

I pounded my fists against his back. His grip slackened, and I slid down enough to swing my leg back and knee him in the stomach.

He stumbled, dropping down to one knee, and I fell out of his arms. My back hit the ground, and the air whooshed out of my body.

I gasped, but oxygen didn't inflate my lungs. Black spots danced in front of my eyes.

Seth knelt over me and breathed in deeply. His cobalt eyes fluttered, and his features morphed until they were completely inhuman. His nose and mouth lengthened into a snout. Razor-sharp teeth filled his jaws. Ivory horns protruded from the top of his head. Azure scales covered his skin. He grabbed my wrists one after the other, holding them in one hand. Then he clutched my neck, squeezing his fingers, cutting off my air completely. Lowering his face to mine, a guttural growl rumbled through him.

My heart pounded against my ribs. The sound roared inside my skull. I felt it pulsing in my neck.

Cash ran over and reached for Seth. I shook my head, and smoke rolled out of his nostrils.

I bent my knees and slammed my feet down into the back of Seth's legs. At the same time, I twisted my hands away from each other, breaking them free from his grasp. He fell forward, slamming his skull into mine.

Scales dug into my forehead. I felt blood well up. Terror clawed at me, giving me an extra burst of strength. I shoved Seth back.

"Enough," Malcolm roared.

Seth stared down at me. I couldn't see any recognition in his inhuman eyes. Talons tipped his fingers. Saliva hung from his lip before dripping onto my cheek. Fire burned in the back of his throat.

Malcolm grabbed Seth by the shoulders and threw him off of me.

He landed in a crouch several yards away, looking even less human. A feral growl ripped out of him.

Malcolm positioned himself between us, ready to defend me at all costs. I scrambled back, knowing that if they transformed with me here I would get crushed.

Cash and Jax each grabbed one of Seth's arms. Seth twisted his body, trying to tear free from their hold. Baring his teeth, he roared. The sound raised the hairs on my neck.

Mavros appeared next to me. He reached his hand down and pulled me to my feet. I backed farther away and morphed into my dragon. Lowering my head, I peered into Seth's eyes. He dropped his gaze and backed away.

The fight drained out of him. The smell wafting off of him changed from something putrid to something delectable. His scales retreated into his body, leaving flesh behind, and his features became human. He hung limply in Cash's and Jax's grasp. "Dacia"—his chin dropped to his chest—"forgive me."

"Of course," I answered before reverting back to my body. "No harm done."

Malcolm turned toward me, and I wondered how he had managed to keep his human form.

I set my hand on his forearm. "I'm okay." I kept my voice soft and was careful not to look directly into his eyes.

"If he was your enemy, you'd be dead." Malus Tribulus looked out at me. His anger was tangible.

Cash carefully sauntered over to us. Even though Malcolm's back was to him, he kept his eyes downcast and his shoulders hunched.

When he was only a couple of steps away, Malcolm spun around, snarling. He blocked me with his body, reaching one arm back, holding me in place.

Cash lifted his hands in a placating gesture. "Go. Hunt. I won't let her out of my sight."

"After I take her home."

Mavros wrapped his arm around my waist, and I leaned into him, not caring anymore that I was supposed to be mad at him.

Malcolm grasped my bicep and teleported us to the middle of my living room. I glanced around, hoping nobody who shouldn't have seen us return that way did. Luckily, the only people in my apartment were ones who knew magic was real.

"Don't go anywhere without Mavros." Malcolm stared at me. As soon as I nodded, he disappeared.

I pulled away from Mavros. "I need a shower. I have dragon drool on me." I walked toward my room. As I reached for the doorknob, I realized that I had left my coat, sweatshirt, and bag in the middle of the desert. I spun around and saw Seth holding them. "Thank you." I strolled over, no longer afraid of him.

"It was the least I could do." He handed them to me, refusing to meet my eyes.

Chapter 8

Faerie Games

$\mathcal{S}$unlight streamed in through my bedroom window. I kept my eyes closed, savoring the feeling of Cody's fingers tracing patterns on my skin. I'd slept through the entire night.

No dreams.

No nightmares.

No midnight rendezvous with Mavros.

Just some much-needed sleep.

I rolled over and snuggled into Cody's chest, laying my head on his arm. He was warm and solid and mine. "Your birthday's Friday."

"Yeah." The word caressed my ear.

I ran my hand along his side, then onto his back, trying to remember what I'd been saying before his breath had distracted me. He moved, and the chain I'd given to him for Christmas brushed against my cheek. When my magic had been corrupted by Argentum, the chain had saved his life twice. It was the best gift I could've given him. My memory came surging back. "I, uh, haven't gotten you anything."

"This is enough." He pulled me closer. "You've had a lot going on."

I kissed the underside of his chin. His stubble scratched against my lips. "We could go anywhere in the world."

"Doesn't matter." He pulled back slightly so he could look into my eyes. "Just wanna be with you."

My door opened a crack, and Mavros peeked in. "Are you two going to classes today, or do I need to kick the dragons out before they forget about their vows and decide just to eat you?"

"Give us a few minutes. We have time before class." I turned my back on him, hoping he would do what I asked. Focusing on Cody again, I said, "If you don't want to get away, we could go to Althea."

He lifted his shoulder. "Won't be alone."

"No, I'll have guards until I figure out this stupid curse." I lifted my arm so that we could see the tree. As far as I could tell, there wasn't any change to it yet this morning, but I still didn't have any answers either. "Then there will probably be something else to deal with." I flopped back on the bed and stared at the ceiling. This wasn't how I had wanted this conversation to go. I'd wanted Cody to understand that I loved him and would do anything for him.

Dr. Yarrow stood in the front of the room. She wasn't one of those teachers who droned on and on, sounding as bored as half of the students. Her voice was animated. Fiction writing was something she was passionate about.

I doodled on the edges of my paper, writing down only the things that seemed like they were important enough to show up on a test.

The door opened, drawing my attention to the far end of the room. None of the other students looked up. Dr. Yarrow didn't so much as glance at Kieran as he bounded in. His dark hair bounced against his face. His eyes were bright, and his cheeks were flushed. A smile danced on his lips.

I expected my guards to move closer, to do something, but they sat motionlessly.

He walked down the aisle in front of me and tugged on one girl's ponytail. Then he flipped a guy's ball cap onto the floor.

The pair of them looked around, searching for the instigator. When they turned toward me, I lowered my eyes, keeping Kieran in my peripheral vision. I nudged Malcolm with my elbow, but he didn't move. Trying to keep Kieran from noticing, I kicked Mavros' foot.

Nothing.

Not a response, not even a startled gasp.

Dr. Yarrow continued her lecture, but I had no idea what she was saying. My attention was fully on the phouka be-bopping through the room. He whistled a jaunty tune as he skipped to my desk.

When he was only a couple of steps from me, he lifted a finger to his lips. "They"—he waved his arm, encompassing the whole room—"can hear everything you say."

Even though I was sure of the answer, I pointed at him and tilted my head.

"No." He threw his head back and laughed. "Where would the fun be in that?"

Calling on my magic, I willed my guards to wake up. They didn't stir, no faint rustling, not even the blink of an eye.

Chaódis Skotádi, I need you. The words sounded almost like a prayer to me, and I couldn't help but wonder what the penalty for praying to a demon prince would be.

Dark tendrils of smoke wafted off of Mavros' hands, answering my call.

Kieran clicked his tongue at me while shaking his finger in front of my face. "Looks like somebody's going to cause a scene."

Fearing that Kieran was right and Mavros would completely vaporize in front of my class, I stopped calling to him. The mist dispersed, and I focused on Kieran.

"Since you won't let me visit your dreams anymore, I needed to come to you somewhere else." He sat on the edge of my desk and fanned the pages of my notebook. "Now, you have no choice but to listen." He stretched his hand toward me and twirled my hair around his finger.

I clenched my pen in my hand. My fingernails bit into my palms. I wanted to say something to him, to scream at him for turning my guards into little more than decorative statues, but I fought the urge.

Kieran flicked Cash in the ear, then twisted some of Malcolm's braids together. He hooked his thumb at Mavros. "How can you bear to have this one in your presence? Do you know the things he's done?" He shivered. "He makes me look like an angel." He focused on me again. "Or do you care? How many deaths are on your hands? Do you still hunger for dragon blood?"

A rush of power surged through me. I remembered the taste of Argentum's blood and how I'd wanted more.

Kieran's yellow eyes danced with merriment. "There are four dragons right here." He patted Seth's head and looked over my shoulder to where, I imagined, Jax had been guarding me. "They wouldn't even wake up before you drained them all. Imagine the power." He leaned in close to me. "Imagine how strong you would be."

Yesss. My magic rose up inside of me.

The power in their blood flooded my senses. My nostrils flared as I pressed closer to Malcolm and breathed in his intoxicating aroma. How could I not have realized how delicious he smelled?

"Just a nibble," Kieran murmured. The words were filled with mirth.

I snapped my head back, snatched Kieran's collar, and jerked him toward me.

He chuckled, and his gaze danced around the room.

A couple of students down the row stared at me. Their heads cocked to the side, and their eyebrows drew together, clearly confused by my actions.

I let go of him, wondering what exactly they saw, and sat on my hands.

He brushed the back of his fingers along my cheek and lowered his face so that he gazed into my eyes. "Oh … we are going to have so much fun together." His hand slid to my elbow, and he tugged gently. "It's time to play."

My body felt like it had been pulled into a whirlpool. I spun, not knowing which way was up or down. The air was sucked from my lungs, and darkness surrounded me.

Kieran's hand never moved from my arm.

Before the spinning stopped, I breathed in the soothing scent of rain. Distant thunder rumbled. My feet hit solid ground, and I swayed. Stretching my arms out to catch my balance, I grabbed onto the only thing in reach to steady myself.

Kieran's laughter made me snap my eyes open.

Green.

Everything around me was green. Like the leaves in springtime after a nourishing rain. But more. The color seemed brighter, more vivid here, almost like it had taken on a life of its own.

Water overflowed from cupped leaves, dripping off their edges, falling to the moss-laden ground, and splashing onto my skin. The droplets were cool, and I shivered. Whether it was from fear, amazement, or cold, I wasn't sure.

Realizing I still clutched Kieran's arm, I dropped my hand to my side and spun around, looking at the surrounding forest. "Where are we?"

"Faerie." He jumped in front of me, splashing my jeans with muddy water.

I glared at him, stumbling back when I took in his appearance. His cheekbones were abnormally high, and he was skinnier, emaciated. His joints bent back at awkward, unnatural angles, and his eyes looked even more inhuman.

He shot me a wild look that made me feel like spiders were crawling along my spine. "Where else?"

My breath caught in my throat. "Faerie?" I stumbled back. How could I be in Faerie? Could he keep me here until the leaves began to fall? "Why?" Panic clung to the word.

He tipped his head. Confusion drew his eyebrows together. "So, we can play." He grinned, a feral imitation of a human smile, showing sharp, pointed teeth, and ran. His laughter floated through the air behind him as he disappeared into the trees.

I darted after him, grateful for all the time I spent training with the dragons. My feet squished into the wet ground. Water seeped in through the sides of my shoes.

At first, his trail was easy enough to follow. His footsteps left a visible path through the mud. Then they disappeared.

I stopped. Spinning around, I searched the trees, trying to figure out where he could have gone. I remembered his other forms, the horse and the dog, but I didn't see any of those tracks either.

There was nothing.

He could have teleported anywhere. As far as I knew, he could have turned into a bird and flown off. There was no way for me to tell and no way for me to find him.

I walked through the trees in the same direction I had been heading, hoping that his tracks would reappear.

The air chilled, and suddenly, the forest seemed more menacing. Branches ripped at my clothes. Something growled, low and deep.

A chill shuddered up my spine. I felt like I was being watched. Anything could be hiding behind the thick foliage. I thought about all the books I'd read in high school and remembered all the faeries who would just as soon kill a human as look at one.

The more I surveyed the area, the faster my heart raced.

A twig snapped. I spun around, searching for the source of the sound. I couldn't see anything or anyone, but I knew I wasn't alone.

Leaves rustled behind me, and a hand clamped down on my shoulder. A scream tore from my throat.

My chest constricted, making my breathing harsh. I grabbed ahold of the wrist, spun away from the arm, and pulled my other hand back into a fist. I stopped my punch right before it slammed into Kieran's face.

He threw his head back and laughed. Then he darted in between the trees again.

My stomach dropped as I watched him disappear.

Mud pulled at my feet, holding them down. I lifted one with a loud squelching sound, then took off running. I felt like I had a ten-pound weight attached to the bottom of each shoe.

A breeze blew through the trees, shaking water from their leaves, drenching me. My wet hair was plastered to my head. I pushed it back, wishing I had a hairband to tie it up.

Lightning flashed, and a second later thunder boomed. Taking its cue, the sky darkened. Rain fell in thick sheets, washing away all traces of Kieran.

I stopped running and bent over with my hands on my knees. My breath came out in heavy gasps. The rain seemed to seep in through my skin, leaving me shivering.

Even beneath the torrential downpour, I felt eyes watching. I couldn't stand still too long or whatever it was would get brave enough to come out into the open.

A tree behind me creaked and groaned like a strong wind had slammed into it. When I turned, I could swear the trunk was closer to me than it had been.

"Okay. This is creepy." My voice shook. While I watched, the tree's roots pulled up, flinging mud through the air.

I turned, practically stumbling in my hurry to get away from it. The fresh rain made the ground slick, but I didn't slow down. I ran until I came to a stream cutting through the forest.

Remembering the books I'd read, I stopped at the edge and stared into the water wondering if kelpies, nixies, naiads, or mermaids inhabited this creek.

"Trees or water faeries?" I whispered, wondering which one would kill me first.

Laughter flitted through the woods and bubbled up from the stream. It filled the air, drowning out the sound of the pouring rain.

"Aaaah!" I lifted my face to the sky. My hands were fisted at my sides. "I wanna go home." A sob followed the words.

"So … why don't you?" Kieran's voice was filled with amusement.

He sat on a branch in the tree that had followed me, somehow, appearing completely dry. His feet dangled down, and a huge smile lifted his lips.

Water splashed behind me. I stepped forward glancing over my shoulder as I did. A dark green, almost black, horse rose out of the stream, lifted by the current. Algae dangled from its lanky body. Its mane and tail were the color of seafoam. The beast was both beautiful and terrifying. It stamped its hoof against the rocky bank but came no closer.

"Come to me, child." The kelpie's voice was ancient, reminding me of water rushing over rocks.

I stepped forward, wanting nothing more than to join this magnificent creature.

"No!" Kieran grabbed hold of my arm.

We spun, twisting and turning through a black void. The smell of crisp, cool air was like a balm to my soul. My feet hit the ground, and I fell to my hands and knees.

Home. He'd brought me home.

Chapter 9

The cold quickly reminded me that I was soaked to the bone. Strands of my hair froze together, and my teeth chattered. As soon as Kieran let go of my arm, I teleported to my bedroom.

I pulled my phone out of my pocket and swiped the screen. 1:13. I had been in Faerie for at least three hours. If Kieran had released Mavros and the dragons from his hold, they would be frantic. *I'm back.* I sent the message out to all of my guards and Cody.

A fist pounded against my door. Without waiting for an invitation, Malcolm stepped inside. His features were somewhere between human and dragon. Smoke rolled out of his nostrils. His eyes took in everything from the top of my dripping head all of the way to my mud-laden shoes. "Where?" There was little doubt that his dragon was doing the talking.

"Fa-Fa-Faerie," I said between chattering teeth. Rubbing my arms, I sent a blast of heat flowing through my body. "I'm skipping class. I need a shower."

He folded his arms over his chest and nodded.

When I finished, Malcolm was still waiting for me in my room. He appeared a little more human, but from his posture and the expression on his face, I could tell it was a fragile hold. He put his hand on my shoulder as I stepped into the living room.

Cody, Liam, Russ, Mavros, Cash, Seth, and Jax stared at me. I stopped walking, feeling like there was no space for me in the room. My chest tightened. The air was too warm. The smells were too strong. I turned around, and Malcolm grabbed ahold of both of my shoulders.

"What is it, Dacia?" The words were a low rumble.

I closed my eyes and took several deep breaths. Fleeing from here wouldn't do anybody any good. Everyone would follow me, and no matter where we were, it would feel over-crowded.

Gentle fingers rubbed my neck, soothing me, helping me breathe easier. "You okay?" Cody's voice was soft.

My muscles relaxed under his touch. I nodded. "I am now."

He slid his hand along my arm and twined our fingers together. Then he led me over to the couch and pulled me down on his lap. Wrapping his arms around me, he said, "What happened?"

Staring into the depths of his sapphire eyes, I pretended like we were the only people in the apartment while I told him about my unexpected trip to Faerie. By the time I finished, my heart had settled down and I could look at all of the people gathered in the room without feeling overwhelmed.

"I heard you call me," Mavros said. "I tried to come to you."

I glanced over my shoulder at him. "I know." His face was expressionless, but I could see the anguish in his eyes. "I couldn't let you vaporize in front of the whole class, though."

"Why didn't you teleport back here?" Liam sat backward on one of the kitchen chairs like he had when he couldn't hide his wings.

"From another realm?" I dipped my head toward one shoulder and felt my eyebrows draw together. "Can I do that?"

Mavros grabbed hold of my hand. "There's only one way to find out."

The room and everyone in it disappeared. Mavros held me against his body, tighter than he needed to. His warm summer nights scent was familiar and reassuring. His hands skimmed over my back. "I thought I'd lost you."

"So did I." I pulled away from him and looked around. We were on the same beach where I had gone to him in my dream to ask for his help. I looked out at the turquoise water before turning back to him.

"I think you should wait to go to Faerie." His voice was soft. "Even in your dreams. Now that you've been there, Kieran might sense your return."

I didn't know what to say, so I just nodded.

"We'll find another way." He held his hand out, and I slipped mine into it. "Now, take us back to your apartment."

Since I didn't know if anybody would have moved after we disappeared, I thought about my room. I pictured the pink and purple comforter, where all the furniture was placed, and the now muddy carpet. Thinking of the space between my bed and dresser, I drew on my magic.

Nothing happened.

Mavros squeezed my fingers. "Try again, Dacia. You can do this."

Focusing on the feeling I'd had right before the kelpie emerged from the stream, I visualized my room again. I concentrated on the lure of home and the comfort of my friends. I felt a tug, but the stretching sensation of teleportation didn't happen. Shaking my head, I looked into Mavros' obsidian eyes. "It's not working."

He pinched his lips together and tapped his index finger against them. "We'll add this to your training." He wrapped his arms around me, and we stood in front of the couch, right where we'd left from.

"Can she?" Cash's voice was nearer to his dragon's than I'd heard it in a long time.

I sat next to Cody and brushed the sand off my socks. I was going to have to vacuum once the mud dried in my room, so I wasn't worried about the mess. "Not yet."

"I'll work with her until she can." Mavros sat next to me. He watched me like he was trying to solve a puzzle.

I felt like squirming beneath his scrutinizing gaze, but I tried to stay still, to not let him see how much it bothered me to be studied like a germ under a microscope.

Liam knelt in front of me, balancing on the balls of his feet. "While everyone's here, I've been asked to talk to you about something." He rubbed his hand over his scruffy chin and focused on my feet instead of my eyes.

My stomach dropped. The only times Liam had ever looked at me like this were when he was ashamed of what the other Nephilim were doing to me or making him do to me.

"What is it?" Malcolm asked the question that was lodged in the back of my throat.

Liam's eyes flicked to him for an instant before returning to my stockinged feet. "The Angelic Tribunal—" he met my gaze, and I nodded "—would like to know if you would restore wings to some other Nephilim."

When Troy and Sebastian had come to my house after I'd returned home, Diana had mentioned that group. I didn't know who or what they were. I didn't know if I could trust them or even if I should. "I …" I didn't know what to say. Several of the Nephilim had wanted me imprisoned. Some of them probably still wanted me securely within their sanctuary. All but a handful most likely wanted Mavros returned to the Abyss. How could I help them and not wonder if they would turn on me as soon as the opportunity arose?

"I understand if you don't want to." He finally met my eyes, and I could see the conflict in his. "My people have wronged you. I don't think I could ever forgive somebody for the things they've done to you."

I tugged my hand through my hair. It was still wet from my shower. "Can I trust them?"

"Some of them."

Leaning into Cody, I pulled his arm tighter around me. I needed some sense of security. "I'll do it for Vicki, Diana, and Olivia if they want it. Maybe a couple others if you know for certain I can trust them." Tears pooled in my eyes, but I couldn't give him more than that. I couldn't inadvertently arm my enemies. I'd learned the hard way that trust had to be earned, and I wasn't about to turn my back on that lesson.

Liam set his hand on my knee. "Dacia, don't feel bad about that. I told them they had no right to ask." He squeezed his fingers before standing up. "They don't deserve your kindness, but I'll let them know."

"Your gramma deserves it." I remembered her telling Sebastian that she wanted a cot and food and water for me. "Things would've been so much worse without you and her."

Since I didn't go to class, Malcolm decided I needed to be training. He teleported all of us to someplace I had never seen before. Tall brown grasses bent in the wind. There were no trees in sight. The ground was flat for as far as I could see. Rocks, yuccas, and cacti broke up the monotony of the scenery. The cool breeze chilled my skin, even though the sun beat down on me.

Malcolm nodded at Liam. "You're up."

Liam stood with his hands behind his back. "Show me what you remember."

Jax attacked me while Seth went after Cody. We went over the moves Liam had already shown us. After having practiced them so many times, the motions were instinctual. As soon as Liam was satisfied that Cody and I would be able to free ourselves, he waved the dragons off. "It's not going to happen very often, but sometimes, somebody will try to grab you in a bear hug from the front, a body lock."

Liam wrapped his arms around Cash. "From this position, I can pull against his body while pushing with my head to knock him off balance." He demonstrated, not allowing Cash to fall. Liam pulled Cash back up. Then they traded positions. "The first thing you want to do is move your pelvis backward to change your center of gravity. While you're doing that, shove your attacker back." He put his hands on Cash's waist and pushed him back. "Once you've set yourself, press your head against his face so that you can poke your thumbs into his eyes." He imitated the movement, and Cash pulled his head back. "Then you can either punch him in the throat with your fist or your elbow. When he goes down, slam your knee into his groin, and hit him on the back of the neck for good measure." They showed us the moves a few more times. Then Liam sent Seth to attack me.

Seth stood in front of me with his chin tucked against his chest. "I vowed to protect you." He shuffled his feet. "I wanted to kill you."

"I trust you, Sapphirus."

At the sound of his true name, he met my eyes. His dragon looked out at me, seeing the truth of my confession.

I grabbed his hand, squeezing his fingers. "I don't think it'll happen again." As soon as the words were out of my mouth, I stepped back so we could train.

When I'd defended against Seth's attacks multiple times, Cash traded places with him. After several rounds, Jax took his turn. Once they were finished, I stood facing Liam. The four of them were similarly built, but their varying heights and weights made it slightly different.

Liam attacked me again and again, coming at me from different angles. I would knock him down, and he would spring back up, ready for more. Finally, he walked over to his duffle bag. After rummaging through it, he handed me a bottle of water. "Good job today."

"Thanks." I rolled my shoulders. My muscles ached, but at least as soon as the collar came off, I would start to recover. "When …" I twisted the bottle in my hands. Fighting dragons would be easier than giving Nephilim wings. "Uh, when do you want me to heal them?"

"If you never want to, I'd understand." He finished his water, screwed the lid back onto the bottle, and tossed it into his bag. "I'm not going to push you on this."

I watched Cody and Cash walk toward us. Even though Cody had said he didn't need to do anything for his birthday, I wanted to spend the day, maybe even the weekend with him. He deserved my undivided attention for at least that long. "Wednesday or Thursday." I pulled my bottom lip into my mouth with my teeth and closed my eyes for a second or two. "Only if you *know* you can trust them."

"We done?" Cody sat next to me and grabbed a water.

"You are," Malcolm answered while Mavros pulled the collar off. "Dacia needs to figure out how to teleport between realms."

I dropped my chin to my chest and nodded. I expected this. I really figured that was the only training I would do until I figured it out, but it had been a long day, and I was exhausted. A resigned groan slipped out before I could stop it.

Cody massaged my neck, and I relaxed into his touch. Magic rushed through my body, recharging it, healing my bruises, scrapes, aches, and pains. I let my power flow into him, hoping to speed up his recovery, too. Then I brushed my lips over his and stood.

Malcolm, Cash, and Mavros stayed with me while the others returned to the apartment. "Can you guys teleport between realms?" I'd never really thought about anybody other than Mavros doing it, but obviously, Faerie was another realm. If the dragons could do it, I wondered why they hadn't used it to escape when Draconian was capturing them.

"We're about to find out." Malcolm flashed his fangs at me, and I remembered when that action had been intimidating. Now, it was just a part of him.

Mavros slid his arm around my waist, and Cash clasped his elbow. Malcolm set his hand on Mavros' opposite shoulder, and the four of us appeared on a beach. This time the ocean was rough. Angry waves beat against the rocky shoreline. Their spray flung into the air, misting us. The sky was gray. At home,

I would expect rain to start falling at any second, but here I wasn't sure what it meant. There was no vegetation or wildlife. In fact, as far as I could tell, there were no signs that this world was inhabited at all.

I stepped away from the others and stared off into the distance. "Do any of these realms have people, life of any kind?"

"No people where I'm taking you." There was a protectiveness in Mavros' voice that I hadn't heard before. "Life happens everywhere. Some you can see with the naked eye, some you cannot. You just need to accept that life doesn't only mean human or animal."

Once again, it wasn't lost on me that I was getting a lesson in morality from a demon.

"The types of creatures, people as you called them, that live in other realms ..." He shook his head. "Let's just say, I don't want them to meet you."

A shiver traveled up my spine while I contemplated all the sorts of beings that could be out there. "All righty then."

"Malcolm and Cash are going to try to teleport back to their apartment." Mavros stood next to me, seemingly looking out at the ocean, but I felt his gaze trailing over me. "If they can do it and come back here, they will try to help you figure it out."

I nodded.

Cash grinned at Malcolm. "First one there and back wins."

"You're on."

They closed their eyes. Strain showed on their faces. The longer they stood there trying to teleport, the less human their features became. Cash reminded me of the creature I'd seen in the cave. Scales dotted his face. Horns jutted out from his head. His fingers were tipped with long claws.

Mavros grabbed ahold of me and ran. When they transformed into dragons, we were far enough away to keep from being hurt.

After a few more minutes, Malcolm roared his frustration. Cash's talons dug into the ground, leaving deep gouges in the rock. "Why?" He narrowed his eyes, focusing on Mavros.

"I am born of another realm." He lifted one shoulder. "I was created to travel between."

Malcolm shifted back into his human form and walked toward us. The beads in his braids clicked together. Most of the time, he kept them silent. That told me more about his level of agitation than anything. His hands flexed and unflexed, over and over again. He stopped about ten feet from Mavros and me and stared into my eyes. His were still completely bronze. "We are born of Earth. How does she escape if he takes her again?"

"You are born of Earth." Mavros turned toward me. He lifted his hand to my face and brushed his thumb along my eye socket. "But Dacia is more." He turned back toward Malcolm. "Demon and angel have taken root inside of her. She has our essence. You can see it in her eyes." He grabbed my hands in his, and a soft smile touched his lips. "If anyone from Earth can do this, it's you. Maybe this is what Khione meant when she said you were becoming more. Maybe you were destined to change so that you can beat Kieran."

I watched Cash morph back into his avatar and stride across the rocky, alien surface toward us. "Maybe." I took a deep breath to settle my nerves. "But, how do I use it? How do I get home?"

"Pull on the part of me that is still inside you."

I saw Mavros' sleeping serpent beneath my skin, but the thought of using it for anything terrified me. What if I woke it up again? What if it was too much, and the silver-haired fairies couldn't remove his taint from me? What if the demon essence took over and I was transformed? How much would it take before I was no longer me?

Mavros must have seen the fear on my face or in my posture. He squeezed my fingers. "You cannot undo what I've done to it, Dacia. The power lies dormant at my bidding. It will be no different than when you used my power to call to me when you were imprisoned."

He was a demon. Kieran warned me about the things Mavros had done, but still, I trusted him. I believed he would do what was right and not just what was right for him but what was right for me. It was that belief that had made the Nephilim so afraid of me, but they didn't know him like I did. So, once again, I put my faith in Mavros.

Closing my eyes, I focused on my power. The massive serpent slithered toward me. Blue, purple, pink, and gold shimmered over its pearlescent scales. My eyes widened, and I took a step back. The hair on my neck and arms stood on end. I imagined the snake attacking me like it had in the past. It wouldn't just leave bite marks on my shoulder. It would consume me whole.

"You've grown." I tried to keep my voice steady, to hide my fear.

You have been feeding me.

I cocked my head. "Feeding you? How?"

Every time you use me, I am nourished. It glided closer, and I held my hand out to it, letting it nestle its head against my fingers. *The dragon form makes me stronger.*

"I'm glad." I was surprised to find that the words were true. With my fingers sliding over the viper's scales, I kept walking. "I need to call on Mavros' power to see if it can help me return to Earth."

Why would you think he can do what I cannot? My magic bristled against the unintended insult.

I stopped moving and looked down into my serpent's black-flecked copper eyes. "Mavros believes that since he was not born or created or whatever on Earth and he is able to travel between the realms that I should be able to if I use his power to do it."

The serpent uncoiled, revealing Mavros' snake. The midnight scales sucked in the light around it. I stared into the shadows and wondered what I needed to do.

Kneeling next to it, I put my hand on top of its head. The only difference I noticed between the two vipers was their size. Mavros' power felt just like mine.

"I need you," I whispered. Thinking about my guards' apartment, I focused on the magic. I felt a tug on my gut like an invisible string was pulling me. My body collapsed in on itself, and I was sucked into a vortex. When everything settled, I was in the living room. A second later, Mavros stood beside me.

He held his hand out. "Now, take us back."

Slipping my fingers through his, I closed my eyes to focus. As soon as I did, I sucked in a deep breath and shuffled back a step.

Mavros slid his hand under my arm. "What is it?"

"I don't know why I didn't see it before. It makes total sense." I looked at him for a long moment before continuing. "I don't need to focus on your serpent to use your power. Your magic felt the same as mine because it's just as much a part of me as my power is."

He nodded at me the way a parent does to a child who has just figured out something that was obvious to the rest of the world. "Right. My power and the Nephilim's are part of you now. That's why you're becoming more."

"But, I've always pictured yours separately. It's always been its own in my mind. " I tugged my hand through my hair. "If it's part of me, I should be able to use it without focusing on it. I should be able to use it like I do my own."

Mavros twined his fingers through mine again. "Right, and you should use it now before the dragons go insane with worry."

Chapter 10

On A Wing And A Prayer

$\mathcal{M}$y foot bounced up and down. I tried to stop it, but my anxiety was too high. I should have skipped. There was no point in being here anyway. Max sat on the edge of his desk lecturing the students, but I didn't hear a single word he said.

The Nephilim were meeting me after class. Vicki, Diana, Olivia, and three others. Liam assured me that I had nothing to fear from them, but my thoughts kept returning to the cell I'd been trapped in. I imagined a faceless man making me drink his gold-flecked blood. I imagined him walking around my cage, placing wards. It wasn't Troy this time. This time the man had wings.

Not just any wings.

Wings I'd given him.

Malcolm held my hand. He hadn't let go of it since we left my apartment, but it wasn't enough. Even with his soothing energy flowing through me, my emotions wreaked havoc on the dragons. Their tension was palpable, but I couldn't stop thinking about being captured.

When Max excused class, my stomach flopped like a fish on the shore. I wasn't ready for this. I knew that the majority of the Nephilim had sided against Troy and Sebastian, but I also knew that several hadn't. How could I be sure I wasn't about to give one of them wings? How could I be sure they wouldn't use them against me?

Cash slung my backpack over his shoulder and led me to the door. As soon as we stepped into the hallway, Liam pulled me aside. "Don't do it, Dacia." He'd traded places with Seth today so that he could go with us to meet the Nephilim. "I'll tell them that you're not ready yet, that they need to earn your trust."

I clutched my hair at the top of my head. "Then they'll hate me even more." My voice sounded so small. Weak and pathetic. Just like I had been without my magic. I couldn't do it again. I couldn't let them take my freedom from me.

"They won't, Dacia." Determination flashed through his steel eyes. "I'll make them understand. I'll make them see what they did to you."

I shook my head. "They won't. They'll never see it that way. All they'll see is that I'm holding them back."

"I never should have asked." He pushed away from me, dropping his chin to his chest. "I should have told them that they don't deserve it." He looked up at me. "They don't. What they put you through …" He scrubbed his hand down his face. "You're going to do it anyway. Aren't you?"

Hoping he wouldn't notice how badly my hands were shaking, I shoved them into my pockets. "Yes."

He nodded, then led me outside to meet with the others. They surrounded me for the walk back to my apartment.

"Dacia."

I stopped at the sound of my name. My guards stepped closer, ready to protect me at all costs. Over Cash's shoulder, all I could see was dark hair. Knowing I couldn't move him, I looked through him like I would a door or a wall that was in my way. "Hey, Justin. What's up?"

"You got Cody and Bryce in there?" He grinned, and my guards eased up. "What about Dan?"

I stepped between Cash and Malcolm. "No, I think they're still in class."

"You guys up for a game tonight?"

Please. I sent the thought to all of my guards. I'd trained until well after dark last night, teleporting to and from other realms, bringing Cash and Malcolm along with me. I'd done it so many times that I could barely stand by the time we finally got back. As soon as I'd eaten supper, I'd crashed.

"Does 4:30 work for you?" Malcolm asked.

Justin nodded. "Yeah, that'd be great. Meet you there." He waved as he walked off.

"They better be quick learners," Malcolm said to Liam as he took ahold of my elbow.

I left a note for Cody and Dan, then teleported high up into the mountains. Judging by the lack of snow on their peaks, we were far from home. I walked to the edge and looked down. Lakes were scattered across the lush, green ground. Backing up, I slumped down on one of the many granite boulders that were scattered over the cliff. Within seconds, I was back on my feet, pacing between Malcolm and Cash.

We didn't have to wait much longer for portals to open up. Malcolm stepped between me and the incoming Nephilim, not hiding me from view, but not concealing the fact that he was protecting me either.

Vicki stepped through the first portal. She met my eyes for a second before searching for Liam. A loving smile covered her face when she found him. "Hello, Dacia," she said without looking away from him.

"Hi." I made no attempt to move toward her. Even if I'd wanted to, I didn't think Malcolm would allow it.

The next person through the portal was a blond man. He hugged Liam, slapping him on the back a few times. My nerves settled a little when I saw their interaction. Obviously, this was someone Liam had spent a lot of time with. Liam put his hand on the man's shoulder, turning him toward me. "Dacia, this is Nathaniel."

"Nathan'll do." He stepped forward and stuck his hand out.

I had to give him points for bravery. Not many people would come near Malcolm when he was in guard mode. "Howdy." I shook his hand. His grip was strong and steady.

As he walked away from me, I realized that he, at least, had come prepared. Long slits had been cut into the back of his shirt. Looking at the bare skin that was exposed, I shivered.

Even in the sun, we were up high enough that it was probably always cold here. I wondered if Nephilim were as hot-blooded as demons and dragons seemed to be.

The next man to step onto the summit was built a lot like Troy. His purple shirt wasn't near as tight, and his skin was much darker. He gave me a two-finger salute and said, "Zed."

I nodded, and he turned toward Liam. The two of them threw several fake punches at each other before shaking hands.

Olivia and Diana waved at me when they stepped through their portals. Liam's eyes seemed to light up when Olivia went to stand next to him. Not for the first time, I wondered what it would take to get the two of them together. I didn't have much time to think about it before the last person strode out. She had long, auburn hair, brown eyes, and a friendly smile. "Hi." She stood next to Olivia. "I'm Izzy." She lifted her hand, and red tinged her cheeks.

I waved back, watching the portals close. "This is it," I whispered. My stomach quivered in response, and I swallowed, forcing the lump in the back of my throat down. Looking at the people gathered around me, I wouldn't suspect any of them to turn on me, but I also wouldn't guess that any of them were something other than human. If I'd learned nothing else in the last couple of years, I had at least learned that looks were most definitely deceiving.

"So, how do we do this?" Vicki rubbed her hands together, ready to begin.

The shadows behind Cash stirred, and Mavros stepped out of them. Olivia took a step closer to Liam, but none of the other

Nephilim moved at all. "Before Dacia bestows this gift upon you, you will all need to make a solemn vow not to harm her."

"Okay." Nathan tilted his head to the side and lifted his hands. "To who? What's to keep any of us from breaking it?"

Mavros chuckled, and the sound reminded me of what he was. "A promise made to a demon is unbreakable."

Nathan and Izzy visibly paled, and Zed shot me an accusatory look.

"I didn't know he planned to do this." I held onto Malcolm's arm, hoping he could sense how much I needed him right now.

He put his hand on top of mine and whispered, "You're okay."

Liam walked to Mavros' side. "Mavros is a demon, but can you sense it on him? He is loyal to Dacia—" he patted Mavros on the back "—and he is a friend to me." Liam unfurled his wings. The tan and cream feathers ruffled in the light breeze. "If you don't promise, you don't get wings. It's as simple as that."

Vicki nodded and stepped forward. "What is your true name?"

"It turns out Mavros Malkin works just fine." He glanced at me, and I remembered promising not to use ice on him. I hadn't even had to say the words while I was awake. Saying them in a dream had been enough to bind me to the vow.

"What is it they need to say?" Liam asked.

Mavros' grin was wicked, and I hoped he wasn't about to cause trouble. "Mavros Malkin, I, insert your full name here, vow upon my honor to never inflict mental or physical harm on

Dacia KayLee Wolf. I promise to defend her from those who wish to hurt her if it is within my ability." He turned toward me. "Is that good enough?"

I nodded. I couldn't believe he'd planned this without saying anything to me about it. It never even would have occurred to me.

The Nephilim made the vow without any arguments and without trying to manipulate the wording. As I walked past Mavros, I grabbed his hand and squeezed it. "Thank you." Tears of gratitude filled my eyes, but I wiped them away before they could fall. Looking at Vicki, I said, "I think I can do this to two of you at a time. So, who's first?"

Vicki and Zed stepped toward me. I grabbed their hands, took a deep breath, closed my eyes, and sent healing energy into them. When I'd given Liam his wings, he had been severely injured. Without having to knit together damaged tissue and mend broken bones, my magic worked much quicker. Before they'd had time to decide if they were making the right choice, they both screamed out in pain. Vicki dropped to her knees as blue-gray, dusty-rose, and white wings burst from her shoulders. The bird that came to mind when I saw them was a great blue heron.

Zed steadied himself against a boulder. His face twisted as pain racked his body, and wings like an eagle's exploded from his back.

Liam grabbed Vicki's hand and helped her to her feet. Then he turned to Zed. "Ready to fly?"

I didn't pay any attention to them after that. My part in their adventure was over. Now, it was up to Liam and the dragons to teach them to soar. "Who's next?"

Diana and Olivia looked at each other and shrugged. They slowly walked over. Olivia slid her hand into mine, and I felt hers shaking.

Diana smiled at me. "Thank you for doing this, Dacia." She clutched my fingers.

I could see the fear on both of their faces, and after seeing how Vicki and Zed had reacted, I couldn't blame them. "You're welcome." Now that I knew Nathan, Zed, and Izzy couldn't turn on me, it was easier for me to say it and actually mean it.

Closing my eyes, I focused on nature and rebirth. Healing energy flowed down my arms, through my fingertips, and into each of them.

Diana screamed. The sound jolted me, but I held on while wings tore through her shoulders. She bent over, panting for a moment before she looked at the ivory and butter-colored feathers like a yellow cockatiel's.

I clutched Olivia's hand in both of mine. Something was straining my magic. With no injuries to mend, this shouldn't be taking so long. It had taken her longer to trust me, and I wondered if something in her was fighting against my power. I pushed harder, forcing my energy into her.

As I watched, her skin gained a healthy glow that I hadn't realized had been missing. She sighed in relief, and a peaceful smile settled on her lips.

My eyebrows pinched together. "Are you okay?" I finally asked.

"I think I am now." She settled her other hand on top of mine. "I've been sick a lot lately." Her grip tightened on my fingers, and I thought she was going to pull me over. The wings that burst into sight were speckled like a flicker's feathers. She let go of me, resting her hands on her knees. "Thank you."

Nathan sauntered across the rocky outcrop toward me. There was something about him that, despite his size, made him seem friendly instead of intimidating. He took in my measure, smiling when his cornflower blue eyes met mine. "I can see why Liam stayed."

Crimson heat burned my cheeks, and I imagined my whole face was scarlet.

Before I could think of anything to say in response, Nathan was continuing, "A beautiful girl who hangs with demons and dragons"—he held out his hand, waiting for me to take it—"the excitement must be unending."

I resisted the urge to run my fingers through my hair and turn away from his gaze. Before he could see how uneasy I was, I grabbed his hand. "Yeah, most days."

"Ignore him." Izzy shot me a conspiratorial grin. "He *loves* to hear himself talk, and if he can be the center of attention, you better believe he will be."

"Ouch, Iz, you're breaking my heart." He placed his palm over his chest and looked deeply wounded.

She shook her head and held my extended hand. "If only you had one."

Their playful banter melted away the last of my concern. The two of them seemed like people I would enjoy hanging out with. I could easily picture them as college students at Phlox University. They would be a blast to have in my classes.

My magic rushed into them, abruptly ending their teasing. Nathan threw his head back and roared at the sky. Massive, white wings exploded from his shoulders. The feathers were tipped with black, like a snowy owl's.

Izzy clutched my hand in a vise-like grip. She barely whimpered when her wings tore through her skin. They were mottled brown on the back. When she opened them, the insides were pale with russet speckles. Immediately, bringing to mind an image of a red-tailed hawk.

Before he walked away, Nathan patted my shoulder hard enough to knock me off balance. "Maybe I'll stop by someday. I could use an adventure."

"I, uh, I'm sure Liam would love to see you."

He laughed and swaggered to the edge of the cliff.

"Thank you for this, Dacia." Izzy held her hand out to me, and I shook it. "It truly is a gift you've given us."

"You're welcome." I smiled at her, then nodded toward the others. "Flying's amazing."

"I can't wait to try it. Are you going to join us?"

I chewed on my lip, glancing at Malcolm. My emotions had taken a toll on him today. Seeing me with angel wings would probably send him over the edge. Glancing back at Izzy, I wondered how the Nephilim would take seeing me as a dragon. "No." I shook my head. "Not today."

Her shoulders slumped, reminding me of a deflated balloon. "Oh, okay. Thanks again." She turned away, and her demeanor changed almost instantly. She practically skipped over to where Liam and Nathan were waiting for her so they could join the others gliding over the mountains.

I plopped down on a boulder. Exhaustion weighed heavily on me. It wasn't from using my magic. Giving the Nephilim wings hadn't taxed my power. I blamed my fatigue on the adrenaline finally leaving my system. I had been dreading this all day. Now that it was over, I could let go.

Bracing my elbows on my knees, I looked around, surprised by the space the dragons had given me after the Nephilim had taken to the skies. As high-strung as I'd been this morning, I imagined they needed time away from me and my emotions. Up here, high above the world, they were probably better able to get away from my scent.

Leaning back, I closed my eyes and let the sun caress my face. I hoped for the day when all of the Nephilim would be able to see me as an ally and not a threat. A gentle breeze blew over my skin, lulling me to sleep.

Feet pounded against the ground, heading toward me. I jolted up and blinked several times until I could see what was going on. A heavy weight settled in my stomach when I saw the bright light that flared between me and my guardians. Malcolm disappeared, reforming in front of me. He reached back, grabbing my arm.

My heart thundered in my chest. "No, no, no." I peeked around his body, needing to be prepared for whatever was about to happen.

The Nephilim flew toward us, and I couldn't help but wonder if it was a result of the vow they'd made or if they were genuinely concerned for me. Nathan, Vicki, and Liam looked like they were prepared to go to battle. The others seemed to be confused as they watched the portal opening.

When they landed and their wings disappeared, all but Liam stumbled forward. He glanced back at the others. "You'll get used to it."

The portal grew until it was taller than me. I clutched Malcolm's sweater in a white-knuckled grip, remembering the agonized cry that had ripped through me when Liam had tried to carry me through one. Troy's blood had stained my lips. Its coppery taste had still been fresh in my mouth, but Mavros' magic had prevented them from taking me to the sanctuary.

A man with thinning white hair and a thick mustache stepped out. Malcolm growled, but the man just shot him a tight-lipped smile.

"Jim." Vicki rushed forward at the same time that Liam said, "Grampa?"

The portal shrunk and blinked out of existence. Vicki jogged through where it had been and stood in front of the man. "Dacia, Malcolm, this is my husband, Jim." She turned toward him and lowered her voice. "You said you weren't coming."

"I know, but I finished." He twisted his wedding band around his finger while watching us over her shoulder. "I decided wings could be fun."

Vicki turned back toward me. "Dacia, would you be willing—"

"He has to swear the oath." Mavros didn't let her finish. "Then Dacia can decide."

Liam strode toward me. Stopping in front of Malcolm whose sweater was still clenched in my hand, he bowed his head and closed his eyes. "He's my grampa, Dacia. He can be trusted." He rubbed his jaw. "It would mean a lot to me if you'd give him wings."

I nodded, and my guardians backed off to give me space.

After Mavros made Jim recite the vow, I took his hand in mine. My magic rushed into him, and his green eyes twinkled with excitement. His grip tightened, and a low groan escaped through his clenched jaw. Gray and black wings like a sandhill crane's tore through his shoulder blades. He pulled me into a quick hug. "Thank you." Tears sparkled in his eyes as he stepped back.

Liam and Vicki hurried over. Liam held his hand under Jim's elbow to keep him steady. "Ready to fly, Papa?"

"I was born to do this." He smiled at Vicki and then at Liam. They jumped off the cliff, and the rest of the Nephilim followed.

Mavros strode toward me from the side. Without turning, I watched him. His hands were shoved in his pockets, and the wind tousled his hair. He stood next to me with his arm touching mine. "They won't be able to harm you. I won't let them out of it."

"Thank you for that." I watched the eight Nephilim race through the sky. "Why didn't you tell me?"

He pulled one of his hands out of his pocket and slid his fingers into mine. They were warm and comforting. I welcomed his touch. "I didn't think about it until they stepped out of the portals. I kept trying to figure out how to help you. Then as soon as I saw them, I realized I could just be myself." His thumb brushed over the top of mine. "Believe it or not, I'm not accustomed to forcing people into binding oaths." He turned so that he was in front of me. "You were the exception." His eyes softened, and my breath hitched in response. "You're always the exception."

ဆ10503

Chapter 11

*L*iam landed in front of me, and his wings disappeared. "Ready?" he asked.

I tipped my head to the side. "You don't have to go back with us. You can stay with your friends and family."

"And miss playing basketball with you?" He rubbed his hand along his jaw. "I think I better be on your team today, though."

Malcolm, Cash, and Mavros walked over to us. I assumed Jax was with them, but I hadn't seen or sensed him all day.

There had been times when Malcolm thought different people would be better suited to be on my team or to be guarding me, but this time, it just didn't make sense to me. "Why?"

"Unless you want to let Justin in on everything, it'll be hard to explain how my scars disappeared." He lifted one shoulder toward his ear. "Sometimes, if I catch my reflection just right, I have to do a double-take. It's hard for me to believe they're not there anymore."

"Okay." I placed my hand on Malcolm's, and the others followed. Malcolm teleported us to his apartment. Everyone else pulled away, but he held onto me, stopping me from leaving. "You did good today, Dacia." He squeezed my shoulder, then left his hand there as he led me across the hall. "You gained four more allies."

"Only because Mavros made them swear." As soon as the words were out, I realized that I sounded ungrateful. Heat blossomed on my cheeks. "I didn't mean it like that."

"No, I know you didn't." Malcolm chuckled as he opened my door. "And, that's not why. You gave them a gift they'd never dared to even dream about. You earned their loyalty." He ushered me inside.

Cassandra and Samantha were nowhere to be seen, but books and paper were strewn across the table. Cody, Dan, and Bryce were playing video games and talking smack to each other. Cody glanced up at me, lifting one side of his mouth in a half-hearted smile. "All good?"

"Yeah." I pointed at my door. "I'm gonna change." I walked into my room and stood in front of my dresser with the drawer open. My hand hovered over the t-shirts I usually wore when I played basketball. There would be no hiding the tree if I had one of them on, but I'd tried playing in long sleeves before. For some reason, they always messed up my shots.

I stood there for too long, debating what to wear. If I could see it, I was afraid Kieran's curse would be a huge distraction, but if my shots were off, I would be frustrated the whole time. Finally, I yanked out a t-shirt and went into the bathroom to change, pulling on sweats over my clothes for the walk to the court.

"Are you okay without me?" Russ asked when I stepped out of my room. His amber eyes met mine. They were filled with hope, and whether I needed him or not, I wouldn't have been able to deny him.

I nodded. "Go. Spend time with your son."

"Thank you," he said before he disappeared.

Cassandra and Samantha sat at the table. Cassandra was shaking her hands. "They're just about dry." She flashed her fingernails at me. From the quick glimpse I got of them, they looked like a professional had painted them. The way they faded from blue to pink reminded me of a sunset.

I looked down at my nails. They were shorter than they had ever been. Before demons, dragons, and faeries, I'd let them grow. I'd painted them. I'd cared what they looked like, but now, my time was spent training, researching, and fighting.

When the guys finished their race, we all got ready to go. Before we stepped out of the door, Mavros threaded his fingers through mine. Cody strode down the hallway and stairwells behind us, but as soon as we walked outside, he moved up beside me and draped his arm over my shoulder. I couldn't help but wonder if people thought we were in a polyamorous relationship. The thought made my stomach queasy. Cody was all I wanted, but I could see how easily Mavros' attention could be misconstrued.

"Yo, Justin," Dan yelled, breaking me away from my thoughts.

"Hey." I could hear a smile in his voice even though I couldn't see it. "Looks like you got enough players. Who are the captains today?" He fell into step with our group.

He had to know there was a reason why certain guards were on my team or defended me, but he never asked. He just went with the flow.

"I'm one," Liam said. "I'll take Dacia."

Mavros squeezed my fingers. "I got Justin."

The teams were set by the time we got to the gym. Mavros' team pulled their shirts off and piled them on the floor next to Samantha and Cassandra. I took my sweatpants off and stood there for a minute, staring into the air, debating whether or not I should pull my sweatshirt off.

"Hey," Samantha got up and placed her hand on my shoulder. "Are you okay?"

"I, uh—" I dragged my fingers through my hair and tried to smile at her "—yeah, sure." I tugged my sweatshirt over my head and threw it down before I could change my mind. The tree covered my skin from my wrist to my elbow. Its branches wrapped around the back of my arm. I pressed my hand to it, splaying my fingers over it to hide as much of it as possible.

Samantha glanced down, then into my eyes. A sad, knowing smile lifted her lips. "It'll be okay."

"Thanks." When I turned around, I realized everyone was waiting for me.

Justin looked from my face to my arm and whistled through his teeth. "Sweet tattoo."

I pinched my eyes shut as I stepped onto the court. "Thanks," I said, trying hard not to grimace.

Everyone but Mavros had a defender on them already, so I took my place in front of him, waiting for him to throw the ball in. As soon as he'd chosen Justin, I knew he would be sticking close to me.

I fought the urge to cover the tree with my hand, lifting my arms into the air instead. Everyone but Justin had seen the curse before. They all knew what it was, and now, he thought I had a tattoo.

I took a deep breath and watched Mavros. Part of the reason I liked playing basketball was because it helped me forget the weirdness of my life, so instead of focusing on the oak, I worried about the game. Mavros threw the ball in to Justin, and I jogged down the court, trying to knock the ball loose a couple of times before giving up and positioning myself between Mavros and the hoop.

When Dan threw the ball to him, I deflected it, sending it bouncing down the court. I sprinted after it, but Bryce got there first. He passed it to Justin, and their team scored.

We'd been playing for nearly an hour when Justin and I both dove for the ball. He gasped and let go of it. I tossed it to Malcolm and looked at Justin. "You okay?"

He stared at my arm. "It's moving. How's it moving?"

"Muscle twitch." I slapped my hand down over the curse, hoping he would believe me.

His eyebrows drew together, but he nodded and helped me to my feet. His laugh was forced. "I thought I was going crazy for a minute there." He jogged next to me until he split off to guard Cody.

Malcolm threw the ball to me, and Cash set a pick on Mavros. I dribbled a couple of steps to my right and sunk my shot. Cash and Mavros ran down the court with me. "Are you okay?" Cash asked.

"As long as it doesn't move again." I chewed on my lip. "I can make it stay like this. It shouldn't drain me too much."

Cash nodded and went to stand at the bottom of the key. Seth waited until we were in position to throw the ball in to Justin.

A half an hour later, Cassandra stood up. She pressed the back of her hand against her forehead and leaned against the wall like a damsel in distress. "I'm wasting away over here," she said with a drawl while fluttering her eyes. "And, I'm in dire need of my man's attention."

Bryce chuckled. "I guess that's my cue. Good game, guys." He walked to her with his arms spread wide. His skin glistened, and the hair on the nape of his neck was soaked.

She squealed and ran off before he could hug her. "Eww. You're all sweaty and gross."

I wrapped my arm around Cody's waist, and he threw his over my shoulders. We were both soaked in sweat, so it didn't bother me at all. We stayed that way as we strolled over to where Cassandra and Samantha had been sitting. Cody let go of me, kissed my forehead, then bent down to grab his clothes.

As soon as my sweatshirt was on, I released the magic that had been keeping the tree from moving. A month ago, holding that form for as long as I had would have worn me out, but my training was paying off. My stamina was building back up to what it had been when I was hiding from the Nephilim and running with Malcolm in the caves.

"Are we too sweaty and gross to eat with you?" I asked. "We can shower first, but I'm afraid you might perish before we finish."

She wrinkled her nose and shivered. "You're all disgusting. I don't know why anybody would want to get sweaty." She hooked her arm through Samantha's and led the way to the door. "Sam will have to sit next to me so I can turn my head toward her and breathe if I have to."

When we stepped outside, the cold air soothed my overheated skin. Gazing up at the star-filled sky, I tugged my sleeves up. "What a beautiful night." I looked down at the sidewalk to make sure I didn't fall, noticed the oak on my arm, and jerked my sleeve down to my wrist, covering as much of the curse as I could. I might have been able to persuade Justin that the tree hadn't moved, but I wouldn't be able to convince a cafeteria full of students.

Mavros stayed beside me while I grabbed my supper, putting foods from the same area onto his plate. Then he followed me to the table, taking the seat next to me. Cody came over and sat on the other side.

From across the table, Justin pointed his fork at me. "Why keep that awesome tattoo covered?"

"I, uh, I never should've gotten it." I ran my hand over my sleeve and wondered if I somehow managed to break the curse, would the tree still be there? "I don't like being the center of attention." I hoped he would let it go at that.

He picked up his glass. "You're going to have to tell me who did it before I get mine done. The detail in it is amazing."

"I did." Kieran pulled a chair over and sat between Samantha and Cassandra.

I hated that he was close enough to my friends to tell what brand of perfume they were wearing. He could easily grab them and whisk them away, and there would be nothing I could do to stop it from happening. "Kieran," I said, fighting to keep my voice steady, "what are you doing here?"

He picked up a grape off of Samantha's plate and popped it into his mouth. "I wanted to see how you were holding up after our game yesterday." He snatched another grape and stood up. "It looks like you're ready for round two." He walked off, whistling a bouncy song.

"Did he really do your tattoo?" Justin turned in his chair, watching Kieran leave.

Holding my head in my hands, I rubbed my temples. "You know there are things I can't tell you, right?"

"Yeah."

I met his eyes. Confusion filled their russet depths. "Stay away from him. He's bad news."

Chapter 12

Waiting

I lay in bed afraid to close my eyes. Kieran said I was ready for round two. I didn't know if he would try to take me in my dreams or if he would drag me out of one of my classes. I knew I would be able to get away from him, but what repercussions would I face if I did?

"Dacia." Malcolm's voice was feral. "Please."

"Help me sleep then." I rolled onto my side and wrapped my arm around Cody. "Don't let him take me, Mavros."

He nodded at me. "Your wish."

A couple minutes later, it was a struggle to keep my eyes open. I fell asleep to the steady rhythm of Cody's breath.

I woke up without the lingering grogginess that usually accompanied me and snuggled against him. His arms wrapped around me, and besides being well-rested, I felt safe and loved.

My eyes snapped open when I realized he was on the wrong side of me. Cody faced me, and a storm raged in his sapphire eyes. I looked over my shoulder, knowing who would be there before I saw him. "What the hell, Mavros?"

He chuckled and slid out of bed. With the warmth of his body gone, I shivered and pulled the covers around me. "Why?" I looked at Malcolm, hoping he could explain why I had woken up sandwiched between Cody and Mavros.

"It was the only way to keep Kieran from you." Malcolm's voice was gruff. He was going to have to leave soon. "He's getting more aggressive."

Mavros leaned against my dresser with his arms crossed over his chest. "You asked me not to let him take you."

"I need to figure this out." I pinched my eyes shut and rubbed the bridge of my nose. "I have no idea how to stop the leaves from falling, and I'm running out of time." I let out a deep breath and looked from Mavros to Malcolm. "Can you guys leave us for a little bit?"

As soon as they were gone, I rolled onto my side, propping myself up on my elbow. "I'm sorry, Cody."

"Yeah, I know." He threw his arm over his eyes, hiding the pain that I'd seen in them. "Can't let Kieran take you, but ..." His words trailed off. He didn't need to finish anyway. It would tear me apart to see him in somebody else's arms. It couldn't be any easier for him, especially knowing what Mavros wanted from me once Cody was gone.

I snuggled up against him, sliding one arm under his pillow and draping the other over him. "I only want you, Cody." I kissed the base of his neck. "I'm supposed to be super powerful, but I can't even fight off Kieran in my dreams. How am I going to beat him?"

He brushed my hair back and held me, relaxing a little as he did. "Don't know, but you have to." He nudged my nose with his until I tilted my face up. Staring into my eyes, he said, "Can't lose you." He wrapped his leg around mine, pulling me closer to him. His hands tightened their hold on me right before his mouth crashed against mine.

Warmth spread throughout my body. Thoughts of Mavros disappeared. My fingers glided over Cody's back, trailing up his spine and over his ribs.

He clutched me to him with one arm and braced his other on the bed, rolling me onto my back. Propping himself above me, he kissed me tenderly, then leaned his forehead against mine. "I love you, Dacia." He brushed his thumb over the exposed skin at my waist, sending a jolt of electricity zipping through my body. "I'll do whatever it takes to keep you safe." His eyes darkened, and his lips pressed into a thin line. "Even seeing you with him."

"I love you too, Cody." I slid my hand from his shoulder to his cheek, holding his face, hoping he could see that I meant it. "Always."

His expression softened. "Should get up." His husky voice made heat coil in my stomach.

"Not yet." I pulled his face down, nudging his arm with my elbow until he lowered his body onto mine. My lips brushed over his, a feather-light touch before I pulled away.

His hands slid into my hair. Ever so slowly, he brought his mouth down on mine. Touching, exploring.

I wrapped my arms around his back, clinging to him, wanting nothing more than to stay here with him all day, but I knew our time alone would end all too soon.

Cody pulled back and rolled onto the bed next to me. He gave me a quick peck on the cheek, then said, "Gotta shower."

I watched him walk out the door, thinking that if he felt at all like I did, it would be a cold shower.

I sat in Introduction to Fiction surrounded by guards, but if Kieran showed up again today, they wouldn't be able to stop him from taking me. They most likely wouldn't even be able to move. My foot tapped a staccato beat, and I spent most of the time watching the door instead of paying attention to Dr. Yarrow.

When class was over, I unclenched my fingers. They tingled as blood rushed through them. I leaned back in my chair for a while, knowing I wouldn't be able to stand on my wobbly legs.

Seth watched me. His expression was stoic, completely unreadable. "This is what he wants, Dacia." He waved his hand at Malcolm and Cash. "They're riled up. You're jumpy. Fairies love to cause mischief. They thrive on mayhem."

"But how do I not let it get to me?" There was an edge to my voice that wasn't normally there. "Just waiting around to be taken—" I ran my fingers through the top of my hair, then clutched my head "—the suspense is killing me."

Mavros held his hand out. "Let's go."

While I put my coat on, Cash grabbed my backpack. He'd started carrying it for me most days. After the first few times, I'd given up on trying to get it back.

As we stepped into the hallway, Mavros draped his arm over my shoulders. Cash, Malcolm, Seth, and presumably Jax surrounded us. Maybe my emotions were a lot for the dragons to handle, but apparently, I wasn't the only one who was concerned.

Tiny snowflakes drifted down, barely visible against the light gray sky. By the time we were halfway back to the apartments, the flakes had grown and multiplied. The wind picked up, whipping the falling snow into our faces.

"Dacia"—Mavros tightened his grip on me—"if this is your doing, relax."

I took a deep breath and slowly released it through my mouth. My emotions hadn't affected the weather in a long time. I wasn't sure if the snow was falling now because of me or not, but if it was, I was determined to put an end to it. I rolled my neck and focused on my mountain lake while letting the dragons lead me. When I opened my eyes, nothing had changed. "I don't think it's me."

"You are far from relaxed." Malcolm didn't look at me when he said it, and a glance at him explained why. His muscles were rigid, his hands were in tight fists, and if he clenched his jaw any harder, he would probably shatter all of his teeth.

Seth opened the door to the apartment building and ushered all of us inside. "Take her to her room."

Cash grabbed hold of my hand, and a blink later, we stood next to my bed. Mavros pulled his arm away, and the three of us walked into the living room.

"What now?" I asked as I pulled my gloves off and shoved them into my pockets.

Cash shrugged. "I imagine we train."

"What if Kieran shows up there?" The last time that happened, Malcolm ran Liam and me until we could barely stand.

Mavros looked at me like I was a puzzle that needed to be solved. "I could take you to another realm to train, but Kieran might be able to find you there."

"How?" I asked at the same time the rest of my guardians joined us.

"He never should have been able to find you that day." He watched me, keeping his words soft and slow. "Malcolm took us somewhere new."

Malcolm folded his arms over his chest and leaned against the wall, but he was anything but relaxed. "He's tracking you, Dacia."

"If he can travel to all the realms that I can, it won't do any good to take you to one."

I let Mavros' words settle in. "Then we need to stay on this one to train." I paced behind the couch, hoping that I wouldn't accidentally run into Jax. "If you take me to another realm and he follows us, he could take you and me and leave the dragons stranded there."

I trained. I went to Graphic Design. I went to the cafeteria for dinner with my friends. I went back to my apartment.

And no Kieran.

Not even a glimpse of him.

Every time somebody had walked by me, I had stared at them through wide, suspicious eyes. Every noise I had heard made me jump around, looking for the source. My nerves were shot, and if it was possible, the dragons were worse.

Cody and I sat on the couch, but I couldn't relax. As much as I didn't want Kieran to take me, I wanted it done with.

Samantha and Dan were nestled together in one of the armchairs. Her legs were tossed over his, and she had an open book on her lap. Normally, her nose would be buried in it, but she watched me instead. "I'm not finding anything helpful in any of these books."

"Neither have I." I rubbed my hand up and down Cody's thigh, trying to bring some comfort to myself. "I think I'll either have to stumble on a solution or live in Faerie."

Cody looked around me at Mavros. "Your cats find anything?"

"Not yet." He shook his head. "I'm either going to have to recruit more help or go back myself."

I thought about the seemingly unending forest Kieran had taken me to. With all of those trees, it would be nearly impossible to stumble on one specific oak. "Wait." My fingers dug into Cody's leg when I stopped moving my hand. "You said you're looking in Spring, right?"

"Yes." An inscrutable look covered his face. "Kieran is a member of the Spring Court."

"But he made it sound like it's always Spring there." I rubbed my arm where the curse hid beneath my sweatshirt. "He said the leaves would turn the color of my hair, then fall."

Mavros looked at me like I'd grown three heads, and I decided it was time to try it. My neck stretched, and a head branched out above each shoulder.

Cody jerked his arm away and stared at me. "What're you doing?"

I nodded at Mavros, and my heads knocked into each other like wind chimes in a strong gust. "Well, he was looking at me like I was a freak, so I became one." I transformed back into myself and rubbed my neck while waiting for Mavros to say something.

"There are places in Faerie"—Mavros stared straight ahead, not focusing on anything in the room but perhaps on a memory—"on the edges of the realms, separating the Seelie and Unseelie Courts. The solitary fae live there, and the seasons change as they do here." He turned to me and shook his head. "That's where I should have been looking all along. Do not go to sleep until I return." He disappeared without another word.

Dan clapped his hands, then rubbed them together. "So, do you wanna watch a movie or play a game, or do you have some other idea to keep you awake?" He wagged his eyebrows at us.

"Dan!" Samantha smacked him on the chest.

He grabbed her hand and kissed her knuckles. "What?" He shot her one of his award-winning smiles.

"If I sit here, I'm more likely to sleep—" I yawned to emphasize my point "—so let's play something."

Cash and Liam joined Cody and me against Dan, Samantha, Malcolm, and Seth in Pictionary. Seth hadn't played it before, but he caught on quickly and even seemed to enjoy himself.

At midnight, I wrapped my arms around Cody's neck and pulled him close to me. "Happy birthday."

"Thanks." He hugged me back. "Gonna be a long day if Mavros doesn't get back soon."

I looked at my friends, feeling guilty for keeping them up so late. Samantha didn't have class as early as the rest of us, but they all needed their sleep. "You guys can go to bed. Malcolm, Cash, and Seth can keep me awake."

Samantha stretched her arms above her head. "I think I'll take you up on that." She stood and looked at Dan.

He pushed his chair back. "See you guys in the morning."

Cody looked at me. His eyes were bloodshot, and he struggled to keep them open. "I'm done for."

"It's okay." I rubbed his arm. "Get some sleep. I'll be in as soon as I can."

The rest of us stayed up until after 3:00, waiting for Mavros to return. When he finally did, my eyes were so heavy I could barely keep them open.

Mavros reached his hand down to me. "The cats are all searching the outlands now." I slipped my fingers into his, and he pulled me to my feet. "Depending on where the tree is, it could be days or months before the leaves begin to turn."

"Days?" I swallowed hard.

Mavros led me to my room, and the dragons disappeared. "Or months."

Chapter 13

When my alarm clock blared at me to get up, I felt like my head had just hit the pillow. I peeled my eyes open and looked up into Cody's face. He had been sound asleep when I climbed into bed with him. "Happy birthday," I mumbled.

"Favorite one yet."

My eyebrows pulled together in confusion.

"First one I woke up with you." His gentle fingers trailed from my hairline, along the side of my face, and down my neck.

A tiny sigh of pleasure broke loose from me, making Cody tug me closer to him. He kissed my forehead, the tip of my nose, and then my lips, gently exploring my mouth.

Footsteps padded across my room. When the door shut, I assumed Mavros had left us alone. The lack of commentary must have been his gift to Cody.

I lifted onto my elbow and drew tiny circles on Cody's chest. Goosebumps trailed my touch. "After class, we're going out."

"No training?" He raised his eyebrows and pinched his lips together.

I shook my head. "Not today."

He grinned and pushed himself up so that our faces were even. Sliding his hand along my spine, he clutched the back of my head and pulled me toward him.

Mavros sat on the couch with his arms spread over the back of it. There were no dragons in sight, but that didn't mean Jax wasn't there.

"What do you want for breakfast?" I asked.

Cody squeezed my fingers. "I'll get it."

"No. It's your birthday. I'll make it." I opened the fridge. "Omelet, bacon and eggs, pancakes, French toast?"

"Surprise me," he said before disappearing into his room.

Cody had always been a meat and potatoes kind of guy, so I decided he would probably rather have a protein-filled breakfast than a sweet one. I pulled out the ingredients for an omelet. "Do you want one?" I held the eggs, ham, and cheese out for Mavros to see.

"If you don't mind." He nodded. "I can help."

"No, I want to do this on my own." Cutting the ham into cubes, I silently thanked my parents for teaching me how to cook. It would never be my favorite past-time, but I was grateful that I knew how. So many students here had no idea how to toast bread let alone make a meal.

While the ham sizzled in the pan, I grabbed plates and forks and set three glasses on the table. I frowned at the third place setting, hoping that Cody wouldn't mind Mavros joining us.

"I'll eat in the living room." Mavros' hand covered the glass. "Give you a little space."

A sad smile tugged on my lips. I didn't know if my life would always be a juggling act or if I would eventually be able to live without someone constantly watching over my shoulder, but Cody deserved better. He deserved a normal life. "Thanks."

Cody's hair was wet, and he was clean-shaven when he stepped out of his room. He pulled on a sweatshirt as he made his way toward me. While I slid his omelet out of the pan and onto his plate, I watched him, wondering how I'd gotten so lucky to have him in my life.

He wrapped his arm around my waist and kissed my forehead, taking his plate out of my hand. "Smells good."

By the time the next omelet was cooked, Cody had finished his. I tried to give the eggs to Mavros, but he shook his head. "You eat it. I'll make my own." I sat next to Cody and took a bite.

"What're we doing tonight?" He leaned back in his chair and watched me.

I held my finger in front of my mouth while I finished chewing, then I wiped my lips off with the napkin before saying, "Going out."

"Okay." He nodded as he drew the word out. "Where?"

"Somewhere." I took another bite, hoping he wouldn't ask anything else.

He pushed his plate to the side and folded his arms on the table. "That's … vague."

"Don't worry. You'll like it." I took a drink of milk, watching him over the rim of the glass.

He waited until I finished, then said, "You'll be there?"

"Yeah."

The smile that spread over his face made the butterflies in my stomach take flight. "It'll be perfect."

When I finished eating, Mavros grabbed my plate and offered to do the dishes while I got ready for class. There wasn't enough time for me to shower, so I got dressed, braided my hair, and brushed my teeth. As soon as I stepped out of my room, Mavros slipped his hand into mine.

Cody clenched his jaw, then looked away while rubbing his chest.

My heart sank. I knew this had to hurt him, but I didn't know what else to do. One corner of my mouth lifted in a sad smile. "Don't forget. We're going out after class."

"I won't." He blew out a breath and walked over to us. "Keep her safe."

Mavros nodded. "With my life."

"Love you, Dacia."

I wrapped one arm around him and breathed in his wintry scent before brushing my lips over his. "I love you, too."

Malcolm and Mavros stared straight ahead. They didn't notice Kieran bounding toward me. Each step he took made his sable hair flop over his yellow eyes, but he never pulled his gaze from me. His lips curled into a mischievous grin. "Miss me?" he asked as he came to a stop right in front of me. "Don't answer that." He stretched his hand out toward me. When I didn't take it, he said, "We have another game to play."

I pinched my eyebrows together, guessing that I couldn't talk without being overheard by all of my classmates.

"Didn't I tell you?" He rubbed his chin like he was deep in thought. "Seven games. Each time you lose, the leaves will get a little closer to falling."

I felt my eyes widen and bit down on my cheek to keep from saying something.

He stared at my arm as if he could see through my sleeve. "I had to save you from the kelpie in our first game, so that's a win for me." He licked his finger and marked a line in the air in front of him. It shimmered before breaking apart into gold dust and sprinkling down on me.

I jerked my sleeve up and watched as red tipped the edges of the leaves. My heart raced, and my breath hitched, but I tried to hide my reaction from him.

He leaned down and whispered, "It's only a matter of time." Then he straightened and held his hand out. "Why delay the inevitable?"

I grabbed my pen and scribbled, "Not today," on a sheet of paper. Before looking up at him, I hurriedly added, "Tomorrow."

He clutched my desk and brought his face level with mine. "You'd better be ready bright and early."

I nodded, and as soon as he turned around, I slumped down in my chair.

Mavros grabbed my notepad, and flames danced in his eyes. "Tomorrow?" The word was growled.

"It's Cody's birthday." I tucked my hands into my armpits to hide their trembling. "I couldn't let him take me today."

He tossed the notebook onto my desk. It slid across the smooth surface and fell onto the floor.

Malcolm bent to pick it up but stopped with his face next to my arm. He grabbed ahold of it and flipped it over, exposing the tree. Staring at the turning leaves, he asked, "When?"

"Apparently, I lost the first game." My voice rose toward the end of my sentence.

Professor Natterjack looked at me over the top of his wire-rimmed glasses. When his eyes met mine, his pinched lips softened. "Are you okay, Dacia?"

The majority of the students turned to look at me. Tears that I hoped they didn't notice slipped from my eyes. I clamped my mouth shut and nodded.

He lifted his eyebrow, clearly not believing me but returned to his lecture.

I tugged my sleeve down, covering the oak, then wiped my eyes.

When class ended, I sat at my desk, waiting for everyone else to leave. Several students glanced at me over their shoulders, but none of them were brave enough to approach.

Once the room was mostly cleared out, I headed to the door with my eyes lowered. I could sense Mavros' disappointment, but I hadn't known what to do when Kieran showed up to take me away.

"Dacia."

I jumped at the sound of Professor Natterjack's voice.

He chuckled. It sounded like it was more to relax the situation than out of humor. "I didn't mean to startle you." His brown eyes softened, making him look much younger. "I know you said you were okay, but … are you?"

I lifted one shoulder and opened my mouth to answer, but the words didn't come out.

"All of us teachers, we know there are things"—he waved his hand at my friends—"about you that you can't tell us, but if you need anything, let me know."

"Thanks." I appreciated his concern, but I couldn't open up to anyone else. There were already too many people in on my secret. "I'll be fine. I, uh, I just have moments." I looked down at my boots. "I didn't mean to disrupt class."

He took his glasses off and cleaned the lenses with the bottom of his button-down shirt. "No worries."

Mavros pressed his hand against the small of my back and ushered me into the hallway. As soon as we stepped outside, the dragons surrounded us. Malcolm set a brisk pace that I had to jog to keep up with. Thankfully, the walk from Quartz Building to the apartment wasn't very long.

"Slow down," Cash growled at Malcolm.

Malcolm turned toward him. The movement was predatory, like a wolf protecting its kill, and suddenly, I didn't want to be between the two of them.

"For Dacia." Cash nodded at me without dropping Malcolm's gaze.

Malcolm slowed, but I wasn't sure if it was the wisest idea. His dragon was too riled for him to be out in the open.

As soon as we were in my apartment, Mavros slammed the door shut. "What were you thinking? You can't make a promise to that phouka!"

"So, you wanted me to go with him?" Heat spread through my body, and a hard weight settled in my chest. Tears burned in my eyes, and I hated that anger made me cry.

Mavros grabbed both of my arms hard enough to bruise.

One of the dragons growled. The sound sent shivers racing up my spine, and Mavros dropped his hands to his side.

He clenched and unclenched his fists, making the tendons pop up on the back of his hands. "I wanted you to be smart."

"I thought I was." The heat in my body flared, and flames flickered over my fingers. "I'm not with him right now, am I?"

He stared at me, and I couldn't remember ever seeing him so angry. "He's a faerie, and you said, 'tomorrow.' Do you know what that means?"

How could he think I was that stupid? "Yes!" I shoved him away, and blue flames danced over his coat. "It means not today." My voice rose with every word. "It means that right now, I am safe. Tomorrow, I will have to figure out how to keep more leaves from turning, but right now, I'm here."

Mavros stared down at me while he brushed his hands over the fire. The flames seemed to be sucked inside of him. His jacket and shirt were ruined, but his skin wasn't marred. "Let's pretend it's tomorrow," he ground out through clenched teeth. "Saturday. What day would Sunday be?"

"What?" I shook my head at him.

"On Saturday, Sunday is tomorrow. On Sunday, Monday is tomorrow. Tomorrow is any day except today or yesterday."

"Oh." All the fight drained out of my body all at once. I stumbled back onto the couch. "Oh." I dragged my hands down my face. *Tomorrow never comes.*

Mavros knelt in front of me. His anger wasn't gone. I could still see it burning in his eyes, but he was holding it back. "He's a faerie, Dacia. He can take words and manipulate them to mean whatever he wants them to mean. You can't be vague when you talk to him. Everything has to be specific."

"But tomorrow never comes." I pulled my lip into my mouth. "You just said so yourself. On Saturday, Sunday will be tomorrow. Can't I use that same word twisting ability against him?"

He rocked back slightly. Malcolm and Cash sat on either side of me, and Seth plopped down in the chair. Their dragons all seemed to have retreated somewhat.

"What do you think, demon?" Malcolm's voice wasn't his own, but it was closer than I expected. "Would it work on you?"

Mavros tipped his head back and stared up at the ceiling. "There's only one way to find out." He looked into my eyes. "You need to answer my question with tomorrow."

How many times had I been reminded that he was a demon? How many times had I been warned not to trust him? He could ask for anything, and whatever he asked, it couldn't be something I would willingly give to him. It had to be something that would test my resolve, that would test the theory. I stared into his eyes. He'd just admonished me for not being smart, and here I was about to give him whatever he wanted … tomorrow. "O-okay."

He took my hand in his and brushed his thumb over the back of it. "Dacia, will you kiss me?"

I tugged on my hand, but he didn't let go. I knew why he asked it. He had to make it something I wouldn't do normally. He could have asked for something else, something worse. "Not with Cody around, not if Cody knows, and not today, but tomorrow."

He lifted my hand to his mouth. His lips were gentle, and I remembered what it had been like to kiss him. Before I could pull away, he pushed my sleeve up, exposing the tree. "Tell me exactly what he said."

"There are seven games." I stared at the tan carpet while I told them everything I could think of. "I don't know if the leaves will fall if I lose all the games or if they'll just keep turning."

"You can't lose." Cash's purple eyes bored into mine.

Instead of saying the first thing that popped into my mind, I sucked in a deep breath and let it out slowly. "I don't want to lose, and I'll do my best not to, but he has the advantage."

"So, take it from him," Seth said as if it was just that simple.

Tugging my hand through my hair, I stood, jerked my coat off, threw it to the floor, and began pacing. "How? He knows Faerie. He's lived there for thousands of years or more. He knows which trees will sneak up on you. He knows what other creatures live in Spring. He knows all of it, and I know nothing." I stopped walking in front of Seth. He looked so comfortable, leaning back in the chair with one leg thrown over the arm. I wanted some of that peace, but all I felt was panic, despair, and anger. "How am I supposed to gain the advantage?"

"Set the rules." His dangling leg swung ever so slowly.

"Yes." The couch groaned as Malcolm leaned forward. "You said his footprints disappeared last time. There's a good chance he changed shapes."

I shook my head. "No, I thought of that. I looked for paw prints or hooves."

"He can take many forms," Cash said. "A raven is among them. He could have flown off to keep you from finding his tracks."

I sank to my knees and slumped over, holding the sides of my head. "Does it ever get easier?" I tried to focus on every detail of that day, but I couldn't remember anything that would indicate he had transformed into a bird. "What else can he be?"

"There are several things." Cash lifted me like I was weightless and set me on the couch next to him. Holding onto my hand, he sent soothing energy into me. "Horse, dog, cat, fox, wolf, raven, goat, goblin, rabbit, maybe more."

I laid my head on his shoulder. "What rules should I set?"

"First, tell him you need to know the rules." Seth sat up, planting his feet. He looked through me and rubbed his hand along his jaw. "Make him tell you what the game is. If he says you'll be playing tag again, tell him he must stay humanoid. Find anything that he might use as a loophole, and take it away from him."

Mavros leaned his shoulder against the wall. "Maybe it won't matter. Maybe tomorrow won't come." An impish smile lifted his lips. "Or maybe it will, and I'll get that kiss."

Chapter 14

Surprise

When I got back from Creative Writing, Cody, Dan, and Liam were sitting on the couch playing video games. Russ sat in the chair watching the screen.

"Why don't you play?" I asked him while I peeled my coat off.

He held his hands out in front of him and flipped them back and forth. "I can't seem to make my fingers hit the right buttons at the right times."

"Me either."

Cody glanced up at me. "Where we goin'?"

I smiled at him and said, "I'd tell you, but then I'd have to kill you." As soon as the words were out of my mouth, I wished I could take them back. I'd killed … more than once, and I would probably do it again.

Malcolm set his hand on my shoulder. His pinky brushed against my neck, and soothing energy flowed into me.

"You should probably change, though." I pulled my bottom lip into my mouth with my teeth. "The sweats won't do."

"Sure." He flicked his eyes toward me, then back to the screen. "Almost done."

I walked behind the couch, kissed the top of his head, and then went to my room to get ready. After I showered, I pulled on a form-fitting dress that shimmered in the light, changing from a deep, rich green to almost black. Its long sleeves were slit between the elbow and shoulder but would still cover Kieran's curse.

I stood in front of the mirror and turned from side to side, loving the way the dress hugged my curves. It only reached to mid-thigh, but since we were teleporting there and back, I wasn't worried about getting cold. I searched my closet for my strappy black heels before joining the others in the living room.

Everyone who knew about my magic was gathered there. Cody turned at the sound of my door opening. He strode toward me, looking fantastic in a cobalt button-down shirt that made his eyes look like polished sapphires. "You look beautiful, Dacia."

"Thank you." Heat flooded my face. I reached up and straightened his thin black tie. Then lifted onto my toes to press a kiss to his lips. "So do you."

"Sarah's here." He raised his eyebrow.

I nodded. "Of course, she is."

Malcolm, Mavros, Liam, and Sarah walked over to us. Sarah pulled me into a quick hug before stepping back. "Thank you for inviting me." She wore a mauve and burgundy pantsuit that sparkled even in the dim lighting of the apartment.

Cash and Jax held onto Samantha's and Dan's hands. Seth threw his arms over Bryce's and Cassandra's shoulders, and Russ followed suit.

"See you there," I said as I watched their groups wink out of existence.

It was another thirty seconds to a minute before my body stretched in and squeezed out. Everything went black, and sound disappeared. As soon as our feet were on solid ground, a room full of people shouted, "Surprise!"

We stood in Cody's living room surrounded by his family, my parents, and our friends. He pulled me into a hug, holding me tightly for a few seconds. "I love you."

I kissed the bottom of his chin. "I love you, too."

"Cody!" Britny's high-pitched squeal filled the room as she skipped over to him. "Were you surprised?"

He lifted his sister, tossing her into the air. She squeaked in delight.

I didn't stay to hear his answer. Mom and Dad watched us from across the room. A year ago, I couldn't have imagined them being involved in my life, but they knew everything about me now.

As I made my way over to them, I tugged my sleeve down. The trunk and roots of the tree could be seen on my palm, but I hoped no one would notice them. I didn't want to use my power to cover it just in case I had to deal with Kieran in the morning.

My parents wrapped their arms around me, then Mom asked, "How are things?"

"Not tonight." My voice was hard, leaving no room for argument.

Dad squeezed my shoulder. "That was answer enough."

"It's Cody's night."

Someone bumped into my side. I turned to find Val nudging his head against me like a cat who wanted attention.

I rubbed his head, amazed again by how soft his blue hair was. "Hey, Val. Thank you for keeping an eye on my parents."

He arched into my touch. "I've been keeping two on them." He grinned at me and sniffed my hair. "You're stronger. It makes you smell so good."

In the past, I would've backed away from him. His need to stand inside my personal bubble, touch me, and smell me had made me uncomfortable at first, but as I got to know him, I realized that besides being the youngest dragon I'd met, he was also the most harmless. I looked over his head and saw Arianna watching us.

She tipped her glass toward me and smiled but didn't come over.

I nodded at her, and Val scrunched his nose up. "But there's other magic on you." He shook his head and backed up a little. "I don't like it."

I didn't want to think about what he said. The other magic had to be Kieran's curse because Mavros' power had been mixed with mine last time I'd seen Val.

"Can I have your attention?" Brent's voice carried across the room. "I'd like to thank Dacia for arranging this." He smiled at me, then turned toward Cody who was still surrounded by his siblings. "Cody, your mom and I are so proud of the man you've grown into. We know that whatever mountain rises in front of you, you'll work hard to reach the summit. Happy birthday, son."

Susan slid her arm around Brent's waist. "Happy birthday." The smile that covered her face could have lit up the room. She pointed at the kitchen. "There's a ton of food, so please eat up. Don't be shy."

Dragons stood next to each entryway into the room. I wasn't sure if anybody else noticed that they looked like a security detail, but as I squeezed past Seth to get to the restroom, I said, "It's a party, loosen up."

He smiled at me, showing fang, and watched as I pulled open the door.

I closed and locked it behind me, and when I turned around, Kieran was appraising my outfit. A startled cry escaped me before I could stop it. My heart thundered in my chest, and I wondered how my guards didn't hear it.

"Stunning." His eyes sparkled mischievously, and he rubbed his chin as if deep in thought. "Though, I would wear something a little more practical tomorrow if I were you."

"What are you doing here?"

He hopped up onto the cabinet and swung his feet. "Making sure you're not trying to weasel out of our deal." He snapped his fingers, and my body shrank.

Tan and ivory fur covered my elongated body, and long whiskers twitched next to my nose. When he snapped again, I stood before him, wearing my dress.

"What the hell?"

He tossed back his head and laughed like a madman. "Oh, we're going to have so much fun in Faerie, you and I." Without another word, he was gone.

I leaned forward, bracing myself against the counter, trying to calm down.

Pounding on the door made another yelp tear from my chest and brought back my panic. I tried to catch my breath so I could answer, but the words wouldn't come out.

"I'm coming in." Malcolm stood next to me a half of a second later. "What happened?"

"Kieran." I stared at my ashen reflection instead of looking at him. "He t-turned me into a-a weasel and left."

Malcolm pulled me against his side, but I think it was more to relax him than me. "Are you finished in here?"

"Give me a minute," I said. When he left the room, I slumped back down again and sucked a breath in through my teeth. Kieran obviously didn't see any loopholes in the deal I'd made with him. He expected me to go to Faerie with him tomorrow, and if I didn't, what would he do?

Chapter 15

Putting On A Brave Face

When I came out of the bathroom, everybody made a point not to stare at me. They glanced at me surreptitiously, looking away again when they caught my eye.

I ignored the adults, focusing instead on Britny. She sat next to Cash, talking animatedly to him. He nodded his head from time to time but kept an eye on me. She got up and twirled in front of him. Her purple dress flared out around her, and a genuine smile lit up his face, softening his features.

"Are you okay?"

I jumped at the sound of Sarah's voice. I'd been so focused on Britny that I hadn't seen her walk over. "It's a little—" I stared up at the ceiling, trying to think of a word to describe how I felt "—disconcerting to suddenly become a weasel. I'm still pretty shaken up."

She gave me a quick sideways hug. "My door is always open, Dacia."

"I know." I dropped my chin to my chest. "I need to come see you more often, but I'm always in class, training, or researching faeries."

Susan strode toward us with a camera in hand. She snapped a couple of shots of Sarah and me, then said, "I need a picture of all of you kids. You all look so nice."

"Sure." As I walked toward my friends, I realized she was right. Bryce wore a black shirt and pants with an ice blue tie that matched Cassandra's eyes and strappy dress. Together they looked like they should be a power couple on the cover of a magazine.

Samantha's copper dress hugged her curves, and with her hair in a braided updo, my studious friend had transformed into a sophisticated enchantress. Dan wore a black jacket, pants, and tie with a copper shirt, but it was his smile that was mesmerizing.

We stood for several pictures as a group, as couples, and with our families. Liam ended up taking a lot of the shots since Susan was in them. When he handed the camera back to her, I said, "Can I get a picture of us with all of our friends?"

My guards lined up behind us. Susan snapped a few photos, then gasped. I looked over my shoulder and saw that Mavros had transformed into Damon. My chest tightened, seeing him standing there. It shouldn't have affected me at all. Mavros and Damon were one and the same. I knew that, but it didn't stop me from missing Damon's rakish smile or his friendship.

Even though I shouldn't be, I was glad that I would have a picture of him.

Cody's grip on my waist tightened. Apparently, knowing they were the same person didn't make things better for him yet either.

Once pictures were done, Cody slid his fingers through mine and led me down the hall. We stopped outside his door. Concern tightened his eyes. "What's going on? What aren't you telling me?"

"Kieran." My shoulders slumped. I didn't want to bother Cody with this on his birthday. I wanted him to have one day to forget that his girlfriend was constantly in danger. "He wanted to take me today, but I asked him to wait until tomorrow."

"Th—"

I held up my hand to stop his words. "Mavros is afraid that Kieran will be able to twist tomorrow into every day. I'm hoping that since tomorrow never comes, the deal can be that I don't have to go, but if I don't, what will happen?"

"What else?"

Dacia, will you kiss me? I couldn't tell Cody about that, not until I knew for sure if I would have to. My hand inadvertently covered my arm. "Isn't that enough?"

He rubbed the back of his neck and looked over his shoulder at his parents. "They want me to stay."

I nodded even though he couldn't see the movement. "You should. If I have to go with Kieran tomorrow, there's nothing anyone will be able to do about it anyway. One of us can teleport you back to campus Sunday."

"Yeah … maybe." He turned toward me. "How'd Mavros get in?"

I flattened my palm on Cody's chest. "Your parents invited him. Malcolm told them I would be safer with him here."

"Don't like him being Damon."

I flexed my fingers, bunching up his tie. As soon as I realized what I was doing, I let go and smoothed it out. "I know. I'm sorry about that." I couldn't tell him that I felt the same. I wouldn't lie to Cody.

Putting his hand over mine, he asked, "Dance with me?"

I looked out at the living room. Nobody else was, but it wasn't like Cody to ask. I nodded. "Someone's got to be first."

He walked to the middle of the room, then pulled me in close to his body. I wrapped my arms around his neck, removing any space that had been between us. As soon as we started swaying, our friends joined us.

"Did I tell you how beautiful you look?" Cody's words blew into my ear, sending a shiver through my body.

"Mmm …" Suddenly, I wanted nothing more than to be alone with him. I could take him anywhere in this world or one of the others I'd been to. Mavros' beach was one of the many places that came to mind. "You did." I tilted my head back to look into his eyes.

He brushed his lips over mine. My grip on him tightened, and I fought to keep from deepening the kiss. He chuckled, pulling back just slightly.

"Think I'll stay." His fingers skimmed along the side of my face. "That okay?"

I leaned into his touch. "Of course." I wanted him with me, but I couldn't keep him from spending time with his family, and if I did have to kiss Mavros, at least Cody wouldn't have to witness it.

"You'll be careful?"

I nodded, a nearly imperceptible movement that showed how spread thin that question made me feel. "Maybe I won't have to go."

"Both know you'll go." He didn't meet my eyes but stared somewhere over my shoulder. "Be worse if you wait."

I stopped moving, realizing I hadn't told Cody about the leaves changing. I stared at my left arm, imagining the crimson foliage beneath my sleeve.

"What is it?" Cody squeezed my waist.

Chewing on my bottom lip, I looked around the room. Our parents and Sarah had moved into the dining room. Cody's brothers sat on the couch playing video games. They had changed out of their dress clothes shortly after Cody had asked me to dance. Britny stood on Cash's toes as they danced across the room. A radiant smile covered her face. The other dragons, Liam, and Mavros stood on the edges of the room. Cassandra and Bryce might as well have been in their own world. Her head was on his chest, and his was bowed over the top of hers. Their eyes were closed. Samantha steered Dan toward us.

"Nothing Cody." I shook my head. "You're right. I need to go with Kieran tomorrow whether the promise makes me or not."

"You're hiding something, Dacia." Samantha kept her voice quiet, but I heard the admonishment in it. "Why can't you just trust us?"

"I do trust you. I trust every one of you here with my life." My eyebrows pinched together in frustration. "But, it's Cody's birthday."

He stepped back from me, still keeping his hands on my hips. "So?"

"So … so you deserve one day." I pulled away from him and threw my hands up. "One day to not focus on me and the mess I am."

Apparently, my voice had been louder than I realized. Everyone stopped what they were doing and watched me. Mom, Dad, Brent, Susan, and Sarah got up from their chairs in the dining room and stood in the doorway, looking at me. The weight of their gazes was too much.

Cody stepped closer, but I backed away, slamming into Bryce and twisting my foot beneath me. "Stupid heels," I said as Bryce steadied me, holding me in place long enough for Cody to grab my hand.

"Dacia, I want to know." He rubbed his thumb over mine. "No matter what day it is. No matter what's going on in my life. You're what matters most." He lifted his other hand to my face, gently caressing my cheek. "So, what is it?"

I closed my eyes and shook my head.

"Dacia lost the first game she played with Kieran." Mavros' silky-smooth voice carried across the room. There was anger simmering in it that would be hard for those who didn't know him well to pick up on. "He showed her the consequences of that today."

Cody raised one eyebrow. "Consequences?"

I tugged the sleeve of my dress up as far as I could. The majority of the leaves were still completely green. The ones that were beginning to turn were just tipped in red. "Seven games." My voice sounded dejected. "With each game I lose, more of the leaves will turn. Then they'll fall, and I'll end up in Faerie."

Val slipped past Arianna and strode across the room toward me. He kept his eyes on the floor, always the submissive dragon. He stood in front of me, sniffing my hair. "Don't be sad, Dacia." He stepped too close, but with Val, that was expected. "The phouka can't keep you there. Can he?"

"I don't know." I put my hand on his arm, knowing it would soothe him. "He said he'd whisk me away to Faerie, but I don't think there was a forever in there."

"So even if you lose, you might just be able to teleport back?" Bryce draped his arm over Cassandra's shoulder. "That doesn't sound so bad."

Could it be that simple? Go to Faerie with Kieran, then just teleport back? He'd said that if I ate there, I couldn't return, but what if I didn't eat? If I tried to come back, could he make me stay? "I don't think I should let him know that I can teleport away from Faerie." I tugged my hand through my hair, not caring if it messed it up. "If he finds out, he'll change the rules."

"Oh, honey." Mom held her hand in front of her mouth. "I wish I could take this from you."

A sad, withered imitation of a smile lifted my lips. "I know, but you can't."

"Speaking of Kieran—" Mavros cleared his throat "—we should get you back before tomorrow." He held his hand out, lifting it into the air to encompass all of me. "You don't want to be wearing that when he shows up."

"No." I sighed. "I don't."

Cody squeezed my fingers. "I'll go back."

"No." I glanced around the room, taking in each of his family members. I remembered the way Kieran had looked at me across the desk and the promise I'd made to Mavros. An ominous feeling settled in my stomach, reaffirming that Cody should stay here. "I think it would be best if you didn't."

His eyebrows dipped down over his nose. "Why?"

"I don't know." I shook my head. "It's just a feeling."

Cody pinched his eyes shut. "Need to trust those." He took hold of my hand and led me to his room. "You'll let me know if something happens?" His gaze shifted from mine to the tree hidden beneath my sleeve.

"Seth seems to think I can set the rules to tilt the games in my favor." I tried to believe it could be true, but I didn't see how. Kieran would've thought of that. For each rule I threw out at him, he would most likely have one to counteract it.

Cody's fingers brushed against my chin, gently lifting my face until my eyes met his. "But you don't."

Even though it wasn't a question, I felt inclined to answer, "No."

Chapter 16

Tomorrow Never Comes, Or Does It?

My eyes popped open, and I was wide awake. My heart raced. Mavros' cat-like pupils glowed back at me from the desk chair. I relaxed a little. Knowing he was there made me feel safe.

"It's tomorrow." His silken voice sent shivers over my skin. He stood and strode toward me, kneeling next to my bed. He brushed my hair off my face, and I swallowed hard, wondering what would happen when he asked. "Dacia, will you kiss me?"

I leaned toward him, focused on his lips, but stopped. "No." The word came out huskier than I would have liked. "Not today."

A laugh filled the room, and Kieran materialized, clapping. "No, but she will come to Faerie with me, demon." He held his hand out, and without any conscious thought of my own, I lifted the covers and got out of bed.

Mavros growled but didn't stop me.

"It's all about intent, you see." Kieran pushed his hair out of his eyes and looked at Mavros. "You should know this. She never intended to kiss you." His smile turned wicked, and he patted his chest. "That must break your poor, demon heart." Cocking his head, he added, "Or do you even have one?"

Mavros stepped between us, but I set my hand on his arm. The warmth of his body seeped through his black shirt into my fingers, soothing me. I needed to go to Faerie with Kieran. Hopefully, I would make it back without any more red leaves. I thought of the trees that had chased after me and the kelpie and revised my thoughts. Hopefully, I would make it back. I gently pushed Mavros out of the way and stepped closer to the phouka. "I'm sorry. I have to go with him."

"That was the intent." Kieran grabbed my hand, and the room spun, disappearing, replaced by a verdant forest. A fine mist was barely visible, but I felt it collecting in my hair and on my clothes.

I glanced down, glad I'd gone to bed in sweatpants and a t-shirt, but I missed my shoes. "You could've given me a minute." I wiggled my toes, making mud ooze between them.

He looked down at my feet. "Manifest them." He rolled his eyes. "You're magic, or have you forgotten?"

He was right. I didn't have to go through this game barefoot. I didn't even have to do whatever it was as a human.

Pointing through the trees, he said, "First one to the top of that mountain wins. Ready—"

"Wait." I grabbed his arm. "Rules." I hoped Seth was right. "This game can be played using only one form. One avatar. One body. One shape." I tried to think of all the words Kieran might use to describe the different creatures he could become.

He narrowed his eyes, appraising me. "Anything else?"

"No illusions. No hindering the other player in any way." I chewed on my bottom lip, wishing I had given this more thought. "If you cheat, I win whether I make it to the top or not."

I could feel anger radiating off of him, and I knew he had to follow the guidelines I'd set. "One more."

"Do tell." He waved his hand through the space between us.

I schooled my features, hoping he was angry enough not to catch onto what I was going to say. "You can't teleport."

He jumped in front of me, baring his fangs. I screamed at the unexpected movement, and he laughed, but it lacked all humor. "Nice try, Princess, but I'm a faerie, not some stupid, love-struck demon. I'm not about to fall for that trick. If I can't teleport, neither can you."

"Fine." I huffed. "You can't blame me for trying, though." I stretched my hand out to him, and he shook it. "Ready." My body grew, shifting, transforming. "Set." My voice was a deep growl. "Go."

By the time the word was out of my mouth, I was fully transformed into my dragon, and Kieran was a raven. We both launched into the air. His lithe body avoided all the branches, not even touching a leaf on his way to the overcast sky.

I busted through the trees. Some of them jumped out of the way. Their roots and boughs creaked as if they were being blown by a strong wind. Some stretched their branches out, tearing at my wings, and tried to grab onto me. Others didn't move. Their limbs cracked, crashing to the forest floor.

By the time I was free of their hold, Kieran was a tiny black speck in the sky. I called upon the wind, using it to push me forward. I flapped my wings harder than I ever had when racing Mavros and the dragons. I couldn't let Kieran win. I couldn't let more of the leaves turn. I needed more time to figure out how to keep them from falling or figure out if I'd be able to teleport away once he brought me here.

Kieran's body grew larger as I gained on him. Lightning flashed across the sky, and Kieran's feathers shimmered, the black turning royal blue for just a moment. He glanced back and pushed harder, but he was no match for me in this form.

Torrential rain pelted against my scales. The tempest pushed me back, and even though, I flapped my wings harder, the wind gusts held me in place.

Kieran flew through the storm unhindered.

I called on my magic to turn the winds so they propelled me forward instead of pushing me back, but nothing happened. Drawing on the serpent's strength, I flapped my wings.

The rules that I had set played through my head. One form. No teleporting. No illusions. No hindering.

This storm had to be Kieran trying to slow me down. Didn't it? Or did Faerie itself not want me to win?

One form. If I made myself smaller, would I be able to avoid this storm the way Kieran was? I started to call on my magic when I remembered a paper I had written about bald eagles. Instead of changing my size, I flew straight up.

The wind pushed me back the way I had come from, but it didn't keep me from ascending. Lightning flashed across the sky before crashing into the ground far beneath me. I continued beating my wings, flying through the black clouds. Finally, I burst through the wispy tendrils. A cerulean sky greeted me.

Thunder rumbled below me. The clouds lit up as they discharged their lightning bolts. The mountain beckoned me. My magic pulsed in my chest, and I drew on it, using it to push me forward. I clutched the peak in my talons and scanned the area for Kieran, wondering if he had beaten me here.

I scented my surroundings, but there was no trace of him. Curling up on the summit, I soaked up the sun's warm rays while I waited.

The raven burst through the clouds. Rain clung to its black feathers. Its yellow eyes narrowed, and its body shifted until Kieran landed in front of me. "You cheated." He pointed his long, misshapen finger at me.

"No." Flames ignited in my throat. "I believe you did, but I did not change forms. I did not hamper you in any way. I did not create any illusions. I did not teleport."

He stepped closer to me, and I stood, towering above him. "Then … how did you beat me?"

"I flew." Thank God for Mr. Chickaree's love for reports. If I wouldn't have researched the bald eagle, I would never have realized that they flew above storms. How many other bits of trivia would save me? Would I remember them when I needed to?

His lip curled up on one side. "You may have beaten me this time, but it will be the last." He snapped his fingers, and I transformed back into a shoeless Dacia.

"How'd—" I glanced around, not sure what had just happened "—how'd you do that?" Standing on top of the rocky peak in a t-shirt and bare feet, I shivered uncontrollably.

He grabbed my wrist and flipped my arm over, showing the oak tree. The leaves looked the same as they had before he brought me to Faerie. "Maybe when you tell me, I'll tell you."

"Yeah, maybe doesn't work for me."

Chapter 17

Intent

$\mathcal{I}$ lay in bed, staring at the ceiling. Scenes from the day kept replaying through my head. There was no way Kieran hadn't broken the rules with the storm, but if he did it again and I didn't win, would the leaves turn? He'd said it was the intent that mattered, so if he didn't intend to follow my rules, would he still be bound by them?

I flipped onto my side, shoving my arm under the pillow. I missed Cody, the comfort I felt from having his arms wrapped around me, the warmth of his body pressed against mine. Knowing I needed to sleep, I closed my eyes, but I pictured Kieran in front of me. I stared at my dresser. I didn't want to go to bed thinking about him. That would be an open invitation for him to invade my dreams.

But I couldn't stop the thoughts spinning in my head. How had he transformed me? He shouldn't have been able to take my magic away like that, no matter how angry he was that I'd bested him. And, if he could do that now, what would happen if I beat him in the end? I closed my eyes and breathed in as deeply as I could. This line of thinking wasn't doing me any good. I exhaled, hoping to relax, but then something else occurred to me. What if I didn't?

If intent was what mattered, I was sure I would be trapped with him in Faerie forever. That was what he intended. No matter what I evolved into, I didn't think I would be able to teleport out. I never should have accepted the acorn.

However, if I did beat him, would he let me go? He was obviously more powerful than I had believed. And, while he might act childlike when things were going his way, I remembered the look on his face and his disjointed finger pointing at me. He didn't handle losing well. How would he react if I stopped the leaves from falling?

After beating him to the top of the mountain, he had been so upset that I had wondered if he would return me to Earth or if I would have to show my hand and teleport out of Faerie myself. Luckily, I still held onto my secret.

Soft footsteps padded toward my bed. I rolled over and looked into Mavros' eyes. "What's going on?" He sat on the edge of my mattress.

"If it's intent …" I stopped. I didn't want to be trapped in Faerie forever. "I have to stop the leaves from falling."

The trees are so green. As far as I know, there's nowhere on Earth where the colors even begin to compare to this. The vivid hue is almost overwhelming. It's everywhere. The leaves, the grass, the moss on the tree trunks, the undergrowth. I spin in a circle, hoping to find something different so I can use it as a landmark, but everything looks the same. There isn't even a gnarly dead tree. I look up at the gray sky. Rain mists down, and I wonder if the sun ever shines in Spring.

I set off through the trees, wondering why Kieran brought me here if not to play another game. After a few minutes, I look behind me. My footprints have already disappeared, and everything looks the same. I wish I had breadcrumbs or string or something to leave a trail.

I can use my magic, but if I damage a tree, I am afraid of how the forest might retaliate. I tread carefully, avoiding low-hanging branches.

A noise somewhere between a growl and a hoot makes my heart race, and my feet plant themselves in the thick mud. I scan the trees, searching for the source, but there's nothing except the constant rain and green.

The desire to teleport out of here is nearly overwhelming, but I fight the urge, hoping to keep Kieran from finding out for as long as possible.

The strange noise sounds again, but this time, I run. The leaves above me rustle, and the branches creek, shifting and groaning underneath the weight of the creature.

I press down with my foot and leap into the air, praying one of the trees won't snag me and drag me back down to the forest floor. I burst through the canopy, expecting the creature to follow, but I never even catch a glimpse of it as I fly higher.

Rain plasters my hair against my head, weighing down my curls until they straighten and fall to my waist.

Kieran appears in front of me astride a dapple gray stallion. "You made it out of the forest." He smiles, but anger hardens his eyes.

"Yes." I stare at the horse, trying to understand how it's flying without wings. Can all fairy horses fly?

Kieran runs his hand through the stallion's mane, and fluffy seeds float up, catching on the breeze. I remember seeing something in my research about faeries turning ragwort into horses and flying on them.

He blows the seeds toward me. Thousands of them. I swat them away, but I still breathe some in. They catch in my throat. I inhale some and cough others back out. When they disperse, I want to ask if getting out of the forest was today's game, but if I do, I'm afraid he'll say no, and even if it was, it won't be anymore. I know faeries can twist words, but I don't know if they can change their intention based on the knowledge of the other person. And, even though Kieran said he can't lie, can he?

Kieran snaps his fingers, and I plummet toward the forest. His laughter seems to grow louder the farther from him I fall.

Angel wings tear through my skin. I spread them wide, jerking to a halt. I flap them enough to hover, watching Kieran, wondering what he will do next.

Something grabs ahold of my foot and drags me down.

I kick, but it only clutches me tighter. Glancing down, I see branches and vines wrapped around my ankles. I call on my magic, but it doesn't answer. There's a chasm where my power should be. It's vast and empty.

Limbs wrap around my waist. They pull on my wings, tearing them from my shoulders. I scream.

Strong hands held my thrashing body. "Dacia, stop." Mavros' voice was edged with something. Fear? Hunger? Pain? I couldn't tell for sure, but it sounded broken. "Stop, please."

Mavros. Why was he here? Where had he come from? I tried to peel my eyes open, to move, but pain ripped through my body. Hot and furious. It pulled the air from my lungs in a harsh gasp.

"Don't move." The words were more a plea than a command.

Claws tore through my skin. Then Mavros pulled me against his body. "Shh. Dacia, it'll be all right."

His warmth seeped into me, dulling the pain.

I woke up in Cody's room. Liam stood at the end of the bed with his arms folded over his chest. No one else was around. "H-how'd I get here?" I dragged my hand through my hair. Knots caught under my fingernails.

Sitting up, the sheet fell off of me, revealing my bandage-wrapped torso. "What happened?" Panic clung to my words. I'd left Faerie after defeating Kieran, but I couldn't remember anything after that.

I didn't remember returning to the apartment, eating dinner, showering, going to bed.

Nothing.

"Your wings were torn off." Liam kept his voice steady, emotionless, but anger sparked in his steel eyes. "There was so much blood." He walked toward me and knelt next to the bed. "Malcolm—"

I closed my eyes, wondering how bad it had been. "He's tasted my blood."

"His bloodlust …" Liam shook his head. "They all had to leave." He held onto my hand, and I knew there was something more.

Squeezing his fingers, I asked, "What else?"

"Your back—" he swallowed hard "—it looks worse than mine did before …" He looked out the door. "Mavros doesn't know if it'll heal or if you'll be like one of the fallen."

I stretched my arms behind me, feeling my back. Stubs protruded from near my shoulder blades. I winced when I touched them. My fingers came away sticky. "Why didn't I heal?"

"Can you use your magic?" He rubbed his chin, and the familiar scratching sound filled the room.

I lifted my hand and called on my power. A spark jumped on my palm, but it didn't flame. "What happened? How'd my wings get torn off?"

"You're the only one who knows." His eyebrows puckered. "You were sleeping. Mavros thought you were dreaming about Cody."

My heart seemed to stop. A weight settled inside of me. "I don't remember anything." I clutched the sheet against my chest and tried to focus on what I'd been dreaming. When that didn't work, I focused on the events of the day, beating Kieran, his anger. He snapped, and I was no longer a dragon.

There was nothing after that. No matter how hard I concentrated, I couldn't remember anything else. Pressing my eyes shut, I pinched the bridge of my nose and looked inside.

The pearlescent serpent didn't glance up at me. It didn't even seem to notice I was there. I slowly inched forward, not wanting to startle the snake.

As I moved toward it, I realized it looked smaller. The bony spines of its vertebrae were more prominent. Its girth had diminished significantly. I knelt down next to it.

My hand shook as I reached forward to touch it. The normal shimmer was missing from its scales, leaving them lackluster. I trailed my fingers along the length of its body, praying it wouldn't attack like it had before. It lifted its head off the floor just barely. Its copper eyes were sunken. Saliva, thick with mucus, stretched from its bottom lip to its top.

"What's wrong?" My voice trembled.

We are dying. My serpent moved enough to uncover Mavros' power. His snake had the same emaciated look that mine did. The normally obsidian scales were gray.

"Why?" I sat next to it, pulling my legs up to my chest. "What happened? Did I do something?" I clutched the hair on the sides of my head, trying to remember anything after besting Kieran. Had he somehow done this to me? "How did Kieran make me transform?"

He cut you off from us. The serpent lowered its head and kept breathing in through its mouth.

Even if it wasn't a part of me, I would hate to see it like this. It was suffering, and without my magic, there was nothing I could do to help it.

Chapter 18

Unexpected Guest

"Where did Mavros go?" I understood the dragons not being here, but my injuries had never bothered Mavros before.

"There was a lot of blood." Liam stared at the wall like he could see through it and into my room. Maybe he could. I had no idea what Nephilim could or couldn't do. "Like a lot." He scrubbed his hand down his face and turned back to me. "He said he was going to check on the cats."

I wouldn't be able to do anything to the tree with my magic gone, but if he could find it … My heart started racing. The idea that there could be an end to this was a bit overwhelming.

"What did you figure out?" He leaned against Cody's dresser.

Liam was a soldier. He just wanted facts so he could come up with a plan. There was no reason to sugarcoat things with him. "It's dying."

"What do you mean? How?" His face fell.

I shrugged.

He paced alongside Cody's bed with his hands clasped behind his back. "I'm not qualified to handle this."

I laughed. I couldn't help it. "So far, I haven't been qualified to handle any of this."

"Fair point." He stopped moving and nodded. "So, phase one of the plan: breakfast." He held up two fingers. "Phase two: figure out what phase three is."

I rolled my head, stretching my neck. "Sure. Give me a few minutes, and I'll make breakfast."

"No." His lips pinched into a firm line. "I'll give you a few minutes, and I'll make breakfast."

I swung my legs over the side of the bed. Pain tore through my back, and the room spun. I clutched the mattress with both hands.

"Are you okay?" Liam grabbed my arm to steady me.

Tears filled my eyes, but I fought to keep them from falling. "I didn't expect it to hurt like that."

He helped me up, and I leaned against him as he led me to my room. "Holler if you need help."

The sheets, blanket, and comforter were all missing, and my room smelled like a gallon of bleach had been dumped in it. I stared at the bed, trying to remember anything. A bottomless, hollow pit that sucked in all that was good and right settled in my chest. I shook my head. This was more than I could cope with right now.

Grabbing my clothes, I stumbled to the bathroom. I clutched the sink to keep from toppling over. The girl staring at me from the other side of the mirror looked like a ghost. The color was completely drained from her face, and even her freckles were pale. Dark circles ringed her eyes.

I scrubbed my hand down my face. As awful as I looked, it was no wonder the dragons had left. I wouldn't blame them if they didn't come back. I was a burden they didn't need.

Taking in the rest of my appearance, I realized that the bandages around my chest left little to the imagination. I lifted my hand to them, wondering if I should look to see how bad it really was, but I stopped, knowing I wouldn't be able to put them back on very easily, and I didn't want to ask for help. Either Liam or Mavros had wrapped my wounds, but it seemed like too much effort to be embarrassed by that right now.

Looking at the girl in the mirror one more time, I wondered how she'd gotten here, but her memories were hidden just like mine.

I grabbed my sweatshirt, putting my hands through the sleeves. Then I lifted my arms to pull it over my head. The muscles in my back tightened, and I bit back a scream. The hoodie pooled around my hands as I clutched the sink and breathed in deeply. Neither brushing my hair nor changing clothes was going to happen until I healed a little.

Not wanting to be alone any longer, I shuffled out of the bathroom, holding onto the dresser, then the wall as I staggered to the bedroom door. My legs shook more than a newborn giraffe's.

"I don't know," Liam said in hushed tones. "She's in bad shape."

"I have seen her in bad shape before." The voice that responded was familiar, but could it really be her, or was it just wishful thinking?

I opened the door and fell against the refrigerator. Liam and Aurelia both turned toward me.

The gold dragon who had been my mentor looked me over from head to toe. "You are more gravely injured than I expected." She strode toward me, cocking her head once she was beside me. "You are not healing on your own." Wrapping her arm around my waist and bearing most of my weight, she led me to the couch.

"I didn't expect to see you." I clutched the arm of the sofa as I eased myself onto it.

She sat next to me and held my hand in hers. Her magic seeped into me. Cool, soothing energy flowed through my veins, driving away the pain and weakness. It weaved around inside me, mending my wounds.

The stubs still protruded from my shoulders, making sitting uncomfortable, but I breathed easily for the first time since waking up. "Thank you."

"You are welcome." She smiled at me and kept pushing her curative power through my body. When it brushed up against my serpent, she jerked her hand back. "What happened to your magic?"

Liam plopped down in the chair and leaned forward with his elbows resting on his knees. "I told you. She said it was dying."

"You did." Aurelia focused on him for a moment before her gold eyes met mine again. "What happened to them, though?"

I lifted my shoulders toward my ears and winced, expecting it to hurt, but when it didn't, I let out a heavy sigh. "I can't remember anything." I tugged my hand through my hair. My fingers caught in a mess of tangles, reminding me that I hadn't been able to brush it this morning. "Can you heal it?"

"I am not sure." She tapped her index finger against her lips, and her flawless skin sparkled in the overhead light. "Focus on your magic so that I can direct all of my healing power toward it."

Closing my eyes, I thought about the serpents. They were in even worse shape than they had been earlier. Skin clung to their scales, peeling away in chunks. I rested my hand on the embodiment of my magic. It was colder than normal. The light that usually shone on it was gone.

A golden beam surrounded the three of us. The room filled with the tranquility that I recognized from Aurelia's aura.

My serpent lifted its head. The scales no longer had a pearlescent sheen. It looked nothing like the snake I had gotten used to seeing, but as Aurelia's magic shone on it, shimmers danced over its body. The loose skin fell away, revealing bright scales.

"You were poisoned." Aurelia's voice filled the room where the serpents resided.

I slumped back, and the nubs pressed into my flesh. "Poisoned? How?"

"I should have looked you over before I healed you." She sighed. "It is too late now. Liam, did you notice any other injuries?"

His gaze immediately went to my legs. Most nights, I went to bed in sleep shorts, but I was wearing baggy sweatpants when I woke up. "Her legs were scratched from her ankles to her knees, and there were several puncture wounds."

"You should have told me." Aurelia's hand tightened on mine.

Liam rubbed his jaw. "I forgot. With all the blood and Mal…" He let his voice trail off. "The scratches seemed insignificant at the time."

"I will do what I can to pull the toxins from your body." Aurelia closed her eyes and nodded. "I may need to seek help."

I chewed on my lip for a second, not sure if I wanted to know the answer to what I was about to ask. "Did, uh …" I let my voice trail off. Liam would've told me if there was something I needed to know.

"What is it?" Aurelia lifted one perfectly trimmed eyebrow.

Releasing a long breath, I asked, "Did anyone get hurt?"

"Nearly." Liam stared at the carpet between his black combat boots. He swallowed, visibly shaken by the memory. "Somehow, Cash held back his bloodlust, grabbed Malcolm from behind, and teleported out of here." He looked up, meeting my gaze. His gray eyes were haunted. "It was … tense." He rubbed his hand down his face. "Terrifying actually."

"That's why you're here." I turned to Aurelia.

She dipped her chin toward her chest. "I have no idea when the others will return."

"Oh … oh." I didn't know what else to say. My heart seemed like it plummeted, and it left me feeling hollowed out.

She scooted to the end of the sofa. "Put your feet up here. If the poison went in through your legs, it may be more concentrated there."

I turned on the couch and pulled my sweats up to my knees. There were no marks on my skin, no scratches, or punctures. They were totally unblemished.

Aurelia placed a hand on each of my legs, midway up my shins. "This will hurt."

"Of course, it will." I breathed in deeply and readied myself for the pain.

She closed her eyes, and her magic entered me. Normally, it was a soothing, revitalizing feeling, but this time, it felt like predators chasing their prey. It tore through my body, hunting, tracking. Once it found what it was searching for, its claws dug in, ripping the toxins from my blood, my muscles, and my bone marrow.

I whimpered and clenched my teeth, trying to keep from screaming. Liam knelt next to me and held my hand in his, letting me squeeze his fingers until they had to have gone numb. He stared into my eyes. "Just breathe, Dacia."

While the poison was torn from my body, I focused on what Aurelia had said. There had been so many times over the past nine months that I had been injured. Why had my blood affected the dragons so much this time, and what exactly had happened? Why wasn't Mavros here with me? There had to be something that they weren't telling me. Something else must have happened, but what?

From the doorway of my room, I saw myself lying on the blood-soaked bed, screaming and writhing. Crimson-coated feathers floated through the air. They were scattered over the mattress.

She's going to die. Liam's thoughts surprised me.

I jolted, and the scene started to fade away. Somehow, I'd gotten into his head and was seeing his memories. Concentrating, I pulled his thoughts back.

Mavros stood over me in panther form. His fangs were bared. Long gashes in his shoulder dripped black ichor. It sizzled on the sheets.

Malcolm stalked toward the end of my bed. Talons tipped his fingers, and horns jutted out of his skull. There was nothing human left in him. He was a predator, and Mavros stood between him and his prey. He growled. The sound rolled across the room like thunder.

Mavros turned, following Malcolm's movements, keeping himself between us. His ears were pinned back, and his hackles were raised. He lunged forward. His claws slashed through the air before tearing through the scales on Malcolm's arm.

Malcolm roared and swiped back.

Mavros stood on his hind legs. Biting at Malcolm's neck. Scratching at his body. Trying to push him back.

Liam walked to the bed never taking his eyes off the fight. He lifted me, pulling me against his body. I kicked and punched at him, screaming.

Malcolm's gaze whirled in our direction. Mavros pushed him back, but the dragon charged.

Liam's grip on me tightened. His heart thundered against my arm. Fear froze my movements, stopping my thrashing.

Mavros pounced, landing between us. His tail whipped from side to side. New wounds covered his onyx fur.

Cash teleported into the room. He breathed in, and purple scales freckled his face. Horns pressed through his skin. Thin slits replaced the round pupils in his amethyst eyes. He shook his head and wrapped his arms around Malcolm, disappearing almost instantly.

Black vapor rose from the panther's body, coalescing in the air. It hovered there for a few minutes before reforming into Mavros. "Hold her tight. This is going to hurt her before it helps her."

Liam's grip had loosened slightly after Malcolm disappeared, but his protective instincts kicked in, and he held me tight, turning my body away from Mavros. "Don't you think she's in enough pain?"

"Yes." Mavros stepped closer, and his fingernails transformed into claws. "But, I am a demon, and this is the only way I can help her." He raised his hand above me. Remorse rippled across his face. Knowing what came next, I pulled out of Liam's memories.

"What did you see?" Aurelia still held onto my legs. Her hands against my skin might as well have been an iron branding me.

The toxins moved through my veins like magma just beneath the Earth's crust. I clutched Liam's hand even tighter.

"She saw my memories." He didn't pull away or look angry. "She saw Malcolm and Mavros."

"I—" The word croaked out, and I swallowed to wet my throat. "I didn't mean to."

He nodded. "I know."

"At least, we know this is working." Aurelia's normally steady voice was strained, and I couldn't help but wonder if the poison was affecting her or if she didn't want me to know what had happened.

"How?" I asked.

Her eyes met mine, and I was surprised to see her dragon looking out at me. "You were using your magic to see his memories."

Chapter 19

I woke up with my arms wrapped around a leg that wasn't Cody's. Jerking them away, I bolted into a sitting position on the couch.

Liam lifted his hands. "Hey." His voice was soft like he was trying to calm a frightened animal. "It's okay. No harm done."

"What happened?" I looked around the room. Samantha's door was open, but I didn't see her or Dan. There was also no sign of Aurelia.

Liam stood and stretched. His black t-shirt came untucked from his cargo pants. Never one to look sloppy, he pushed it back in. "Well, we have to redo my entire plan."

My mind whirred, trying to remember what his plan had been. I felt out of sorts. After a few seconds, my thoughts cleared like fog melting away in the morning sun.

"Even though you're technically breaking your fast, it's more like lunch." Walking into the kitchen, he looked at the clock on the microwave. "Or, maybe lunch and a half if that's a thing. What would you like?"

My stomach grumbled in response, but I wasn't about to let him get away without answering me. "What happened? Where's Aurelia?"

The defeated look on his face threw me off. I'd never seen him look like that even when he couldn't make his wings disappear. "Can we eat first?" He rubbed his jaw. "Something quick and easy. I'm starving."

"Fine." I let out a long breath. "How about grilled cheese? I think there's some shaved ham you can add to it if you want."

He started pulling the pan out before I finished. "Sounds good." He went to the fridge and grabbed the butter, cheese, and ham. "How are you feeling?"

"Better." I shrugged and realized that the stubs of my wings didn't catch. I reached my hand back. Gone.

He spread butter over the bread while watching me. "What about your magic?"

"I don't know." I chewed on my lip. "I'm afraid to check."

He turned around and put the first sandwich into the skillet. "I get that." He grabbed another slice of bread and buttered it. "But you need to anyway."

"Yes, Mom." As I closed my eyes to focus on my powers, I heard him chuckle.

The room was darker than normal, but a beam of light shone down from some unseen source.

My serpent's scales shifted from blue to purple to pink as it undulated within its coils. There was no sign of death like what had clung to it earlier. Its ribs no longer stuck out through its skin. It looked healthy.

I sank down beside it, letting my breath whoosh out of my lungs. Mavros' serpent's scales were so black that they seemed to swallow up all of the light surrounding it.

Skimming my fingers over my powers, I said, "How are you doing?"

He tried to kill me. The snake's indignation was palpable. Its body continued to ripple until its head was under my hand. Copper and black flecked eyes stared up at me. *I was dying.*

"I know." My stomach sank. Was Kieran trying to kill my magic, or was he trying to weaken me to keep me from winning? I wished I could remember something to help me figure out how this had happened and how to keep it from happening again.

The serpent yawned, making its fangs descend. They were longer than my fingers, and I shuddered at the thought of how painful its bite would be now.

Standing, I looked down on the snakes again. "I'm glad you're all right."

I opened my eyes just as Liam put our plates on the table.

"Well?" He pulled a chair out and sat.

I plopped down across from him and took a swig of lemonade before answering. "It might need strengthened again, but it's not dying."

"As soon as we finish, we'll work on that."

Without dragons or Mavros to go along with us, Liam and I went to Sarah's office. She stood at the door waiting for us. "Is everything okay?" she asked.

I couldn't stop the snort that slipped out. "No." I glanced around, making sure nobody else was around before explaining this morning's events.

Liam broke into my diatribe multiple times to add his perspective, and Sarah interrupted with several well-placed gasps and oh, nos. When I finished, she tilted her head to the side. "Did you scar?"

"I, uh—" I cleared my throat. It shouldn't matter. People lived with terrible scars, and many of those had memories, lessons that were attached to them, reminders to keep them from making those mistakes over and over again, but I had no idea what had happened to me. I didn't know who or what had ripped the wings from my back, and I didn't want to be reminded that my memories could be erased so easily. I dropped my gaze to the floor, not wanting to see their reactions. "I haven't looked."

"You will when you're ready." Sarah's voice was filled with understanding. "You can use my office or any of the bigger rooms down here. The outside door will be locked. I'm going to visit my grandkids."

I looked up at her with wide eyes. "I didn't know you were a grandma." I shook my head, realizing how one-sided our relationship was. "To be honest, I didn't even know you had kids. I should've asked."

"I have a son, Jake, and a daughter, Brooke. He has three kids, and she has two." She smiled warmly. "They are my pride and joy."

Guilt clawed at me, but I tried not to let it show. "Have a good time."

Liam put his hand on my back and led me to one of the rooms on the main level. Even though it was illuminated from the row of windows along the far wall, he flipped the light switch up before taking his jacket off and throwing it over the back of one of the few chairs in the room. Each one was pushed up to a desk. The tan and black mottled carpet was made to hide any dirt. The walls were a cream color that wasn't quite as stark as white paint. In the front of the room, there was an open space that was large enough for sparring.

Rubbing his hands together, he asked, "How do you want to do this?"

"First, you're going to tell me where Aurelia went." I sat at one of the desks and folded my arms over the top of it. "You've stalled long enough."

He stopped stretching his arms, letting them fall to his sides. "I was hoping you'd forget."

"I have a lot on my mind." I traced the woodgrain pattern on the desk. "But, I need to bring Cody back, and I doubt you want me to go on my own."

He chuckled, but it was humorless. "If I let you out of my sight today, they'll probably kill me." He spun a chair around and sat, looking at me over the back of it. "You know we all want to protect you, right? Even from your thoughts or feelings or whatever."

"Yes." I drew out the word, wondering what was going on. My stomach churned, and I suddenly wished I wouldn't have eaten lunch.

He rolled his neck. "So … is there any way you can wait?"

"What's so bad?" I flattened my hands on the desk, feeling the indentions from years of being written over rub against my palms. "I need to know. I need to know if I'm supposed to be afraid that something worse is coming. I need to know if something like this is going to happen again." I tightened my hands into fists. "I need to know what happened to me."

His chin dropped to his chest. "I can understand that." He loosed a long, low sigh. "Aurelia went to see if she can bring Malcolm back."

"He'll come when he's ready." The tension unexpectedly released from my body. Why had he been afraid to tell me this?

Staring at the floor between us, he shook his head. "He's not planning to, Dacia. Even though he made an oath, his instincts almost won last night."

"No." I stood up so fast that the chair fell over, hitting the floor with a loud crash. "He wouldn't have." I remembered what I had seen in Liam's memories, but those were tainted by his fear. He didn't know Malcolm the way I did. He didn't know that Malcolm had tasted my blood, felt its power, and still hadn't killed me any of the times he could have. I stalked away from him. My hands shook. I flexed and unflexed my fingers, hoping to release the flood of anger that was threatening to drown me.

A hand came down on my shoulder. I grabbed ahold of it and spun so that I was facing my attacker. Liam's eyes were wide. Releasing his hand, I backed up, feeling like an absolute idiot. I should have known it was him. I should have realized he was trying to comfort me, but adrenaline from fear and anger had been racing through me, stopping all cognizant thought.

"I'm sorry." I folded my arms over my chest, trying to hide my embarrassment.

He smiled at me, but it wasn't a happy look. There were too many other emotions fighting for dominance in his eyes. "Don't be sorry. That's what I trained you to do." He stayed back from me.

"He wouldn't have hurt me, though." My voice dropped. "He would've come to his senses."

Grimacing, he rubbed his chin. "Think about it, Dacia." He turned away, shaking his head from side to side. "Okay." He smacked his hands together. "How do you want to train?"

"Uh-uh, think about what?"

His shoulders lifted to his ears. "If Malcolm wasn't going to hurt you, why isn't Mavros here? Why haven't any of the other dragons come back?"

"You said Mavros was with the cats." I reached behind me, feeling for a chair. My knees wobbled, and I needed to sit before they gave out on me. "There was a lot of blood. The dragons just need time." I plopped down so hard that my teeth clanked together.

He leaned one shoulder against the wall and crossed one foot over the other. "They do. Mavros needs time away from Malcolm so that he doesn't kill him. The dragons need time away from the power in your blood." He pinched his eyes shut, and I realized what he meant earlier. It took a lot out of him to hurt me. "Malcolm has been pushing himself too far, trusting on the vow to keep you safe."

"Why didn't he tell me?" With my elbows on the desk, I held my head.

His steps were quiet on the carpet, but I heard them moving closer. He knelt in front of me, so he could hold my gaze with his. "He feels an obligation to you, Dacia. You freed him and the others from Draconian, and he promised to protect you." His gray eyes were filled with sympathy. "I doubt he realized he was pushing himself too far until …"

"Until his dragon decided to eat me instead of protect me."

He nodded. "Well, to put it bluntly."

"Let's jog through the halls." Standing up, I took my coat off. Then I put my foot on the chair and leaned over my leg, stretching out my muscles. After a few minutes, I walked out into the hallway, held my hand out in front of me with my palm facing up, and lit a fire in it. My chest lightened as I stared at the blue flames. Once upon a time, I had wished my magic away, but I realized now that it was a part of me, and without it, I was lost.

"Dacia." Liam's voice was a gentle prod.

I jogged down the corridor, slowly picking up speed. With only Liam here with me, I wanted to make sure I didn't overdo it. He couldn't teleport me back to my apartment if I collapsed or used all of my energy. When the flames didn't flicker or die, I turned my skin the same shade of blue as my dragon scales.

The hall turned to the right, and we followed it. I hadn't been back here before, but I figured that when it ended, we would just turn around and run back the way we'd come from.

I turned my hair cobalt and changed it to a spiked pixie cut. Liam chuckled at me, so I made his skin fuchsia. He flipped his hands over in front of him and shook his head. "Nice."

"It looks good with the black uniform."

When we got to the stairs, Liam ran up them two at a time, and I followed. Looking over the banister, I had the sudden urge to test my wings. I stopped and pulled off my hoodie. The t-shirt I was wearing was old and frayed. I didn't care if it got ruined. I climbed up on top of the railing and wondered if I was being stupid.

Liam stopped and looked back at me. "What are you do-ing?"

I grinned at him as I stepped off into open air. The ground rushed up to meet me, and my wings didn't respond. For a brief moment, I wondered if I would splatter on the hardwood floor-ing, but then I remembered I could fly without them.

Liam jumped off the balustrade, diving toward me. His tan and cream wings opened as he reached for me.

My feet touched the ground, and his skin blanched.

"I'm okay, Liam." I tried to make my voice sound sooth-ing, but I was freaking out a little, too. Would my wings ever come back? "I can fly without wings."

"Don't ever do that again!" His voice trembled.

Chapter 20

Breaking Inside

$\mathcal{L}$iam and I were only alone in my apartment for a few minutes before Dan and Samantha came in. They stopped talking as soon as they saw us sitting there. Samantha gave me the once over. "Are you okay?"

"Mostly." I shrugged. "I don't remember what happened, but I hope it wasn't too terrifying for you two."

Samantha's eyes looked haunted as she turned away from me. "We didn't come out." Her voice was so soft I barely heard it. "We made sure you were okay this morning and then thought it would be best if we disappeared for a while."

Dan took Samantha's coat from her and hooked it on the rack by the door. "Did you do anything fun today?"

Liam rolled his eyes. The action was so unexpected that I had to hold back a chuckle. "She jumped off the railing by Sarah's office."

"You what?" Dan hung his coat up and spun to look at me in one fluid movement.

"Oh, geesh." I shook my head. "It wasn't like that. I knew I would be fine."

Samantha waited for Dan to sit in the chair. Then she piled in next to him, flinging her legs over his. "So … why would you do that?"

"To scare the hell outta me." Liam glared.

If I had realized he would be this upset, I never would have jumped. Hopefully, he would eventually decide to forgive me, but it didn't look like it would happen today. "I wondered if my wings would unfurl. They didn't." I shrugged, hoping nobody would read the dismay that I was sure was written all over my face.

Liam twirled his finger. "Turn around. Let me see your shoulder blades."

I faced Samantha and Dan and lifted the back of my shirt. Liam's fingers skimmed over the place scars would be, and I slumped forward. The only reason he would touch me like that was if I hadn't healed. "How bad is it?" I kept my voice low, thinking it might make the trembling less noticeable.

Samantha shot me a weak smile and leaned toward me.

"They look like mine did." Liam's voice was solemn. He tugged on my shirt, and I dropped it, letting it fall back down.

To keep from looking at anyone, I turned. I didn't want to see the sympathy on their faces. "Why?" I folded my hands in my lap and stared at them. I needed to cut my fingernails. They were getting so long that if I hit them wrong, one would snap off. "I healed you. I healed the other Nephilim. Why haven't I healed myself?"

"Give it some time, Dacia," Dan said.

He was right. I knew he was, but fear hardened inside of me, heating up until it twisted into anger. I opened my mouth to respond but snapped it shut before I said something I would regret. Jumping to my feet, I stormed into my room, slamming the door behind me.

As soon as I looked around, I wished I wouldn't have. The stripped-down bed and smell of chlorine were reminders that I had no idea what had happened to me. I slid down the wall until I was sitting on the floor with my arms wrapped around my legs and my forehead resting on my knees.

Focusing on my power, I called on my healing energy. I thought about life, about renewal, about growth and spring, and terror settled in, clutching at my heart.

An image of a tree flashed through my memories. Vines broke through its canopy, stretching through the sky until they wrapped around my ankles.

My eyes popped open, and I stared at the tree on my arm. How long did I have, and how much more could I take?

A soft knock startled me. "Yeah?"

Samantha opened the door just enough to peek in. "Are you okay? Do you need anything?"

"My memories." I waved at my bare mattress. "New bedding."

She looked around my room. "Do you want the same thing?"

"Not necessarily the same, but similar." I thought about Malcolm coming back with that comforter. He wanted something bright and cheery for me because of the darkness and despair that had lived in me after breaking out of prison.

She perched on the edge of the bed. "There's not a lot that Dan and I can do to help you." Twirling her bracelet on her wrist, she said, "I've been reading about faeries and researching all that I can, but I haven't found anything that you can use to defeat Kieran. If something like this has happened before, I haven't found a record of it." Her voice sped up with each word, and she paused to suck in a deep breath. "We can get you new bedding, though."

"I'd appreciate that." I smiled at her. "I haven't been able to find anything either, but I wonder if something happened to make him do this to me."

She tilted her head. "What do you mean?"

"He's a really sore loser." I chewed on my lip while thinking things through. "I wonder if I beat him in another challenge so he tried to take my magic to keep it from happening again." I shook my head. "But I don't know. Maybe I'm just making things up to make myself feel better. Maybe it was just a nightmare or a premonition. But, then why can't I remember anything?"

She watched me, making sure I was done talking. I nodded, and she said, "That sounds quite plausible. If it was a premonition, it would want you to remember it so you can face it when it happens." She sat next to me and threw her arm over my shoulders. "I think you're right. I think Kieran's got to be behind this."

"I don't know what to do."

She leaned her head against my arm. "I know, but you'll figure it out. I have faith in you."

"I hope you're right." I reached up and squeezed her hand. No matter how much I wanted it to be true, something told me that things were about to get much worse.

Aurelia made it back before Samantha and Dan returned. She appeared in the middle of the living room in a swirl of gold mist. Not a hair was out of place, and her cornflower blue pant-suit was crisp. Not even a single wrinkle marred its surface.

"Well?" I stopped tapping my foot and flipped my hands up. "What did he say?"

She glanced at Liam, pursing her lips. "He will come back once he gets his dragon under control." She sat in the armchair where Jax usually positioned himself to keep his vigil, and I couldn't help but wonder if he'd left, too. For just a moment, her stoic expression slipped. She looked worn out. "I have no idea how long that will be."

"Are you okay, Aurelia?" I leaned toward her.

Her mask slid back into place, and she smiled at me. "Of course." She sighed. "I will stay here until Malcolm is ready to return."

"Thank you." There was something more, but I knew it wouldn't do any good to press her. She would tell me if she wanted to. "Can you help me heal?"

She tilted her head to the side, taking me in. "What happened?"

Liam told her about our trip to Sarah's office. His voice deepened as the anger and betrayal returned to him.

I waited until he told her about my scars. Then I jumped in. "I tried to heal myself, but when I thought about spring …" I tugged my hand through my hair and told them about the scene that had flashed through my mind and about the conversation I had had with Samantha afterward.

Aurelia stood. "Come with me." She pulled out a chair at the kitchen table and waved at the one across from her. Once I was seated, she held her hands out, and I placed mine in them. "I want you to try to heal yourself again. Go through the same motions as before, but open your mind to me so I can see what you do."

I sucked in a deep breath, trying to calm myself. The fear that I had felt earlier pooled in the pit of my stomach. I closed my eyes and pictured my mountain lake. The image was so real that I could feel the breeze raising goosebumps on my skin. I let the peacefulness enter me, and once I no longer felt my terror building up, I nodded at Aurelia. "Okay."

Focusing on the scars on my back, I called on my healing energy. As soon as I thought about renewal and spring. The image flashed through my mind again, but this time, the scene transformed. I was hovering above the trees. Angel wings flapped slowly, holding me in place. Something grabbed my ankle. I tried to kick it away, but it pulled tighter, dragging me down. Branches wrapped around my waist, and other limbs tore the wings from my shoulders, leaving just the bloody nubs behind. Kieran floated above me astride a dapple gray stallion. His laughter followed me into the void.

Aurelia let go of my hands. "Those vines could have been anything." She rubbed her forehead. "I have no idea what they are. I have never traveled to Faerie."

"I wish I could say the same." I wrapped my arms around myself protectively, rubbing away the goosebumps.

She watched me for a little bit. Then shook her head and said, "Let me see if I can help you heal. This time, think about growth and renewal, but try not to think about spring."

Holding onto her hands, I felt her energy flow into me. Instead of focusing on healing, I remembered all of the times she had done this before. Before I even knew she was a dragon, she had been my personal medic. How come she wasn't affected the same way Malcolm was? Why could she sit here with me? Had I done something to make things harder on him?

"Dacia, you are supposed to be healing yourself." Her voice sounded strained.

I shook my head, trying to release those thoughts. "Right. Sorry." I thought about life, the twin baby moose I had seen last year. Their long legs wobbled with every step they took away from their mother.

Aurelia's power merged with mine. Together they trekked through my body, searching for any weakness and repairing it. My eyes shot open as energy surged through me. I tried to pull my hands away from Aurelia's, but she held on tight.

"Whatever did this to you is resisting."

I focused on my back, sending the healing there. It edged down my spine and over my muscles like a massage, kneading and rubbing out the knots as it went. It glided over my back, smoothing out the stress that collected there.

After several more minutes, Aurelia let go. "I believe that should do it."

Standing up, I turned so that Aurelia could see my back. I edged my shirt up and peered over my shoulder at her. "Well?"

She smiled and nodded. "Try to conjure your wings."

An overwhelming sense of relief flooded me as they burst from my shoulders. The tips of my feathers extended from wall to wall.

"It's a good thing Malcolm isn't here," Mavros drawled in his silky-smooth voice. "Seeing those wings would send him into a rage."

My wings folded in before they disappeared. "Where've you been? Why'd you just disappear?" It wasn't what I had planned to ask. The words had just come spewing out without my consent. I smacked my hand over my mouth. "Sorry. You don't need to answer. I'd like to get Cody now that my magic seems to be healed."

"Dacia"—Mavros strode toward me—"I needed to get away." He looked over my head at Aurelia. "I could have tracked the dragons, and without you there, I would've killed him."

I crossed one arm over my chest, grabbing hold of my other elbow. "Liam basically said that. I didn't mean to ask. I'm not used to you guys not being around."

"Sorry about that." He held his hand out. "Let's get Cody."

Aurelia and Liam joined us, and the four of us teleported into the wooded area outside of his house. No light shone through the trees. If there was a moon out tonight, it was blanketed by thick cloud cover. As soon as we started walking, I realized I should have grabbed my coat. We stepped out of the timber, and I heated my skin. Mavros glanced at me and started taking his leather jacket off.

"No." I held my hand up in a stop gesture. "Cody doesn't like to see me in your coat, and I'll be fine for a while."

When we neared the house, the motion detector light came on, and Bo charged the window, barking a warning. Cody opened the door, walked out onto the porch, and shoved his hands into his hoodie's pouch. Tilting his head to the side, he asked. "Where's your coat? It's freezing out here."

"I wasn't thinking." I quickened my steps. "It's been a long day."

"What—"

I reached him and covered his mouth. "Please, please don't ask right now." When he nodded, I pulled my hand away.

"Hey, guys." He waved at Aurelia, Liam, and Mavros as he ushered me inside. "Want a sweatshirt?"

Susan gave me a hug while Brent led Bo down the hall. "Where's your coat? Why didn't you just teleport to Cody's room?"

"I wasn't thinking about a coat since we didn't go outside." I returned her hug. "I didn't want to surprise anybody who doesn't know about my powers by just showing up."

She stepped away. "Cody, get her a sweatshirt."

Saluting his mom, he strolled down the hallway toward his room.

I stepped back. "This is Aurelia."

"We met at your birthday party." Susan nodded at her. "I didn't know about all of this then, so I had no idea you were protecting Dacia. Thank you for that."

Britny tore into the living room, squealing at the top of her lungs. She slid to a stop when she saw us, and her face fell. "Where's Cash?"

"He's with Malcolm." I took my shoes off and stepped onto the plush carpet. "They needed to leave for a little bit."

She tilted her head and looked at Aurelia. "I thought you were a fairy, but you're not, are you?"

"I am not." Aurelia smiled at Britny.

Is Arion here? I sent the thought directly to Aurelia. I didn't want anyone else to hear in case he wasn't.

She nodded.

Will he show himself to her?

"Didn't he want to see me?" Britny looked up at me. Tears brightened her eyes, making them look glassy.

I knelt in front of her. "I'm sure he did. He didn't plan to go away, but something came up, and he had to leave unexpectedly."

"This have anything to do with you?" Cody asked as he handed me a hoodie.

I pulled it on and breathed in his wintry scent. It was my favorite smell. Fresh and clean. "Yes."

"Britny," Aurelia said, "would you like to meet my friend? You will have to put your coat and boots on."

Britny turned toward her mom. When Susan nodded, Britny asked, "Is your friend like you?"

"No." Aurelia shook her head, and Cody's brothers who had just entered the room stared at her. "He is pretty amazing, though."

Britny looked up at me, and I could see the question written on her face before she asked it. "You'll love him."

"Can we meet this amazing friend?" Brandon asked.

Aurelia tilted her head to the side, and I knew she was communicating with Arion. "You may, as long as it is okay with your parents."

"You'll keep an eye on them?" Brent asked.

She nodded. "They will be safe."

When they stepped outside, Susan turned toward me. "Her friend isn't something we need to worry about, is he?" She looked from me to Liam and then to Mavros. Her face fell slightly. "Is she something we need to worry about?"

"No." Understanding her concern, I smiled. I'd brought dragons, a demon, and a Nephilim into her house. I could see how she would be worried. "Arion is a pegasus, and Aurelia is a dragon. The first one I ever met."

"A pegasus." Susan hurried over to the window and pulled the curtains to the side. "Oh, my. He's magnificent."

Brent nodded. "I remember now. She helped train you when you faced the magician guy."

"Draconian ... yeah." I walked over to Susan's side and looked out at Arion. As if sensing us, he turned toward the window and bowed at me.

"He's beautiful." Susan's shoulders dropped, and her mouth fell open.

Brent stood behind her with his hand on the small of her back. "You have the most amazing friends."

"I do." There was a lot in my life that was screwed up, but I had made some magnificent, if unconventional, friends. "I'm sure he wouldn't care if you went out there."

"He's not very fond of me," Mavros said, "so I'll stay in here if you don't mind."

I remembered how Mavros had nearly killed Arion and figured that would be for the best.

Susan and Brent stuffed their feet into shoes, grabbed their coats, and practically skipped outside. I understood their giddiness completely. The first time I had met Arion, I'd felt the same way.

"How bad was it?" Cody asked as soon as the door shut.

I plopped down on the couch. "Bad enough that Malcolm might not come back."

"Not good." He sat next to me, pulling me against his side.

Liam crossed his arms over his chest and leaned back against the wall. He told Cody about my day spent in Faerie and what had happened since.

Anger darkened Mavros' face with each word. His hands were clenched tightly at his sides. I patted the couch beside me. His steps were wooden, but he settled next to me. I twined my fingers with his. "I'm fine."

"But will you be?" His obsidian eyes sliced into mine, and his nostrils flared. "Can the three of us protect you from Kieran? Do you think we can keep you safe?"

"No." I jerked away from him and jumped to my feet, pacing in front of the couch. "Not at all. You basically told me there's nothing any of you can do against him. You told me it was up to me. Are you telling me that it's not, that there's something you can do?"

He shook his head. "No, there isn't." He leaned forward, resting his elbows on his knees, stared down at the carpet, and let out a long, gusty sigh. "The only help I can give you is to find the tree and hope you can stop the leaves from falling before it's too late."

Chapter 21

$\mathcal{E}$very day that passed without seeing my dragon companions left me feeling more despondent. I knew they were trying to keep me safe, but I missed them. They were so much more than protectors. They had become family, a huge part of my life, and I wasn't ready to let them go.

The only good thing was that Kieran had been absent, too. I still couldn't obtain my memories, so I wasn't sure what kept him away. Had something happened to him that day in Faerie, or was he waiting for something?

"Dacia," Max said my name like it wasn't the first time he'd called on me.

Warmth crept up my neck and over my ears and cheeks. "Yes?"

"Will you please indulge us in the first few paragraphs of your story?" He smiled at me, and I knew I was right about not hearing the first or maybe second or third times he'd called on me.

I took a quick sip of water before I started reading. Last time I'd read something in his class, Troy had harassed me. I didn't have to worry about him anymore, but I still hated having everybody looking at me.

With a shaking voice, I stood and began reading what everybody else in this classroom thought was a work of fiction. When in fact, it was my real life. Magic, demons, dragons, a pegasus, a unicorn, silver-haired fairies, Nephilim, and a phouka. How could it be real? No one would ever believe it if it was written as an autobiography, but as a novel, it was quite thrilling.

When Max nodded at me, I finished reading the paragraph I was on and sat down again. "Very good, Dacia. Your hook is astounding. It draws the reader in right away and leaves them wanting more." He scanned the classroom, meeting the gaze of several students. "This is what I'm looking for when I say I want a strong first line. You need to write something that will make your reader invested from the very beginning."

The door creaked open, and I no longer heard anything he said. My attention was solely focused on whoever pulled it ajar. The student hustled across the room and into an empty desk. "Sorry," she muttered as she grabbed her notebook and pen out of her bag.

I slumped down in my seat, breathed deeply, and willed my heartbeat to slow its racing. Both Aurelia and Mavros watched me from the corners of their eyes. Liam sat in front of me, unaware that my emotions were wreaking havoc on the others.

By the time class ended, I was ready to go looking for Kieran if he didn't show up soon. The reprieve was nice, but not knowing was killing me. I was jumpy and out of sorts. I expected leaves to start dropping off the branches at any moment. Every morning when I woke up, it was the first thing that I checked.

I didn't pay attention to anything on the walk from Quartz Building back to the apartment. If someone would have stopped me to ask if it was snowing or sunny outside, I wouldn't have been able to tell them.

Mavros touched my shoulder as I walked past him into the living room. "Dacia?" His voice was laced with concern.

"When's he going to take me again?" I plopped down on the couch without taking off my coat or boots. "When are they coming back? What don't I remember?" I leaned my head back and stared up at the ceiling. "And why can't I remember?"

Aurelia sat next to me and pulled my glove off. She held onto my hand and sent soothing energy into me, taking the edge off of my anxiety.

We were still sitting that way when Samantha walked in. "Hey." She smiled, and it was warm and caring. "I'm glad you're here. Dan and I were wondering if you and Cody would want to go to dinner in Althea. Cassandra and Bryce are going."

Mavros didn't give me a chance to answer. "They'll go. The change would be good for her. She needs to get out and have some fun."

"The panther has spoken." I rolled my eyes at him. "Apparently, my simple yes wouldn't have been good enough." Glancing at my fleece-lined leggings and wet boots, I decided that maybe I should change before leaving. "I'll be ready by the time the guys are here."

As soon as I opened my door, last weekend plowed into me again. The purple comforter Samantha had found to replace my other one was nowhere near as cheery as the one Malcolm had gotten for me. Seeing it reminded me that he wasn't here, and I didn't know when he would be again.

I sank down onto the edge of the bed. *Malcolm?* Several times over the past week, I had sent my thoughts out to him, but he hadn't responded. *Cash, is Malcolm okay?*

He will be. The growled voice that answered told me that Cash was in dragon form. *His bloodlust has diminished.*

Will you come back?

He didn't hesitate to answer. *I will, Dacia, but right now, Malus Tribulus needs me to help keep his wildness contained.* He growled at someone. *Give him time.*

Yeah. I sighed. *I keep hearing that.*

The roar that followed cut off quickly, and I realized that Cash had more to deal with than a pouting teenager. I pushed off the bed and searched through my dresser for something nicer to wear. I pulled out my favorite pair of jeans and a jade sweater.

Then I went into the bathroom, changed clothes, fixed my hair, and even applied some makeup. Just because I felt hopeless and broken on the inside didn't mean I needed to look like it on the outside.

I tugged a pair of knee-high brown boots out from under my bed and pulled them on before I went back into the living room. All eyes turned toward me. A hard lump formed in the middle of my chest. I wasn't the main exhibit in a freak show. I didn't need everybody gawking at me.

My reaction softened when Cody got up and strode toward me. He lifted his fingers to my face, caressing my cheek with his thumb. "You look beautiful, Dacia." He leaned down, not as far as he normally would have to because of the heels on my boots. "That sweater makes your eyes sparkle like emeralds."

"Thanks." A thousand butterflies took off all at once, reacting to the husky timbre of his voice, if not his words. "You look pretty good yourself." I pulled my lip into my mouth and instantly regretted it. This was one of the many reasons I didn't wear makeup often. "You always do, though."

He chuckled, and the butterflies fluttered uncontrollably.

Cody drove to Althea. Liam rode along with the six of us while Aurelia and Mavros took their own ways to town.

A light dusting of snow covered the road, shimmering like diamonds in the headlights. My friends and I sang loud and off-key. Sometimes, we knew the words, and sometimes, we made them up.

When Cody pulled into a spot at The Avalanche, my sides hurt from laughing so hard. Mavros had been right. I needed this. If I had stayed in my apartment, I would have spent the evening worrying about the dragons and Kieran. Stressing over things I couldn't control. Instead, for the first time in a long time, I was genuinely having fun.

We stayed until they closed. Shoveling in food, talking, and laughing. I glanced at Aurelia, wondering if she had done something to make me loosen up, but before I asked, I decided that it didn't matter. It wouldn't hurt anything, and I'd needed this more than I needed to worry about everything that I couldn't control.

When the manager subtly let us know it was closing time, we piled back into Cody's SUV and headed to campus. Tiny flakes landed on the windshield, melting before the wipers could scatter them.

The headlights reflected in a creature's eyes. "There's something in the road." I pointed ahead, and Cody slowed down.

"Where?" He clutched the steering wheel, waiting for it to run in front of him.

I leaned forward, searching the darkness. "There."

The lights passed over the black body, and my stomach plummeted. The horse had midnight fur and yellow eyes. His long tail nearly brushed the rocky shoulder.

Kieran was back.

Chapter 22

C'est La Vie

$\mathcal{L}$ying in bed, I stared up at the ceiling. Just when I thought sleep would welcome me into its embrace, I saw the massive horse standing on the shoulder of the road, watching us as we drove past. His yellow eyes turned more sinister every time the memory jolted me awake.

Aurelia sat at the foot of my bed watching me. Her golden skin reflected the light from the full Snow Moon shining in through the open curtains. Even after a week, seeing her there still came as a shock to me. It was Malcolm's spot, and at times, when he couldn't be here, it was Mavros'.

She stood and walked past my bed, silently opening my door. "Come out here."

Hoping not to wake him, I slid out from under Cody's arm. He mumbled something before grabbing my pillow and flipping over onto his other side.

The apartment was chilly, so I picked up a blanket on my way out of my room. Throwing it over my shoulders, I wandered to the kitchen table where Aurelia sat. "While you are tired but unable to sleep, I would like to try to access your memories. Maybe in this state, I will finally be able to."

Pulling out the chair across from her, I perched on the end of it. She slid her hands across the table with her palms facing up. I slipped mine over them, and she held onto them in a loose grip.

Staring into my eyes, she said, "I want you to think about the last thing you remember from Saturday. Focus on that memory, and we will try to work our way forward from there."

"Kieran snapped his fingers and turned me human." I shivered, and the blanket slipped off my shoulders. "He was angry that I'd beaten him, but I swear I didn't cheat."

She squeezed my hands. "I know you did not. If you would have, the leaves would have turned." Her gaze slid to my arm, to the oak with the beginnings of autumn's kiss shading its foliage. "There is no stopping that. The magic would have known."

"He brought me back to campus." The urge to run my fingers through my hair made me tug my hand back, but Aurelia held onto it. I bit on my bottom lip instead, trying to organize my thoughts. "I don't know why he did. He could have kept me there. As far as I know, he doesn't have any idea that I can find my own way back."

"Is that the last you remember, then?" She tilted her head to the side, watching my reaction.

I started to nod but stopped the movement short. "No. I remember coming back to the apartment. Mavros was waiting for me." I looked around. "Where is he anyway?"

"Your apartment is a little too small for the two of us to comfortably coexist." Her lip pulled up, exposing her teeth. "He tried to kill Arion."

This time, I squeezed her fingers. "I know, and for that, I'm sorry, but he's not the same person he was then."

"Memories, Dacia, not the demon."

I closed my eyes and thought back to Saturday. Mavros had been pacing in the hallway when I ran up the stairs. As soon as he had seen me, he opened the door. I didn't remember stepping inside. There was nothing after the creaking of the hinges. "That's it," I said.

"Okay, I want you to keep your eyes closed and focus on my voice, nothing else." Her words were soft and melodious. "Listen to the sound, and let your consciousness drift back to that day."

I did what she said, and my mind floated like I was in a dream. Kieran as a raven flew through the air in front of me, growing smaller and smaller as the storm beat against my body. Defeat seemed imminent. The journey to the top of the mountain played out as if I was seeing it through somebody else's eyes. I remembered everything up until stepping through the apartment door. After that, there was nothing.

Aurelia walked me through it multiple times. She stared into my eyes, searching my memories for something, but she hit the same block that I had.

Finally, she leaned back in her chair, pinching her lips together for a moment before she said, "Kieran must have done something to you. If your mind put the block there, I should have been able to break through it."

"Why? What's he trying to keep from me?" I slumped down and pulled the blanket tighter around me. "There must be something from my dream that he doesn't want me to remember, but what?"

She stood and pushed her chair under the table. "Let me help you get some sleep. Maybe you can break through the block in your dreams."

"It's worth a shot." I walked into the bedroom and looked at Cody cuddling my pillow. Instead of taking it from him, I rolled up the blanket that I'd been wrapped in, lay next to him, and shoved it under my head.

Aurelia set her hand on my shoulder, pumping her magic into me. I relaxed instantly. My muscles loosened, and my eyes drifted closed.

"Sleep well, Dacia."

The horse stamps his hoof and whinnies. His mane flops down over his yellow eye, blocking it from view. He tosses his head and transforms into Kieran the man. "Are you ready to tell me how you cheated?"

He reaches for my arm, turning it so that he can see the tree. The branches sway in a breeze that nobody can feel.

"Why have the leaves not turned?" He throws my arm away from him in disgust. Pain grips my shoulder.

I step back. "They haven't changed because I didn't cheat. You did when you conjured up that storm to stop me."

"You won't beat me." His expression turns feral. Sharp teeth jut out between inhuman lips. "You may have bested me in two competitions, but I will prevail in the end. I always do." He turns and storms away.

I jolted awake and tugged my hand through my hair. "He said I beat him in two trials."

"Two?" Mavros materialized next to my bed.

Aurelia's eyes narrowed at him before she focused on me. "If you bested him in two competitions, that means you beat him in your dreams."

"No." I shook my head. It was bad enough that I had to deal with him while I was awake. I didn't want him to be able to invade my sleep, too. "How do I stop my dreams from being reality?"

Cody rolled over and looked at me through barely slitted eyes. "What's goin' on?"

"How, Mavros?"

His obsidian gaze bored into me. "I don't know, Dacia," he said while Aurelia answered Cody, "Kieran can enter Dacia's dreams."

"I don't know if he's doing the same thing I can do or if it's something different." Mavros tucked his hands into his pockets and leaned against the dresser. "I thought my power was unique to me."

"Of course, you did, demon." Aurelia's growl surprised me. She'd been around Mavros since he attacked Arion. They'd been cordial. She knew he protected me. There had to be something more to her animosity, but what?

Cody trailed his fingers down my arm from my shoulder to my elbow, then over again and again. "What if Mavros went into your dreams and pulled you out first?"

"Kieran has blocked him before." I held my hand over his, stopping its movement. "And, they can't interfere."

Aurelia pinched the bridge of her nose, and I wondered if the dragon council met in their human forms. When I'd first met her, she hadn't fidgeted at all. She'd sat so still that it was obvious she wasn't human. I never suspected that she was a dragon, but several other types of creatures had come to mind. "Anything we do will potentially make things worse for Dacia." She folded her hands in her lap and smiled softly at me. "You must be vigilant. Even in your dreams. Compete in every challenge as though you are awake."

"Yeah." I blew out a breath, lifting the hair off my face. "No problem." Sarcasm dripped from the words that slipped out of my mouth before I could stop them.

The smell of coffee cake baking saturated the air, making my stomach growl in anticipation. Samantha stood at the kitchen window while it cooked, looking outside at the heavy, gray clouds that filled the sky. "I know we're in the mountains, and it's wintertime, but don't you think the clouds could disappear for a day or two?"

She glanced over her shoulder, and I shrugged. "Probably not until I get this figured out or the dragons come back."

"This is you?" Dan asked from his position on the couch. As intently as he was focused on the game he and Cody were playing, I was surprised he had heard us.

I closed the book I'd been skimming through and leaned back in the chair. Wobbling my hand from side to side, I said, "I'm like eighty to ninety percent sure, yeah."

"Basketball," Cody said as his car drifted past Dan's. "If Samantha wants the sun, that's gonna be the only way."

The idea of playing without Malcolm, Cash, and Russ tugged at my heart. "You'll have to find one or three extras." Tears pricked at my eyes, and I got up, taking the book into my room before anybody noticed. I sat on my bed and pulled out my phone. There were no cell towers on campus, so it was basically useless while I was here, but Susan had sent me the pictures she took at Cody's birthday party. I scrolled through and found one with all of us in it.

It amazed me how quickly everything could change. We'd been happy. We'd been having fun. Then, poof, everything was messed up.

A light knock had me wiping my tears away. "Yeah?" The single word came out hoarser than I would have liked.

"Hey." Samantha opened the door just wide enough for her to scoot in. Sitting next to me on the bed, she rubbed my back. "They'll be back, you know?"

I lifted one shoulder to my ear but didn't trust my voice enough to respond otherwise.

"The blizzard is beautiful." Pointing out my window, she nonchalantly added, "A bit unexpected, though." She grabbed the box of tissues off my nightstand.

Setting my phone on my lap, I tugged one out, dabbed at my eyes and cheeks, and then blew my nose. "Thanks." I hung my head. "Sorry about the snow."

"It's okay." She looked down at the picture of all of us. "It's the mountains. It happens, but it would be best if it stopped."

"I'll try."

She nodded at my phone. "What other pictures did she send you?"

Knowing that if I scrolled to the right any further I would see photos of Damon, I moved the images the other way. Seeing him would make me sadder, and it would probably make Samantha angry. The shots of Britny standing on Cash's toes while they danced melted my heart. The way she gazed at him—her eyes wide and filled with awe—would have made for a perfect picture even if he wasn't looking at her like she was the most precious thing in the world.

Seeing the expression on his face, I wondered how I had ever been afraid of him. Flipping through the photographs made me feel lighter.

By the time the oven buzzed, the snow had diminished. A few flakes still drifted down, but it was nothing like it had been.

Cody was waiting by my door when we stepped out. "You okay?"

"Sure." I linked my arm through his, leading him into the kitchen. "It's just hard."

The smell of cinnamon strengthened when Dan pulled the cake out of the oven. Samantha and I poured drinks for everyone. She handled the coffee while I got the milk and orange juice out. Liam and Mavros came in just as Dan finished dishing up breakfast.

He pointed the spatula at them. "Basketball? Dacia needs to relax a bit."

"Sure." Liam grabbed a plate off the counter and sat in one of the armchairs. "Who else is playing?"

"Bryce, Justin, and Drew," Dan answered as he sat at the table with Cody, Samantha, and me. "And the five of us. We'll do four on a team."

I stared at the door, waiting for Aurelia to come in. I hadn't seen her since I'd woken up in the middle of the night.

Mavros cocked his head, watching me for a second. "She's hunting." He pointed his fork at his chest. "She was kind enough to let me know I'm in charge until she returns."

"What's going on with the two of you?" I wiped my mouth with my napkin and waited for him to answer. When he didn't say anything, I added, "Last time you two were together, it wasn't this tense."

Flames flickered in his irises. "She thinks we're getting too close."

"Really?" Maybe that was part of it, but I didn't think he was telling me everything. "What else?"

Liam covered his mouth with his hand. "Leave it at that, Dacia."

"Why?" Cody asked. "She has a right to know."

Dan and Samantha both set their forks on their plates and watched. If I wasn't worried about everything going on, I probably would have thought it was cute how in sync they were.

"Last time, we were trying to save you from a common enemy." Mavros walked to the sink, filled it with hot, soapy water, and started washing the dishes.

I stared at his tense shoulders, wondering what he meant by that. "And you're not this time?" I huffed out a humorless laugh. "Which one of you is on Kieran's side then?"

"Is he your only enemy?" Mavros spun around, pinning me with his intense stare. "Nobody else has tried to kill you lately?"

My appetite completely gone, I pushed my plate away. "Malcolm wouldn't have hurt me."

"Malcolm would have killed you if Cash and I hadn't stopped him."

Chapter 23

Death On My Doorstep

My head wasn't in the game. Passes flew by me without me even realizing the ball was being thrown my way. All of my shots were off. Bricks, air balls, and rimshots. The other team dribbled by me without me trying to steal the ball from them. I even made a shot at the wrong hoop one time.

Mavros took full advantage of my preoccupation. Passing and shooting the ball around me when I was playing defense and slapping the ball out of my hands when I was on offense.

Justin ran down the court next to me. "Are you all right, Dacia?" He didn't know the truth about me. He thought I had bodyguards because I'd seen something I shouldn't have.

"Yeah." I glanced toward him and saw genuine concern on his face. I couldn't help but wonder if it would be there if he knew the truth. I shook my head. I shouldn't think that way anymore. I had more friends now than I'd had at any other time in my life. Sarah, Samantha, Dan, Cassandra, and Bryce had all accepted me. Maybe given the chance, more people would. "I need to get my head in the game."

He reached toward me but didn't touch me. His hand hung in the air between the two of us. "Not what I meant. Your guards …"

"Yeah, I'm good. No worries." I shot him a look that I hoped passed as a smile. He waited at the top of the key for Liam to dribble down the court, and I ran to the right wing.

Mavros took his position between me and the basket. As soon as I looked at him, I saw him in the kitchen. *Malcolm would have killed you if Cash and I hadn't stopped him.* "Would he?"

He didn't even ask what I was talking about. He just nodded. "I promised not to lie to you, Dacia." His voice was softer than an angora rabbit's fur. "I'm sorry."

The air was sucked out of my lungs, and I stumbled. Mavros caught me before I slammed into the ground. He picked me up, pressing me against his bare chest, holding me tighter than was necessary.

"Dude," Drew's voice followed behind us, "he's stealing your girlfriend."

Cody chuckled. It sounded a little off, but I couldn't tell if it was jealousy or concern. "Nah. Already tried that. She chose me."

"I'm okay." I flattened my hand against Mavros' pecs. His skin was always hot. I assumed it had something to do with being a demon, but after playing basketball, it was even warmer. "Put me down."

He set me on my feet but held my arm under my elbow, making sure I could stand on my own. "What do you want to do, Dacia?"

"I thought you were just angry." I looked over his shoulder at my friends. "I didn't realize you were serious."

He rubbed my arm with his thumb. "I'm sorry."

Aurelia's aura neared me. Her tranquility brushed against my mind, soothing it. I felt her hand on my shoulder and tried not to let anyone else know she was there. She smoothed the hard edges of my emotions, taking away a lot of the pain that came with realization.

"I'll play." As I walked back onto the court, I whispered, "Thank you."

Mavros cocked his head to the side but didn't respond.

"You okay?" Cody's eyebrows were pinched together in concern.

Red tinged my cheeks as I realized how pathetic I must have looked to Justin and Drew. "My leg gave out, and Mavros took his bodyguarding a little too seriously."

Staying in place, Liam dribbled the ball. "Do you want me to start from up here or throw it in?"

"There's good." Bryce moved between Cody and the basket, and Justin took his place in front of Liam.

Dan and Drew stood at the bottom of the key. Dan gave a thumbs-up, and Drew lowered into a defensive position.

Liam nodded at me, and I ran up behind Justin, setting up a pick just as Liam drove past him. Bryce moved to block him, and he passed the ball to Cody. Mavros jumped between them but missed the ball by a hair when he swiped at it.

Seeing the opening, Cody passed it to me, and with no one guarding me, I shot. The ball swished through the hoop. Nothing but net. "Yes!" I did a fist pump, feeling like myself for the first time since I woke up.

Dan ran over to me and gave me a high five before we took off down the court. "She's back." The smile he shot me could have melted all of the ice off the Snowfire Mountains.

The rest of the game went that way. After Aurelia took the edge off my emotions, I was able to focus on playing basketball and burn off some of my frustration.

By the time we finished, I was breathing hard, my muscles felt used and abused, and my stress level was lower than it had been for quite some time. I pulled my sweats on, and we walked out of the gym into the sunlight.

Drew shielded his eyes with his hand. "What happened to the snow?"

"It wasn't supposed to storm anyway," Justin answered. "The weathermen never get it right."

Mavros patted me on the back. "I bet it cleared up about the same time Dacia's game came back."

I looked up at him surprised he would just come out and say that. When my gaze met his, he winked.

"That was pretty impressive." Drew looked over his shoulder at me. "You were like a new person after Mavros carried you off."

Mavros wagged his eyebrows. "I have a way with women."

I swatted at him, but he dodged the blow.

"Lunch?" Cody threw his arm over my shoulders, pulling me against his side and away from Mavros.

I slipped my hand around his waist. "We should let Samantha and Cassandra know."

"We'll get 'em." Bryce slugged Dan's arm, and the two of them took off at a jog toward the apartment while the rest of us headed to the cafeteria.

Liam and Mavros stuck close to me, and even though I couldn't see her, I felt Aurelia's aura. I let the tranquility of it sink into me so that I didn't think about Malcolm and Cash. As we walked along, I noticed another aura, and I didn't bother hiding the smile that his illuminating energy brought to my lips.

Hello, Arion. I sent my thought out to only him. *I've missed you.*

His breath lifted the hair on the back of my neck. *And I you.*

With him behind me, my mind drifted back to last Sunday. While I'd rehashed my weekend to Cody, Arion had entertained Cody's family. Britny could barely contain her excitement after flying through the night sky on Arion's back. His brothers tried to mask their exhilaration, but it was obvious in their faces. No matter how much they bit on their cheeks to hide their smiles, they couldn't conceal the gleam in their eyes.

Susan had walked inside the house and pulled me into a tight hug. "Thank you, Dacia, for bringing this magic into our lives." Joyful tears leaked out of her eyes. "A pegasus. I flew on a pegasus!"

Mavros held the door to Sedum open, and Cody ushered me inside. Drew and Justin made a beeline for the grill. Liam and Mavros surveyed the area before looking down at me. "Where to?" Cody asked.

"You guys can get what you want." If Kieran was waiting for me, they couldn't stop him from taking me anyway. When nobody moved, I said, "I was thinking chicken tenders and fries."

Cody looked at me, then at my guards. "I was thinking burger."

"I'll be fine." I squeezed his fingers before walking away from him.

Mavros trailed behind me like a stray puppy. I had a feeling he would growl at anybody that came too close to me.

"You know Aurelia's here, right?" I said it louder than I would have in the gym. There were a lot of people around, and I could have meant anywhere in the cafeteria.

He sped up so that he walked next to me. "Yes." He grabbed my forearm. "But after what I told you, what would make you think I would leave your protection to a *dragon*?"

The growl that I'd been expecting came from my other side. It was loud enough that a few people looked in my direction before quickly turning away. Their fear and confusion brought a smirk to Mavros' lips.

Mavros filled his plate with everything that I put on mine and then some. We walked to the table without saying anything to each other. The tension between him and the dragons was something that would need to be dealt with, but this was not the place to have that conversation. It would have to wait until we were alone.

Cody and Liam had pulled two tables together along the back wall. We sat there, facing the doors, waiting for Dan and Bryce to show up with Cassandra and Samantha. Drew and Justin were still waiting in line, so Cody leaned close to me and whispered, "What really happened?"

"It seems I was wrong." I pushed my plate away suddenly having no appetite. "Malcolm did want to kill me."

"Wouldn't've." Cody took a bite of his burger and watched for my reaction. "He loves you like you're his little sister."

"Yeah, well, apparently dragons will eat those if they're bleeding and helpless." I leaned my chair back on two legs until it rested against the wall and stared at the ceiling, trying not to think about Malcolm and his instincts. Instead, I wondered how many times I'd been yelled at for tipping a chair back like this.

Mavros pushed on the back of my seat, propelling the chair back onto all four feet. "You have to eat, Dacia."

Aurelia's hand settled on my shoulder, but I didn't feel her normal reassurance. She pushed more magic into me, and I finally relaxed enough to eat something. I was just about to take a bite when four people walked into Sedum. The sunlight streaming in through the wall of windows silhouetted them, but even if their massive bodies hadn't given them away, I would have known them anywhere.

I dropped my chicken. It bounced off my tray and onto the floor. Gripping the edge of the table, I held myself in place.

Liam wiped his fingers on his napkin, stood, and pulled another table over to join with ours. Before he sat down again, he watched me, waiting for some reaction or expression or something.

Cash, Malcolm, Russ, and Seth stopped across the table from me. I assumed Jax was with them, but like most of the time, if he was, he was invisible. Cash's smile was warm. He nodded at me but said nothing.

Malcolm stared at a spot above me, not meeting my eyes. "I'm sorry, but you should not forgive me."

"We're not alone." Liam's eyes darted to the side.

I pointed at the seats across from me. "Sit or don't." The chairs scraped over the linoleum as I reached a shaking hand for my chicken. I needed to eat. I needed to be brave. But there was no way they didn't sense my fear, anger, and betrayal. I chewed, but the food could have been cardboard for all I tasted of it.

"Man, you guys should have been here earlier." Justin set his tray on the table and pulled out a chair next to Liam. "We coulda used a couple more in our game."

"We were out of town." Cash glanced away from me just long enough to respond to him. Malcolm, on the other hand, looked everywhere but at me.

Liam tipped his glass toward them. "It's good to see you back."

"That's yet to be determined," Malcolm said in a low voice meant for only me.

The rest of my friends joined us a few minutes later. Samantha's smile broadened as she neared the table, covering her entire face by the time she reached us. "You're back! It's been a long week without you here."

Russ nodded. "Really long."

Once I finished eating, Cody pushed his chair back, but I set my hand on his, stopping him. I wasn't ready to go back to the apartment and have it out with Malcolm.

I scooted my chair closer to Cody and pulled his arm over my shoulders, leaning into him. We talked and laughed with our friends, and I did my best to ignore the tension rolling off of Malcolm.

Chapter 24

*M*alcolm stormed down the sidewalk in front of me. His muscles were rigid. His hands were fisted at his sides. Every student who neared us on our trek back to the apartment veered off. They kept their eyes averted, not daring to glance at him.

Could they tell he was other? Or did they think he was just an enraged human that they didn't want to cross? Whatever the answer, I was glad for the instinct that kept them from looking into his eyes.

Cody held onto my hand. His grip was strong and reassuring. I knew that no matter what, he would be there for me, but he was no match for a livid dragon.

Mavros strode on my other side, glaring daggers at Malcolm. Flames burned in his irises. I elbowed him in the side.

When he looked at me, I pointed at my eyes. He blinked, and the fire burned out, leaving glowing embers behind. I pulled my sunglasses off and handed them to him.

He shook his head and reached into the inside pocket of his coat. Pulling out a pair that I knew hadn't been there before, he slipped them on.

When we neared the dorms, Drew and Justin veered off. "Let me know next time you play." Drew waved. He kicked at piles of snow as he walked.

Justin nodded at Malcolm's back. "You're okay with him, right?"

"Yeah." I folded my arm over my chest, gripping my other one just above the elbow. A weight had settled in my stomach, but I needed to get this over with. "I'm fine."

He pressed his lips together and shook his head. "If you say so." He turned and jogged to catch up to Drew.

With every step, my chest tightened more. If Malcolm wanted to go, there was nothing I could do to make him stay. And, if he really had intended to kill me, I shouldn't try to keep him here anyway. My pace slowed. My feet dragged through the snow. Malcolm didn't notice. He charged forward, glaring at anyone who dared to step too close to him.

"You should have seen Dacia try to play basketball today." Mavros smirked at me. "She couldn't catch, couldn't throw, couldn't make a shot to save her soul."

Knowing what he was doing, I tried to shake it off, but I felt anger burn away all of the other emotions inside of me anyway.

"Most of the time, I wasn't even sure she knew she was supposed to be playing." He lifted his sunglasses so I could watch him roll his eyes at me. "I'm not sure why we let a girl play with us. Somebody else had to have been available."

I should have been grateful for what he was doing, taking me from smelling like prey to predator, but the rage simmered inside of me.

Malcolm's shoulders relaxed, and that movement sent another surge of frustration rolling through me.

"You guys should go to Cassandra or Bryce's dorm," I said through clenched teeth.

Bryce turned toward me. His eyebrows were pinched together. "And miss this?" He waved his hand between Malcolm and me. "Don't think so."

"Don't blame me if you get hurt." I picked up my pace. The reluctance I had felt earlier had been washed away. I wanted to have it out with Malcolm. I wanted to get this over with and move on with my life. Whether it was with him in it or out of it didn't matter anymore. I wanted it over.

I stormed up the steps to my apartment and held the door open, impatiently tapping my foot, while everyone took their sweet time shuffling in. The door slammed shut behind me, and I stood in front of it with my arms crossed over my chest. Mavros was close enough to me that I could feel the heat radiating off of his body, fueling my anger.

Dan, Samantha, Bryce, and Cassandra sat at the kitchen table. Liam was in one armchair, and Cody was on the couch. I glanced at the other chair. "Jax." I nodded, and for the briefest of moments, I caught a glimpse of his dark skin and blond hair.

Waving my hand at Aurelia, Russ, Cash, and Seth, I said, "You might as well sit. I'm not going to."

Russ plopped down next to Cody, and Aurelia perched on the end, positioning herself so she could see both Malcolm and me.

He leaned against the cabinets between the sink and the stove. His hands clutched the countertop. His eyes were his dragon's, completely bronze with a thin slash of pupil dividing them. "I don't want to hurt you." His voice was the rumble of thunder, deep, resonating. I could feel it inside of me at the same time I heard it. "If I stay here, I will."

"You made a vow!" I stabbed my finger through the air. "Does that mean nothing to you?"

His expression darkened further. "Don't, Dacia."

"Why not?" Tears burned in the back of my eyes, but I tried not to let them fall. "You promised to protect me." I clenched and unclenched my fists. The cabinet doors rattled as my anger shook the apartment.

Cash strode toward me, but Mavros moved between us. Cash held his hands up. "I don't want to hurt her. I want to calm her."

"If she's calm, what will *he* do to her?" Mavros nodded at Malcolm without taking his eyes off of Cash.

Cash looked over his shoulder. "There is no blood. He will not hurt her." He stepped closer and entwined his fingers with mine.

"Why did you leave me?" I asked Cash as he poured calming energy into me.

He looked down at our joined hands. "I am the only one who can still his dragon. I am the only one strong enough to fight him."

"Was it really that bad?" I knew it was. I had seen Liam's memories, but I needed to hear it from Cash. I needed to know what he thought. I needed to know if I should want Malcolm to stay or if I was being stupid.

He didn't need to answer. The way his grip loosened on my hand, slipping until he barely held onto the tips of my fingers was enough. "Yes." The word was spoken so softly that I almost didn't hear it.

"Should he stay?" I met Cash's gaze. His dragon wasn't riled, so I didn't see any harm in it. "Should I want him to?" The rest of the room was silent. The only noise was the humming of the refrigerator. "Will you stay if he doesn't?"

He rubbed his hands down his face. "He is your friend. Of course, you want him to stay, but I think you need to let him go."

"Oh." My legs shook. I slid down the wall and looked around the room. That wasn't what I'd expected him to say. I thought he would tell me that he could keep Malcolm in line. I thought he'd tell me that it would be all right now.

"He shouldn't be with you while you're training to fight." He knelt in front of me. His amethyst eyes were filled with sorrow. "He shouldn't be with you while you sleep, but he could guard you in your classes and on your way to them." He looked over his shoulder at Malcolm. "He could play basketball with you and keep training your magic."

"Kieran almost killed my magic." I tugged a trembling hand through my hair. "He poisoned me somehow. It … it needs strengthened again." I leaned to the side, peering at Malcolm. "I could use your help. You can leave whenever you need to. You can leave now if you want. I'll"—tears slipped out of my eyes—"I'll understand. I won't stop you."

Chapter 25

For the second time today, we sat in the cafeteria. Nobody felt like cooking, and we all had meal plans. I listened to the students around us. Conversations were usually quite varied, but today it seemed like everyone wanted to talk about the blizzard and the earthquake. It seemed I'd done more than just rattle the cupboards in our apartment. I held my head in my hands and wondered how bad things would have been if my magic had been at full strength.

"Looks like we'll be working on control." Malcolm pointed his fork at me. "Again." His expression was still hard, and his muscles were tense, but at least he was talking to me. He was here.

I peeked at him through my fingers. "That's probably for the best. It's been a long week."

He flashed his fangs at me, and for the first time in a long time, the action made me shiver. He shoved a practically raw piece of meat into his mouth without taking his gaze off of me. Even though he never looked away, I had no doubt that he knew where everyone in the room was and what they were doing.

I pushed the noodles around my plate. I had been hungry when we'd gotten here, but I couldn't force myself to eat.

For once, nobody tried to compel me to shove it down my gullet. When everyone else finished their dinner, we left. Without the moon's glow, millions of stars dotted the cloudless sky. The cold was biting, but there were too many other students around us for me to warm the air. I snuggled down into the warmth of my coat and pressed into Cody's side.

As we neared Dracaena Hall, I noticed a figure leaning against a lamppost. Even if I wouldn't have recognized his carefree stance, Malcolm's growl would have told me it was Kieran.

"Not today, phouka." Malcolm shifted to the side Kieran stood on.

Kieran lifted his hands and stared directly at me. "Tomorrow, Dacia." His thick, dark hair fell over his eyes, and he shoved it back. "We'll find out if you can best me again. This time without cheating."

My stomach dropped, souring what little I had eaten. The smug look on his face made it obvious that it wouldn't do any good for me to argue with him about it. I kicked at a chunk of ice on the sidewalk. "Fine. What time? Where?"

His head snapped back slightly before he was able to hide his surprise. "Outside your apartment. 8:00 in the morning." He didn't wait for a response before he turned and walked into the trees.

"I wonder what it will be this time." My arms and legs felt heavy as we trudged to the apartment.

Samantha patted my shoulder. "Whatever it is, you've got it. Just remember to do what you did last time."

I looked back at her to see her smiling reassuringly at me. Even though I tried, I couldn't return the expression.

Malcolm held the door open, made sure I went inside, and then turned around and walked to his room. I watched him disappear with a sinking feeling. I knew it was what we had agreed on, but it still felt wrong for him not to be here.

Cash squeezed my shoulder. "Give him some time. He wasn't sure he should come back at all."

"Then why did he?" I closed the door, and the click sounded so final.

Cash walked across the room. "It was time for me to return."

The serpent slithers closer. Its pearlescent scales glint in the light that shines down from nowhere. Even though it looks healthier, it's still not back to its previous size.

"Tomorrow, we have to go back to Faerie." I kneel next to it. "Do you think we can beat him?"

It lifts its head to rub on my fingers. *We must.*

"Are you strong enough?" I slide my hands along the scales, wondering what will happen if I win. Or worse, if I lose.

The snake puffs up, rising above me. *Even diminished, I am stronger than most.*

The room fades away, and I sit on the grass. Three full moons light the night, making it almost as bright as day.

A girl dances through the meadow. Her green dress twirls around her legs. The wind catches her dark hair, whipping it around her face.

She tosses her head back and laughs, never missing a step.

Her bare feet pound against the ground in an ever-increasing beat. Her arms wave through the air.

Suddenly, she stops and stares into the trees across from me.

Kieran steps from the shadows. The moonlight emphasizes his too sharp features, accentuating his cheekbones and extra joints.

The girl turns, running from him as fast as her feet will carry her, but she's no match for him.

He catches her, grabbing her arm and spinning her around. He lifts his hand, showing her an acorn like the one he gave to me.

She's mesmerized. She lifts her hand, brushing her fingers over the acorn's cap.

A bright light flashes.

My alarm went off. I looked at the clock and groaned. I shouldn't have set it for so early. I lay in bed, staring at the ceiling, wondering why I'd dreamed about that other girl. Was she Kieran's next victim? Did it have anything to do with today's challenge?

Running my hand over my face, I looked at the clock again. 6:36. I let out a long sigh. I shouldn't have given myself so much time to stress about going to Faerie. I threw the covers to the side intending to get out of bed, but Cody tugged me back. "Not yet."

Giving in to him, I snuggled against him and tried to relax, but I was terrified of what this day would bring. If I lost, how much more would the leaves turn? When would they begin to fall?

Cody kissed the tip of my nose. "Gonna be okay." His sapphire eyes were soft and sure.

I wanted to believe him, but last weekend's injuries were still too fresh in my mind. When I closed my eyes, I pictured my magic dying. Its skin peeling off its emaciated body. "I hope so." I pulled away. This time, I got out of bed and grabbed my clothes. In the bathroom, I changed into comfortable leggings, a sports bra, and a t-shirt.

When I finished, the bedroom door was open, and I heard Cody talking to Liam. The two of them were sitting at the kitchen table. Cody was shoveling food into his mouth. Liam waved at the stove. "I made breakfast."

"Thanks." I looked at the food, but the thought of eating anything turned my stomach. "I don't think I should, though."

Sitting on the couch, I stretched my legs out in front of me and stared up at the ceiling. By now, I should have had the patterns of the spackling memorized. I also should have realized I would find no answers there, but I kept gaping, keeping my eyes open until everything blurred together and the ridges and valleys formed images. I blinked them away when they formed the kelpies and moving trees that I'd seen the first time Kieran took me to Faerie.

The cushions on the couch sank, and I glanced over at Mavros. He slid his hand over mine, and I welcomed the warmth of his fingers.

"Don't forget you have my power at your disposal," he whispered into my ear. His words were only for me. "It's in you if you're just brave enough to use it."

I nodded, sure that if I tried to talk the words would catch in my throat.

"Do whatever you need to do to win." Jax's disembodied voice came from the armchair closest to Samantha's and Dan's rooms. "Lie, cheat, steal."

I stared at the place where I assumed his eyes would be. "I'm hoping to set the same rules as before. One form, no cheating, no hindering the other opponent, no teleporting to the end." I tugged my hands through my hair, clutching it at the back of my skull. "Am I forgetting something? What if I forget something?" My breath came out in harsh gasps, keeping my lungs from filling. My chest tightened. The air in the room was too thick to breathe. It was too hot. The walls closed in, trapping me with no oxygen.

Leaning forward and holding my head in my hands, I tried to focus on my breathing and not on defeating Kieran. The oak glared at me from my arm, taunting me. There was no way I could get away from this. There was no way for me to win.

Kieran would change the rules. He wouldn't let me beat him again.

The room spun. My heart pounded in my ears, drowning out all other sounds. The drumming was too fast.

I rocked back and forth, trying to calm myself, fighting the panic that stole my breath, my vision, and my hearing.

A hand rubbed small circles on my back, but it did nothing to soothe me. The terror had dug its claws in too deeply, clutching my heart and my mind.

Aurelia knelt in front of me. Her golden hair shone, practically glowing, as she took my hands in hers. Her magic rushed into me faster than ever before. It surged through me, but the panic acted like a dam, keeping her soothing energy from reaching my core.

Cody sat next to me. He slid one arm behind me and one under my knees and pulled me onto his lap, pressing me tightly against his body. Then he leaned down and sprinkled kisses along my jaw, my neck, and my forehead. Between each peck, he whispered something that I couldn't make out. His breath caressed my face. The tenderness in his motions drew me out of my darkness.

Aurelia's power burst through the dam. It flooded my body. My heartbeat slowed. My breathing relaxed.

"It's okay, Dacia." Cody's voice was low and husky. "You're going to be okay." He kissed just below my ear. "You have to. I need you."

I wrapped my arms around him and buried my face in his neck. "Thank you." The steady rhythm of his heart drowned out my despair. I didn't feel confident, but the hopelessness that had consumed me was gone.

Cody brushed my hair back. "Anytime, Dacia."

I looked at Aurelia. "Thank you."

"You are welcome." She smiled at me, but it didn't reach her eyes.

There was a sharp knock on the door right before it opened. Malcolm looked in. "It's time."

"Can you control yourself?" Mavros didn't hide the disdain in his voice.

Malcolm looked down. The self-loathing on his face surprised me. "My hunger is sated." He glanced back up at me. "If you don't want me with you, I will stay here."

"No." I shook my head. "You can walk down with me. I'm sure as soon as I get there, he'll whisk me away."

"Unless he taunts us." Mavros stood in front of me, holding his hand out.

Cody started to stand, but I shook my head. "Please stay here, Cody. I don't know what he would do if he got his hands on you."

"Fine. Whatever." He sat back with a huff.

I knew that being weaker than my enemies and allies had to wear on him. If there was a way for me to transfer some of my power to him to keep him safe, I would gladly do it.

Knowing that I might not come back, I bent down and kissed him. I didn't care that we had an audience. I didn't care what my emotions would do to any of them. I just wanted Cody to know that I loved him and wanted to make it back to him.

As I walked by the door, I looked at my coat. If I took it with me, there was a chance I would lose it, but if I didn't, would Kieran decide to stay on Earth?

"If you need one, you can take this." Mavros grabbed the front of his coat and held it out from his body while he opened the door for me. As soon as I stepped into the hallway, he took ahold of my hand and gently rubbed his thumb over mine. "You can do this, Dacia. Establish the rules. Don't just use your magic or your strength. Use your head."

"Try to remember everything that you read in the books about Faerie, no matter how unimportant they may seem." Liam walked on the other side of me.

Malcolm and Cash led the way. Their bodies were a solid wall in front of me. Seth and, I assumed, Jax followed behind us. Aurelia and Russ had stayed behind to make sure that Cody, Dan, and Samantha stayed safe.

We stepped outside into the frigid mountain morning. The sky was a brilliant blue, but frost floated down off the branches, making it look like it was snowing. I wrapped my arms around myself and wished I had on something more than my t-shirt.

Seeing my discomfort, Mavros took his coat off and handed it to me. As soon as he did, another one appeared on him. I shook my head, and he smiled, a sly curling of his lips.

Kieran bounded out of the trees that surrounded the apartment building. "It is time." He held out his hand.

"No." I took a step back, keeping my guardians around me. "First, I want to set the rules."

He narrowed his eyes and tipped his head forward slightly.

"No cheating. After the game is declared, we must each choose a form and remain in that manifestation until it is completed. No using magic or nature or anybody or anything else to hinder the other player. If this is a race of some sort, no teleporting to the end." I closed my eyes, hoping that I hadn't forgotten anything.

He tapped his chin thoughtfully. "One form? So, your magic has returned."

"What do you mean?" I didn't want him to know what I'd been through. I didn't want him to know that whatever he'd done had nearly killed my powers. I shook my head. "It doesn't matter. Do you accept?"

He rocked his head from side to side like he was thinking or trying to crack his neck. I wasn't sure which. "Deal. Tell your guards to back off."

I squeezed between Malcolm and Cash, brushing my hands against theirs, letting their soothing energy sink into me.

Just as I took Kieran's hand, he grinned wickedly. "You forgot a rule."

Chapter 26

Illusions

As I plummeted through the realms, fear clutched my heart in its icy grip. I had forgotten a rule. I knew I had been missing something, but what?

What would Kieran be able to do with my omission?

Too soon my feet were on solid ground. The vibrant green of Faerie and the heady smell of petrichor threatened to overwhelm my senses.

Leaning over with my hands on my knees, I breathed deeply. My mind raced with the implications. What had I forgotten? How would he take advantage of it?

"Is all of Faerie this green?" I asked Kieran, hoping he'd give me a few minutes to shake off my fear and collect myself.

His eyes danced with merriment as he grabbed hold of my upper arms and spun me around. A massive body of water sprawled out in front of us. Blue as far as I could see. Raindrops sent ripples dancing across its surface, growing bigger as they moved from the epicenter. I strained my eyes but couldn't see the end of the enormous lake or ocean, just a line where the sky and water met.

Kieran stepped to the edge, wetting his toes in the lazy waves that met the shore. "First one to swim to the other side wins." He waved his hand impatiently, motioning me closer. "Choose your form."

Thinking of all the nature documentaries I'd ever watched, I said, "Sailfish."

"If that's what you want." He smirked at me. "I'll go with hippocampus."

I mentally smacked my head. Transforming into a mythological creature hadn't even crossed my mind. I closed my eyes and pinched the bridge of my nose, hoping I hadn't made a horrible mistake. "Hey! I thought phoukas could only take specific shapes."

"Don't tell me you believe everything you read in books." He clicked his tongue against the roof of his mouth several times. "I thought you were smarter than that." He shook his head, and his dark hair flopped over his eye. There was a playfulness in Kieran's voice that I hadn't heard since I'd beaten him. "Step into the water."

The lake wasn't as cold as I'd expected, but it still made goosebumps rise on my flesh as I walked forward until the water reached my waist. As I shifted my body into a sailfish, I tried to remember which rule had eluded me. No cheating, no hindering, one form, no teleporting. What else had I told him before?

Gills cut slits through the side of my neck, and I gasped for air that I could not find. My nose lengthened into a sharp point. My spine cut through my flesh, forming a dorsal fin. My arms pulled in, turning into pectoral fins. When my legs morphed into a caudal fin, my body splashed into the water. Blessed air filled my lungs.

With eyes on the sides of my head, I saw Kieran without looking for him. He was stunning, a massive blue, black, and purple amalgamation of a horse and a sea creature. Easily three times the length of my body, he didn't fit without his caudal fin lying on the shore behind us. His front legs stamped the ground like a thoroughbred ready to dart out of its gate. The action made his mane flop down over his luminous yellow eye.

I heard his voice in my head. *Ready.* He lowered his body. *Set.* He glanced at me, and the mirth dancing in his eyes was infuriating. Something was up. *Go.*

I wiggled my caudal fin, hoping it would drive me forward. While I tried to figure out how to move as a fish, Kieran's hooves kicked up dirt, and he galloped off. There was no other way to describe his movements. His front legs tore through the water, racing toward the far shore, while his fin sliced from side to side pushing him faster and harder than I would ever be able to propel myself.

By the time I figured out what I was doing and began cutting through the water, Kieran climbed onto the shore. The magnificent water stallion transformed into the man. He shook, and water flew off of him in all directions.

Reaching the edge of the lake, I had to stay underwater until I morphed into my body, holding my breath until my fins changed into arms and legs. As soon as I could stand, I trudged onto the shore. Looking over my shoulder, I saw the other side of the lake maybe twenty feet away.

I spun around to face Kieran, and he lifted his hands into the air. A mischievous smile tugged at his lips. "I told you that you forgot a rule." He turned, striding into the trees. "This wasn't going to be the game at all, but you made it so easy when you set the rules on Earth … and left one out. All I had to do was bring you to a body of water and create an illusion that it was vast."

My legs gave out, and I fell to the rocky ground. Stones dug into my knees and the palms of my hands. Blood mixed with the water that still clung to my body and dripped onto the shore.

Mavros had told me to use my head, but I couldn't even do that right.

Illusions.

How could I have forgotten to ban illusions?

Shivering uncontrollably, I sat up, pulled my knees to my chest, and wrapped my arms around my legs.

"Faerie will love you forever for feeding her." Kieran nodded at my torn leggings and the bloodied skin underneath. "She may never let you leave."

I looked from my knees to him. "What do you mean?"

"You gave her an offering of blood." The rain slowed to a light sprinkle as Kieran sat next to me. "Either way, it won't be long now. Think of all the fun we'll have once you're in Faerie permanently." He grabbed my arm and flipped it over. Blood dripped from slices on my palms. He reached for it, but I closed my fists.

I knew what my blood did to dragons. I didn't need to see what it would do to a phouka.

He laughed and drew a line in the air. Together we watched as more of the leaves turned a fiery red.

A giant hollow space opened up in my chest, threatening to suck everything into it. A black hole of despair. I drew in deep breaths, but they did nothing to stop the panic that was taking over again. I pressed the palms of my hands into my eyes, trying to shut everything out. "Take me home, Kieran."

"You are home." He pulled away from me. His feet crunched on the rocky shore.

I glared up at him as he danced along the water's edge. "This is not my home. It's yours, and even if you make me live here for the rest of forever, it will never be mine." Hot tears rushed down my cheeks. "Take me home."

"I'll make you a deal." He tapped his chin with his finger. "Fly with me over Spring. See the land from above. Then, if Faerie lets me, I'll take you home." He bowed, keeping his gaze locked onto mine. "I promise no harm will come to you."

I narrowed my eyes. "First, Faerie cannot keep me. We have a bargain that precedes any claim that she might have. Second, you told me I can't believe everything I read, yet you expect me to believe that faeries can't lie."

"Everybody knows faeries can't lie." He shook his head like I was an idiot. "How many people even know what a phouka is?"

Since I didn't want him to know that I could leave on my own, I really didn't have a choice. "What form would you like me to fly in?"

"That one's fine." He pulled a ragwort stem out of his pocket and whispered something to it. A tiny dapple gray stallion formed in his palm. He set it down on the rocky ground, and the beast grew until it stood at least sixteen hands tall.

I held my hand out, and he nuzzled against my fingers. I petted his face, neck, and ears. When I touched his mane, seeds flew into the air, drifting lazily on the breeze. Using my magic to boost me, I jumped up onto his back, and when Kieran tried to hop up behind me, I nudged the horse forward. "Get your own."

"You think you can ride a fairy horse?" He lifted one eyebrow in question.

I stared down at him from my seat atop the stallion. "It seems so."

That aggravating smile turned his lips up again as he pulled another ragwort stem out of his pocket. This time the horse was a light gray dapple with black stockings and a white mane and tail. It was about the same height as the horse I rode. "Have you ever flown on a horse?"

"Does a pegasus count?" I looked over my shoulder at him. This time I got to be the smug one.

He kicked his steed, making it gallop across the rocky ground. When it was almost to the trees, it lifted into the sky. I followed behind him, talking to my horse as he ran. "Don't make me look bad. Please." He leapt into the air, soaring over the tops of the trees.

Unable to stop myself, I laughed with delight. I was flying above Spring on a weed. Of all the things that had happened since I came to college, this had to be one of the weirdest experiences.

The green territory spread out beneath me. The sun peaked out from behind gray clouds, and a rainbow formed. It was brighter than any I had ever seen. Fairy mounds dotted the landscape. In the clearings, flowers covered nearly every available space. Purples, pinks, yellows, whites, reds, and oranges. It was surreal. Beautiful.

We flew to the end of Spring and turned where it met Summer. The trees were still green here, but they looked drier. Their trunks weren't covered with moss, and the sun was hotter.

Our horses took turns taking the lead, chasing one another through the clouds, galloping on air. Somehow, their hooves still made clopping noises.

As the horses ran, Summer turned to Autumn. The trees there were all wearing stunning fall foliage. Reds, oranges, yellows, and purples. The leaves were beautiful, but they reminded me of the one on my arm. I resisted the urge to look at the oak.

We curved again, never leaving Spring. Animals with their offspring foraged through the grasslands and forests that we flew over. Some of them were creatures I'd seen before, ones that I knew of from back on Earth, and some were fantastic, amazing things that I could never have dreamt up on my own. Others were horrible, terrifying monsters that would probably visit my nightmares.

Kieran led us from Autumn to Winter. The snow was pristine, pure, beautiful. Thick icicles hung from the trees' branches and rocky outcroppings. The wind blew the snow into massive drifts, picking it up and swirling it around before dropping it down again. Even well within the borders of Spring, it was chillier here. My breath puffed out in front of me, frosting the air.

I used my magic to warm my skin and to dry my still wet clothes from my time in the lake.

We turned again. Winter changed into something totally different. Green trees were mixed with ones in their autumnal dresses. I looked for oaks with red and green leaves, hoping I would see something that resembled the one on my arm. Hoping to catch a break.

Kieran slowed his horse. "If you would still like to go back, I will take you now. It seems that Faerie agrees with your argument. She cannot keep you yet."

"I should." I smiled at him. "Thank you for this. It was actually kind of amazing."

He reached his hand out. "You know you should never thank a faerie, don't you?"

Chapter 27

As soon as we were above Phlox University, my horse turned into ragwort seeds and blew away. Falling through the sky, I felt a profound sadness at the loss. I knew that was what the stallion was from the beginning, but he had been beautiful and alive. To have his life cut so short was tragic.

I turned myself invisible so nobody would see me free-falling. Then before Kieran could grab ahold of me, I teleported into my bedroom.

My feet had barely touched the carpet when somebody knocked on my door. "I'm back. I need to change clothes."

"The clock's ticking," Malcolm growled through the wooden barrier that separated us.

A shower would have been nice. It could have chased away some of the chill and washed the lake water off of me, but there was no way anybody would be okay with me taking that long. I huffed as I grabbed a pair of fleece-lined leggings and a comfy hoodie. I changed as quickly as possible. Before I went out into the living room, I threw my wet clothes on the bathroom floor and took a few seconds to look at the oak tree on my arm.

Roughly half of its foliage was the color of my hair. A bird hopped along one of the branches, and I said a silent prayer that it wouldn't knock any leaves off. I pulled my sleeve down and turned the handle.

Malcolm and Mavros both stood right next to my door. Aurelia was nowhere to be seen. "What rule did you forget, Dacia?"

I looked across the room at Liam, surprised it was him that asked. A lump formed in my throat, and I didn't know if I could talk around it.

Mavros slid his hand around my waist and deposited me on the couch next to Cody. "What rule?" he asked as he stepped away.

"Illusions." That single word was all I could force out before tears streamed down my cheeks. I held my face in my hands, fighting the hopelessness that had found me again.

Cody wrapped his arm around my shoulders and tugged me against his side. His hand brushed from the top of my head to the middle of my back. "How bad?"

"Obviously, it's bad." Samantha smacked the table. "Why don't you all just give her a few minutes?"

As much as I appreciated Samantha standing up for me, I knew I needed to at least show them even if I couldn't say anything right now. I tugged on my sleeve and lifted my arm so they all could see it.

"No." Cassandra gasped and covered her mouth.

Malcolm growled, and Mavros moved so that he was standing between the two of us. "She is safe from me, *demon*."

"I wouldn't know." Mavros folded his arms over his chest and lifted an eyebrow.

Dan cleared his throat. "So, you've both won twice, right?"

"Yeah." I pulled my sleeve back down, not wanting to see it anymore. "If—" I sucked in a deep breath and tried to calm myself "—if I lose two more, the leaves will turn faster, but either way, they'll start falling."

Cash strode to the couch. Standing in front of me, he reached his hand down. "Enough with the self-pity. Let's go train."

"Hasn't she been through enough today?" Cassandra asked.

I looked over my shoulder at her. She sat next to Samantha, examining her fingernails, not meeting anyone's gaze. "No, I should go." I tugged my hands through my hair. Some of the strands were still damp. "Training might actually help. If nothing else, it'll take my mind off of everything."

We flew, soaring on currents, racing across the sky. Mountains stretched up beneath us. Their rugged peaks were buried beneath snow. The sun was setting in front of us. Pinks, purples, oranges, and reds painted the gold-lined clouds.

Steam rose from my body as the cold air brushed against my hot scales. Catching the dying rays of the sun, it turned pink before dissipating.

Malcolm darted through the sky in front of all of us. I smelled fear and doubt rolling off of him, and my stomach rumbled in response.

Mavros was between the two of us. His distrust of Malcolm ate at me. They were all my friends, and I wanted them to get along. I didn't want this rift between us to continue to grow.

Liam and Cash flew to my sides with Russ and Seth behind us. If Jax had come along, I didn't know where he was. I hoped he had stayed at the apartment to make sure my friends were safe.

"Where's Aurelia?" The resonant tone of my voice always surprised me when I was a dragon. It was so much richer than that of my human form.

Cash turned his long neck toward me. "She was called back by the dragon council. She will return as soon as she can."

"Oh." I knew she had responsibilities other than me, but I would have liked the chance to say goodbye to her.

Malcolm sped up, and the rest of us followed suit, pushing ourselves harder. I glanced at Liam. He had cut slits in what looked like one of Mavros' leather jackets. His tan and cream wings jutted out through them. A stocking cap was pulled over his auburn hair. His face was bright red from the wind and the cold.

As if he sensed my gaze, he looked at me and smiled. "Next time, can I bring some of the other Nephilim to fly with us?"

"Yes." I had been terrified that they would turn on me once I gave them wings, but I no longer feared that. Even if they wouldn't have promised Mavros, I think their joy would have prevented them from hurting me. I remembered Malcolm telling me that I had made more allies, and I wanted to make sure they stayed that way.

We landed on a rocky outcrop. Malcolm's bronze eyes met mine as he took his human form, but he quickly looked away. As soon as he transformed, he started jogging through the coniferous forest. With the rest of my guards surrounding me, we followed.

Branches hung low, their needles catching on my sweatshirt and snagging my hair, so instead of fire, I created a ball of blue light. It hovered in front of us, guiding us over the treacherous ground.

With every step, the forest around us darkened. The shadows lengthened, and I shivered. Not from the cold, but from not knowing what was out there. I remembered the imp that had wanted to rip my heart out and eat it while it was still beating.

"Dacia." Cash's growl was a low warning.

I looked ahead, instead of into the deepening shadows. "Sorry." Scales formed over my hands, face, and neck, hiding my exposed skin. I straightened my hair and made it green with blue roots.

Mavros glanced back at me, and a smirk pulled his lips up.

"What?" My voice came out as a high-pitched squeak.

He chuckled as he turned around. "You remind me of a pixie." He shook his head. "You've already got their temperament down."

"What's—" I slapped my hand over my mouth, trying to stop the shrill noises coming out of it "—that supposed to mean?"

His shoulders bounced, and I knew he was silently laughing at me. He slowed until he was running right next to me. I tried to recall when if ever he'd run with me in his human form, but as far as I remembered, he'd always transformed or stayed behind. "It means you think you're a panther, but you're really a lap kitty."

I smacked his arm at the same time that I rolled my eyes.

"Thank you for proving my point." He picked up his pace, moving back between Malcolm and me.

I glared at his back, pretending not to enjoy the view. "You know house cats are one of the deadliest creatures on the planet, right?" Again, with that voice. I shook my head and removed the transformations, heating my skin instead.

"Keep telling yourself that, pussy cat."

Knowing it wouldn't hurt him, I shot a blast of blue fire from my fingertips into his firm derriere. It made me feel better until he turned around and wiggled his eyebrows at me. "I'll get you back for that."

Heat rushed my cheeks, and Cash growled again. Grabbing my arm, he held me back. "You have to control your emotions, Dacia. Lock them down, or he will leave."

"Okay." I jerked away from him. Hot tears burned my eyes, but I tried to hold them back. He was right. I was just making things harder for Malcolm, maybe for the other dragons, too.

Malcolm looked over his shoulder. "You've gotten soft. Can't you run any faster?" He flashed his fangs at me and sprinted into the darkness.

The challenge was exactly what I needed. My emotions were buried beneath a heavy desire to win. I ran after him. The light stayed just in front of me, showing me where boulders jutted up through the snow. I tried to follow in Malcolm's footprints, but his strides were longer than mine.

Mavros and Cash matched me step for step. Neither of them was willing to let me gain ground on Malcolm without them nearby.

I summoned a gust of wind to push me along. Sweat dotted my forehead and temples, cooled instantly by the wintery air. I moved to the side, ready to pass Malcolm.

Mavros stuck his arm in front of me. "Do you have a death wish?" Flames exploded in his eyes, and he laughed. It wasn't a laugh that invited anyone to join in. Instead, it made the hairs on my neck stand on end and chilled me to the bone.

He slowed us and grabbed both of my arms above the elbow. "You are prey, Dacia." He stabbed his finger through the air at Malcolm. "His prey." He rubbed the back of his neck and breathed in deeply. "The lamb does not play with the lion."

"Then what am I doing with any of you?" Molten lava flowed through my veins, heating my core, ready to erupt out of me. "At one time or another, you all saw me as prey!" I tried to pull away from him, but he clutched me tighter.

The urge to freeze my body nearly overwhelmed me. I stumbled back, but he held on. "Let go, Mavros." I glared at him, grinding out through gritted teeth, "Let go of me before I do something I'll regret."

He pulled his hands back and held them up, showing me his palms. "Easy."

"Easy?" I shoved him back. "Easy?" Ice coated my fingers, covering my palms. I clenched my fists, trying to fight the spread. The anger was all-consuming. It surged through me, begging me to hurt him. "I'm sorry," I said before I disappeared.

Chapter 28

Anger Management

$\mathcal{I}$nky blackness surrounded me. I spun in a circle, wondering where I was. My heart raced as the anger drained out of me, leaving only dread in its wake.

I called on my magic to teleport me to my apartment.

Nothing.

I tried to go back to the mountainside.

Nada.

I held my hand up in front of me. With my palm facing the sky, I summoned fire, but it didn't answer.

Terror gripped me, running its cold fingers up my spine, clutching my heart.

Something moved in the darkness. Its footfalls scuffled over the ground.

My eyes hadn't adjusted at all. Everything looked the same.

Black.

In every direction.

I couldn't even see darker shadows. It was as if Mavros had pulled me into the Abyss again, but this time, something was here with me.

My breath rushed out of me in short, shallow bursts. I turned constantly, waiting for something to jump out of the darkness. Waiting for an attack, wondering when it would come.

Another noise. Closer this time.

Something grabbed hold of my arm.

I screamed.

The sound seemed to be swallowed up by my surroundings.

The grip tightened. I tried to pull free. I swung my other arm around and connected with something. I struck out again and again.

"Stop!" Malcolm roared. He grabbed my hand. "Use your magic. Get us out of here."

"I can't." The whimpering, feeble voice that came out of my mouth sounded like it belonged to a frightened child, not an adult. "You do it."

I heard the crack, crack, crack of him popping his neck. Since I still couldn't see anything, I imagined that his pupils were slits and that scales most likely dotted his face. "I can't get us back to Earth."

"Back … to Earth?" The words choked out of me. "Where are we?"

There was a long pause while he moved around me. "I have never been here before, but I could feel it when we moved between realms."

"How did you get here?" I asked before realizing what else he'd said. "Wait. You can see? I can't see anything. Everything's pitch black."

He sucked in a breath, and I tried not to think about why. "I lunged for you, trying to stop you from going. Somehow, I got sucked into your vortex." He stopped talking.

I counted to ten.

Waiting to see if he would answer.

Not wanting to push him.

Not wanting to think.

Now wasn't the time to let myself feel fear.

Alone.

Vulnerable.

Trapped in the dark with the dragon who had tried to kill me a week ago.

"I can see the pulse in your neck." His voice was strained. "It's much too fast." He swallowed loud enough for me to hear, and I wondered exactly how close he was to me. "I wonder if it's fear of me or fear of the wretched darkness that you're in. I can see your eyes darting from side to side, searching for a miracle. A way out."

"Hold my hand." I reached for him, hoping I was doing the right thing. "Walk somewhere, anywhere. Get us somewhere where I might be able to see something."

His fingers entwined with mine. He didn't grip them too hard. It didn't feel like he had talons instead of fingernails. His skin was smooth and not scaly.

I breathed easier and squeezed his hand gently. Hoping he would understand that despite everything, I trusted him. It might make me the biggest fool to have ever lived, but we'd been through too much together for me to give up on him.

The pace he set was slow, and I wondered if it was to keep me from tripping and hurting myself. "There's a root here. Step high."

"What does it look like?" I turned my head from side to side, searching the darkness for anything.

His voice was soft as if he was worried there might be something around to hear him. "There are trees everywhere. Deciduous ones. We're on a path that cuts through the forest."

There was a loud creaking noise followed by a ground-shaking slam.

"And that tree just took a step toward us."

My grip on his hand tightened. "Run!" When he didn't move immediately, I screamed again, "Run! We're in Faerie. Run!"

He took off at a sprint, dragging me along behind him.

The creak thump noise followed us, gaining speed.

"Jump." As fast as we were running, he should have sounded out of breath, but he didn't seem fazed at all.

I did what he said, hoping that my hold on him would keep me from falling or overshooting my mark. My feet hit the ground, snagging on a root. I stumbled, and he caught me, lifting me into his arms like I was a ragdoll. He held me close, and I hoped the smell of my fear didn't overwhelm him.

The tree was falling behind. Malcolm ran harder, striding out, clutching me to his chest.

He stopped so fast that I nearly flew out of his arms. Centrifugal force kept my body moving when his stopped.

"What?" I asked still unable to see anything for myself.

He set me down but didn't let go of my hand. Dragging me with him, he inched forward. "This is your tree, Dacia."

I held my hand out in front of me and took a couple of tentative steps. The bark was rough beneath my fingers. It felt every bit like a normal tree. Like all living things, life thrummed through it.

All of the tension whooshed out of my body, buckling my knees. I choked back a sob, not wanting to cry in front of Malcolm even if it was in relief. "Thank you," I whispered to God as I leaned my head against its trunk.

Flattening my palm against the bark, I turned my head so that my ear was against the tree. Closing my eyes, I listened to the steady beating of a heart.

Images flashed through my mind. A young girl in a green dress, dancing in the woods. Kieran holding an acorn in his outstretched hand. A bright flash of light. Then darkness.

The feelings of loss and sadness that consumed me were not my own. I stood back, looking at the tree, trying to figure out what had just happened, and pressed my hand to my chest.

The creak thump of the walking tree pulled my attention away. "We need to lead it away from here." Panic replaced the relief I'd felt moments before, making my voice rise as the words rushed out of me. "We can't let it knock any leaves off."

He picked me up again and ran. "Do what you did before, and get us out of here."

I pictured my room, the new bedspread, my dresser, and desk. Imagining Mavros mad with worry, I let the magic that had been his call out to him. I felt a tug. "Stop," I said to Malcolm.

"It will catch us." He kept running.

I lifted my hand to his face. "I need you to stop. If you're moving when I teleport us, you'll still be running. My room isn't that big."

He slowed to a jog before coming to a halt. I concentrated more, seeing Mavros' face in my head, picturing every detail. His black hair, obsidian eyes, his flawless olive skin, his cleft chin, his perfectly kissable lips. A jolt of desire shot through me, and I wondered if it was because I was calling on Mavros' power or if he had found us.

Our bodies squeezed in and stretched out. When Malcolm's feet touched the ground again, we were in my room. The lights were off, but I could see. Raised voices came from the other side of the door.

"She's here," Mavros said. The door pushed open, and he stared at us. "Put her down, *dragon*."

He didn't argue. He just set me on my feet and backed away.

I stood between them, not wanting to take sides. "We found it, Mavros."

He cocked his head, focusing fully on me.

"I don't know how we ended up in Faerie, but we found the tree." My insides practically vibrated from the rush of saying it out loud. "We're one step closer."

Cody pushed past Mavros and ran to me. He lifted me, and I wrapped my legs around his waist while he spun the two of us. "That's great!"

Everyone else looked at us from outside of the door. Their expressions ranged from excited to relieved.

"Take me there," Mavros said. "Before you can't get back, take me there."

Cody stopped moving, and I slid down his body until my feet were firmly on the floor. "Why wouldn't I be able to go back?"

"Do you remember what happened to your wings?" Mavros shoved his hands into his pockets like he always did when he knew he was winning an argument. "Do you remember how you got poisoned?" He stepped forward and glared over my shoulder. "Do you remember that you should fear that beast behind you? Do you remember that he tried to kill you? That he still would kill you?"

I chewed on my bottom lip, pulling it into my mouth. "Mavros, I love you, but you need to understand that I love everyone here, and I am not giving up on any of them." I glanced at Malcolm. "Malcolm could have killed me. For some reason, Faerie was as black as the Abyss. I couldn't see anything. He saved me from the tree that was following us. I wouldn't have made it out on my own."

"Take me to the oak—" his lips turned up in a mischievous grin "—love."

I took a step toward Mavros, but Cody grabbed my wrist. "Everyone out."

"Cody, she has to take me there." Mavros stepped toward us.

Cody shook his head. "Give us five minutes." The tone of his voice made me wonder if he would drop down onto his hands and knees to beg if he needed to. "Please. Thought I lost her again. Please."

Malcolm scooted past us and put his hand on Mavros' shoulder. Mavros jerked away before walking out the door. "Five minutes," he said as he pulled it closed.

Cody turned toward me and cupped my face in his hands. Ever so slowly, he leaned his forehead against mine. "Don't do that again."

"I'm sorry." I held onto his arms. "I didn't mean to go there. I meant to come back here." I closed my eyes, and my chin would have fallen to my chest in shame if Cody's head hadn't held mine in place. "I thought I was going to kill Mavros. The anger …" I pulled away, tugging my hand through my hair. "I've never felt anything like it."

His hand slid to my chin, tipping my head back. He leaned in, and his mouth crashed down on mine. His thumbs brushed over my cheeks as he kissed me hungrily.

I clutched the back of his head, running my fingers through his hair, never wanting to let him go.

His hands slid down my neck and over my shoulders. Then he was lifting me, holding me while I wrapped my legs around his waist, pressing our bodies closer together. His lips moved off of mine, trailing kisses over my chin and along my neck to my ear.

I leaned my head back and moaned.

He stumbled to the bed, laying me on it, following with his own body. "I love you, Dacia. I need you to stay safe." His finger traced along my hairline and down my neck, moving over my arm until he clutched my hand in his. "He's going to knock any second."

"Yeah." The word came out breathy.

"Stay safe." He kissed my cheek, then my forehead. "Come back to me." He kissed my other cheek before moving back to my lips.

The kiss was gentler this time. I held onto his shoulders, realizing how much they had broadened since he'd started training with me. I slid my hands into his sleeves, running my fingernails over his skin.

He groaned, and Mavros knocked on the door. "Time's up."

Cody rolled onto the bed next to me, his hand searching for mine. "Come back to me." He squeezed my fingers.

Chapter 29

Return To Faerie

"Is Kieran going to be expecting me?" I swallowed hard, hoping I was worrying over nothing.

Mavros held his hand out, wiggling his fingers impatiently. "He might. There's a reason I wanted to get there quickly. In and out. As soon as I know where it is, I'll send my cats to guard the tree until you figure out how to stop it from dropping its leaves."

"Okay." I slid my hand into his.

I pictured the tree. My one chance to beat this curse. If I could just figure out how to stop it from shedding its leaves. Was there a way?

Our bodies stretched and squeezed. Pulled and pinched.

Blackness surrounded us.

Back to Faerie.

For the third time today.

My own personal hell.

Our feet touched the ground, but I was still surrounded by the impenetrable darkness. "I can't see."

A breeze blew my hair back. It took me a few seconds to realize it was Mavros waving his hand in front of my face. My eyes darted from side to side, trying to see the movement, but there was nothing.

"You're still under his illusion." He grasped my face in both hands.

I sucked in a startled breath at the movement. "I thought we were leaving. In and out, remember?"

"I need to remove this or it will still be here next time he takes you." His breath brushed against my face, warm and closer than I'd expected. "While I do this … did you mean it when you said you love me?"

That was the last thing I ever thought he would ask me. I considered making a joke or deflecting his question somehow, but he sounded so vulnerable. I had to tell him the truth. Placing my hands over the top of his, I said, "I do, Mavros. Not like I love Cody, but I do love you."

"Nobody—" his voice caught on the word, and he started over "—nobody has ever loved me before." He slid his hands from under mine, down to my shoulders.

Everything around me lightened. The forest surrounding us was still swathed in shadows, but it wasn't the absolute darkness I'd seen before. "I find that hard to believe." I pulled my lips up in a sympathetic smile. "I can see now."

"Sometimes, I think you forget that I'm a demon." He brushed my hair back behind my ear. "Let's get out of here."

I glanced at the tree before he teleported us back to the apartment. It was identical to the one on my arm. I didn't know how I'd gotten lucky enough to find it, but I was grateful to be one step closer. I felt like I might actually be in charge of my fate for once.

As soon as we reappeared in the living room, Cody stood. His gaze traveled from my head to my toes, taking in my appearance. The tension in his shoulders eased, and he wiped his hand down his face. "You're okay."

I nodded. "Mavros, are you going back right now?"

"Yes." There was something in his eyes that I'd never seen before. They seemed to shine a little brighter. "I want the cats to guard that tree night and day until you figure this out."

I glanced at Malcolm, knowing this wouldn't go over very well at all. "Can you take Malcolm or Cash—"

"No." He shook his head. "I can do this without them."

Pretending like he hadn't interrupted, I continued, "—or both of them to see if they can erase my trail like they did when I hid in the caves."

"Not a bad idea." Cash nodded his agreement. "If we can keep Kieran from finding out she was there, it could buy her some time."

Malcolm strode toward Mavros. "I will go. I will do whatever I can to keep Dacia safe."

"Don't let her out of your sight." Mavros pointed at Liam.

Liam stood at attention and saluted him. "Yes, sir."

Cash, Malcolm, and Mavros disappeared.

The air shimmers. Everywhere I look, it's like a mirage. Three waxing moons hang in the sky, brightening the night nearly as much as if it was daytime. I stare at them, mesmerized. The largest of them shines with blue light. The craters on its face are unrecognizable. The smallest moon reflects pink light, almost like how our moon looks when the sun is setting. The third is the one I can't quit staring at. Everything about it looks like the Earth's moon, but how can it be? How can there be two other moons in the sky that are not ours, with one that is?

Kieran strides toward me, skipping every so often, whistling that same jaunty tune. His movements are lighter than they've been the last few times I've seen him, and I wonder if he thinks he's won.

He hops, landing right in front of me, and his hair falls over his eyes. Pushing it back, he grins at me. The smile of a kid on Christmas morning. "The nights are beautiful here. Are they not?"

"Why don't you cut your hair?" I ask, ignoring his question. "Don't you get tired of pushing it out of your eyes?"

He shrugs. "It is what it is. Every phouka takes something of its true form through all its manifestations with them. At least I'm not stuck with furry ears like some of my brethren."

"Furry ears?" I try to imagine furry ears jutting out through his hair. It would make it difficult to blend in.

"We all have obstacles to overcome." He reaches for my hand, but I back away before he can grab hold of it. "You, for instance, are human. Even with your extra special abilities, you'll never measure up to a faerie."

I tip my head to the side and purse my lips. "Then why do you want me here with you?"

"Because of the fun we'll have together." He shoves his hair back again. "Faeries don't like to play my games."

"Huh." I look at him pointedly, hoping he'll understand what I'm saying and maybe care. "I guess I do have something in common with faeries then."

Quicker than I've ever seen him move, he grabs my hand and turns my arm so we can see the tree. "But you accepted my gift."

"Your curse." I try to pull my hand away, but he won't release it.

He snarls at me. Rows of pointed teeth fill his mouth. "If you didn't want it, you shouldn't have taken it." He throws my hand down. "I could have given it to your pretty, *little* friend." Tapping his finger against his lips, he adds, "Actually, I still could. What would it be like to have you both with me?"

"We still have three games to play."

"And then you'll be mine."

Not wanting to see the smug expression on his face anymore, I look up at the moons. Even though they're beautiful, I hope to never see them again.

My eyes fluttered open. I gazed toward my window, wondering if the moon looked the same here tonight as it had in Faerie. Then remembering what Kieran had said, I jerked up.

Cody's arm fell off of me, waking him. "You all right?"

I focused on my dream, trying to memorize every detail of it, trying to figure out for sure who Kieran meant. The way he had emphasized little led me to believe he meant Samantha, not Cassandra. The more I thought about it, the more I believed I was right. "He wants Samantha now, too." I clutched the covers. The chair at the end of my bed was empty. At the very least, I expected to see Liam sitting there. I threw the blankets off and walked out into the living room.

"Everything okay?" Liam asked.

Shaking my head, I said, "They're not back. Do you think I made a mistake asking Mavros to take Cash and Malcolm?"

"No." He rubbed his hand over his jaw. "I think it was a good idea. It would be best to cover your trail, and this mess between them needs fixed. You need them to at least be cordial to each other. You can't be fighting battles on two fronts. You'll just end up losing them both that way." He glanced at my room—his steel eyes looked weary—then at me. "But that isn't what brought you out here, is it?"

I looked at Samantha's closed door and hoped she was sleeping and wouldn't hear me. "Kieran wants Sam. I need to figure out how to beat him so I can end this."

"Do you have any ideas?" He leaned forward, planting his elbows on his knees.

I plopped down on the couch and held my head in my hands. "No. How do you make a tree quit doing what trees do?"

"A question for the ages." He shot me a smile. "You should get some sleep. They'll buy you as much time as they can, and you'll figure it out. Look at how many trials you've already overcome."

I wanted to feel his optimism, but this time, I wasn't sure if I would.

Chapter 30

The Man With The Plan

When Samantha came out of her room and saw me sitting at the table thumbing through books, she shook her head. "Shouldn't you be in class?"

"I'm skipping." Knowing she would feel this way, I'd almost gone to the library, but I wanted the privacy of our apartment. "What's the point of sitting through Arthurian Legend and Creative Writing when I'll be trapped in Faerie if I don't figure this out?"

She poured herself a cup of coffee and added creamer to it before sitting next to me. "If you're not going, you should at least let Sarah know so she can get you excused." She reached for my hand, squeezing it affectionately. "I know you don't need the degree because you'll never have to work, but if you're not going to quit, you don't want to fail either."

"Yeah. I'll see if I can meet with her before I train."

She looked around the room. "Where are they?"

"Herding cats."

Jax's voice startled both of us.

"Geesh, Jax." Samantha clutched her chest. "Don't do that."

His rumbling laughter filled the room, and without being able to see him, it was eerie. "Until this mess gets sorted out, plan on me being here."

"Were you?" I stared at the chair, wondering if he was still sitting in it. "When they left. Did you stay?"

"No." He showed himself. His pale eyes wouldn't meet mine. "Malcolm ordered us all to leave. We didn't want to make things worse, so we followed."

"Where's Liam?" I asked. When I'd woken up and he was gone, I assumed Jax was here watching over me or Seth and Russ were keeping an eye on me from their room.

"I sent him across the hall to sleep."

Samantha took a sip of her coffee. "So, herding cats."

"Apparently, faerie cats can be just as difficult as house cats." Jax flashed a smile our way.

Samantha tipped her head toward her shoulder. "Mine are pretty easy to herd. You get out the jar of treats, and they'll do just about anything."

"Maybe Mavros needs to figure out what kind of treats they like." I turned a page in the book, then lifted my head as a thought occurred to me. "How do you know? Can they communicate with you from Faerie?"

He stood and stretched. "I've met a faerie cat before. It was just an educated guess." He bent over and touched his toes, then walked across the room. "What's more, every time Mavros goes to Faerie to deal with them, it takes him a long time." He strolled back to the chair. Before he sat, he made himself invisible again.

They still weren't back when Samantha had to leave for her class. I pushed the book I'd been reading away and got up, I walked around the furniture several times before looking at the seemingly empty chair. "Do you want to go to Sarah's with me? We could teleport there invisible."

"If it will stop your incessant worrying, let's go." He grabbed my hand, and it took everything I had to hold back my scream.

As soon as I could talk, I said, "I need my coat so it looks like I walked over."

Boulders lined the walkway to Cacomistle Hall. We teleported behind them, and when it was obvious that nobody was around, we made ourselves visible. If anybody thought about it, they would wonder why the footprints appeared out of nowhere, but I wasn't too concerned about it. Too many other things were already on my mind.

Alicia sat behind the desk. Her purple hair was short and spiky. The stud in her nose sparkled up at us when the light shone in through the door. "Just the two of you?" she asked before I told her why we were there.

"Yeah." I stood at the desk while she called Sarah.

Jax wandered over to the seating area and looked out the massive windows.

Alicia hung up and whispered, "Where do you find these guys? He's gorgeous."

"They've pretty much all found me." I glanced over at him and noticed his shoulders shaking slightly.

She sighed. "If you ever have a spare lying around, you can send him my way."

Jax sauntered by her and winked as he passed her desk.

I swore I heard her swoon. "You're incorrigible," I said when we were out of earshot.

"She didn't know I could hear her." He grinned at me. "I just made her day."

Sarah met us at the door. She looked from Jax to me and lifted her eyebrows in question. "When Alicia said it was you and one guy, this wasn't who I expected."

"Malcolm and Cash are in Faerie with Mavros trying to get some cats to guard this tree." I pointed to my arm. "Cody's in class which is where I should be. That's what we're here to talk to you about."

"Well, come on in and have a seat." She waved us toward the couches.

I sat on the same one that I always did. It had the best view of the mountains. Then I told her about last weekend, about the challenges with Kieran, finding the tree, and about last night's dream. "I have to figure out how to stop the leaves from falling before he decides to go after Samantha. If I don't, it won't matter how well I do in my classes, so I need to skip. I need to train. I need to read books. I need to brainstorm. I need to do whatever it takes to keep Samantha safe and to not wind up trapped in Faerie."

"I know that your circumstances are quite unusual, but after this, I can't keep making exceptions for you." Her expression was stern. "The board will not approve."

"Some of my teachers will probably be okay with me missing, but Professor Shrike won't be." I chewed on my lip. "I can try to go to some of them, or maybe I should just drop my classes for this semester."

She leaned back and grabbed her mug. "No, I don't want you to do that, but I also don't want to put myself in a position to be reviewed. You need me here. You need somebody who knows what's going on and tries to make things easier for you." She spun the mug. "The trouble is, when the teachers set rules for attendance, I can only overrule them by so much before I'm overstepping my boundaries."

"Okay." It wasn't the answer I wanted to hear, but I understood where she was coming from, and the last thing I wanted to do was get her in trouble.

She stared at me intently. "Have you come up with anything to stop the leaves?"

"No. I have no ideas at all." I slumped down, feeling defeated.

She shot me one of those you've-got-this smiles and said, "If memory serves me, you didn't know what to do about Nefarious, Draconian, Mavros, Argentum, the Nephilim, or your powers, yet you survived each of them. You will figure this out, too."

"That's what everyone keeps saying, and I wish I had that same faith." I pulled my hands through my curls. Red hairs snagged under my nails, and I wiggled my fingers, letting them fall to the ground before remembering that Aurelia had told me not to do that anymore. "But I have no idea how to stop a tree from being a tree."

Mavros, Cash, and Malcolm showed up within minutes of our return. "How was herding cats?" I asked them.

"More fun than being chased after by trees," Cash answered.

I laughed at the look of horror on his face. "Yeah, that's pretty scary."

"We are going to train." Malcolm appeared a little less aggressive, and I hoped that his journey into Faerie with Mavros had settled some of the animosity between the two of them. "We've decided that you need to spend every second of your free time trying to stop trees from losing their leaves."

Mavros nodded. "We don't know how long Kieran will wait to take you away for another challenge. All of your other training can wait."

"What if Kieran finds me and figures out what we're doing?" This was what I wanted, but I needed to know if they'd thought through all of the angles, all of the ways that Kieran could thwart our plans.

Cash shrugged. "We have no idea how he's tracking you. We believe it has something to do with the tree on your arm, so we can't keep him away, but there's no reason to tell him what you're training on."

"Speaking of tracking"—I focused on Mavros—"why couldn't you tell I was in Faerie last night? I … I thought you could find me anywhere."

Mavros folded his arms over his chest and leaned against the doorframe. "The only reason I can think of is because your magic was blocked." He nodded at Malcolm. "While we were in Faerie, he told me you couldn't use your powers, and you told me you couldn't see anything."

"Okay." I stared at him for a while, thinking things through. Then I turned back to Cash.

"Won't Kieran figure it out, though?" I felt like I was running out of chances to beat him, and I didn't want to give him any information he didn't already have.

He held onto the back of the couch, digging his fingers into the cushions. "There is the distinct possibility that he will, but you'll be using your magic, so he might just think you're strengthening it."

"Sounds like a plan to me." I held my hand out, waiting for them to join me. "Let's go, then."

One of them, I assumed Malcolm since it was his plan, teleported all of us to a hot and humid forest. I had never seen trees like these before. Buttress roots crawled across the ground, and massive, thorny trunks reached for the heavens. I felt like an ant standing next to a giant. Green seed pods clung to the branches. Some of them had burst open, and cotton-like fluff poked out of the shells.

Since the canopy was still filled with green leaves, I assumed we were in the southern hemisphere. Strange noises emanated from the woods. Cries I'd never even heard on my many trips to the zoo. They raised the hairs on my arms. I spun around, searching for the source but not seeing anything.

Malcolm held his hand up. "You're okay. They're just Howler Monkeys. They aren't going to hurt you."

"Especially not with us here." Cash shot me a grin that showed his fangs.

I looked at all of the trees surrounding us and tried to decide how to begin. "What do I do?"

"That one"—Mavros pointed to a massive tree—"will not survive to see next year."

I followed his gaze. "Why not?"

"See how the bark is peeling away, and sap is oozing out of the gashes on it." He waited while I looked more closely at the tree. "It is dying."

"Okay." I closed my eyes and tried to decide on the best way to stop it. When I opened them, I lifted my hands, and blue flames erupted, covering the tree's canopy. The leaves ignited, shriveling and turning to ash, but before the fire consumed all of them, some fell to the ground.

Seth pointed out a tree a few yards from us. "That one."

While we trudged toward it, I tried to figure out what to do. The leaves on the eastern branches were wilted. It made me sad to see this towering tree so near death. It had lived through centuries. So much had happened in its lifetime, and here I was to end it.

Ice streamed from my fingers. Covering the tree, but before all the leaves were coated, some of them fell from their branches, fluttering to the ground.

For hours, we wandered through the forest searching out trees that weren't going to survive the long winter ahead of them. I used whatever magic came to mind to keep the leaves from falling, and every time, I failed.

When Malcolm finally decided we could return to campus, I was relieved. There were only so many times you could fall short before you felt like giving up.

Mavros held onto my hand after we appeared in my apartment. "When Thomas Edison created the light bulb, after several unsuccessful attempts, he said, 'I haven't failed—I've just found 10,000 that won't work.' He also said, 'Our greatest weakness lies in giving up. The most certain way to succeed is to try just one more time.' You can do this, Dacia." He squeezed my fingers before letting go. "You didn't learn how to keep the leaves from falling, but you learned several ways that won't."

"All it takes is one right way," Jax said before he sat in the armchair and turned invisible. "You've got this."

"But, what if I don't?"

Chapter 31

Learning What Not To Do

The next three days passed the same way. We traveled to some distant forest, and I killed trees. To a lot of people that wouldn't have mattered in the slightest, but their deaths weighed heavily on my conscience. A life was a life, no matter how seemingly insignificant others thought it might be.

I came back to the apartment every night feeling like an absolute failure. My disappointment weighed on everyone else, too. Tonight was no exception. When we teleported into the middle of the living room, Samantha, Cassandra, Dan, Bryce, and Cody all looked at me. Their faces were filled with hope.

"Figure it out?" Cody stood from the couch, stretching as he walked over to me.

I shook my head, and their faces fell.

Samantha fiddled with her necklace. "Well, you're getting closer. You'll get it."

"Maybe we should get out of the apartment and get your mind off things." Cassandra stood, ready to go that very second.

The only things I wanted were a warm shower and divine intervention. "I don't know. I'm exhausted."

"Oh, come on," Bryce joined in. "You can't just sit around here and wallow."

Samantha smiled at me, nodding emphatically. "It'll be fun."

"Where are we going?" Dan rubbed his hands together, and his angelic smile lifted his lips.

Cody entwined his fingers with mine. They were warm, and without meaning to, I pulled some of his strength into me. "Bowling," he suggested.

"Sure." There was no point in arguing. They wanted to ease my mind, but I knew nothing would. "Can I at least get cleaned up first?"

I'd been to the bowling alley in Althea one other time. Cash, Russ, Val, and Arianna had proven to be excellent bowlers after they figured out how to throw the ball without launching it halfway down the lane.

The teams were set before we left the apartment. Cody, Bryce, Cassandra, Dan, Samantha, and Liam were the Mere Mortals. Mavros, Malcolm, Cash, Russ, Seth, and I were the

Fire Breathers. The team names were ones that Dan had come up with last time we had bowled. I tried to explain that it would make more sense for me to be one of the Mere Mortals since Liam wasn't human, and even if I was evolving, I had at least been born one. My guards had made it quite clear that I would be on their team if we were going to do this.

I didn't see what difference it made since they couldn't prevent Kieran from taking me if he wanted to, but it wasn't something I wanted to argue about. I wanted to bowl a few games and go back to the apartment to search through books before I curled up for bed.

As soon as we walked into the bowling alley, Bryce and Dan went to the counter and ordered pizzas, cheese sticks, French fries, and pitchers of pop. Then they went to the counter and rented their shoes.

We were in our third frame by the time the food arrived. Cody brought a slice of pepperoni pizza over to me. "Eat something, please."

"Thanks." I tried to smile at him, but the motion felt flat. "I think you're up."

He walked away, grabbed his ball, and lined up his shot. His shoulders were stiffer than normal, and it was obvious in his release. The ball went down the side of the lane and didn't curve back in like it normally would. Only three pins fell. The second time, he knocked over the opposite three.

When he sat next to me, I leaned my head on his shoulder. "I don't mean to stress you out."

"What?" His eyebrows pinched together in confusion.

I waved my hand toward the pins. "You haven't bowled this bad since you were like eight. You're tense because you're worried about me, and it's throwing your game off."

"Can't help it." He pulled me closer. "Know you've got this." He kissed my forehead. "Wish it was over, though."

"Yeah." I sighed. "Me, too."

The Fire Breathers ended up winning all three games we played. It really wasn't fair to have all of the dragons on one team. They rarely left a pin standing. Their accuracy was uncanny, and their strength sent pins catapulting into each other.

While everyone was turning in their shoes, I wandered to the little girls' room. When I was washing my hands, movement in the mirror made me look up. Kieran stood by the paper towel dispenser. He waved his hand in front of the sensor, ripped off several sheets, and handed them to me. "I noticed you've been skipping class. You're not trying to avoid me, are you?"

"Well, since you're willing to follow me into the bathroom, I don't think that would work very well, do you?" I dried off my hands, hoping he wouldn't notice how badly they were shaking.

He grinned as he moved in front of the doorway to block my exit. "I love that you know me so well."

"I really don't." I leaned back against the counter and shoved my hands into my hoodie's pocket. "I know that you're persistent and don't like losing."

His face darkened. "I don't lose."

"That's exactly what I mean." Antagonizing him was the last thing I should be doing, but I didn't want him to think he could cow me.

He tilted his head as if he was listening to something. "*To-morrow*. Either come to Faerie to meet me, or I will come to you." The last word had just rolled off his tongue when he disappeared.

Samantha and Cassandra opened the door and stopped as soon as they saw me. "She's fine," Samantha shouted over her shoulder. "She's alone."

"Sorry." Cassandra walked over to the mirror and touched up her lipstick even though it already looked perfect. "Your guards thought they sensed Kieran in here."

"And, they sent you two in here alone?" They knew I was trying to protect Samantha from the phouka.

Samantha watched me, no doubt noticing the anger flash across my face before I could stop it. "No. We told them we would check first. We didn't want them to cause a scene."

"So …" Cassandra turned and faced us. "Was he in here?"

I nodded. "I'd rather tell you all at once."

"I'm sorry." Samantha's brown eyes softened, and she rubbed my arm.

I looked at the door, wondering how long until Malcolm or Mavros burst through it. "We better go out before they come in." I stepped out of the restroom, and six burly bodies stood in the hallway. I lifted my hand, silencing all of their questions. "We'll talk about it outside."

Cody pushed through them and handed me my coat. "Okay?"

"For now." I slipped my arms into the sleeves and led them outside. The night was cloudy and cold. The wind blew, whipping up snow and ice pellets. They beat against my skin. I tugged the collar of my jacket up to protect as much of my face as possible.

When we reached Cody's SUV, one of my guards put a shield around all of us, protecting us from the elements and most likely making it impossible for people to eavesdrop on us.

"He came in while I was washing my hands," I confirmed. Once the dragons stopped growling, I told them what he'd said.

"Did he give you any hints?" Samantha leaned in closer to Dan.

I shook my head. "No. Hopefully, I remember the rules tomorrow." I slid down the SUV until I was squatting just above the snow-covered parking lot. "I need more time."

Chapter 32

I tossed and turned until Cash helped me sleep. His magic flowed into me, soothing my concerns, and letting my mind take a break from all my fears.

The leaves drift slowly to the ground. One after another, they fall, coating the forest floor. The red foliage stands out against the vivid green like blood in an open wound. There's nothing I can do to stop them, so I watch, feeling my stomach plummet with each one that drops.

I am sorry. A feminine voice drifts through my head. *I held onto them for as long as I could.*

I look around, but I'm alone with the tree.

Kieran places his hand on my shoulder, and I stifle a scream. "I told you. Nobody beats me."

"I don't want to stay here." My voice is whiny, and I hate myself for sounding like a petulant child.

He lifts his shoulder to his pointed ear. It sticks out through his hair. Where the light hits him, blue streaks show in the black strands. He's taller and thinner.

I stagger back at his alien appearance. Fear thrums through my body, urging me to run, but where would I go?

"Too late for that, isn't it?" His voice is mocking. He rubs his hands together. The extra knuckles in his fingers make them bend at awkward angles. "Oh, what fun we're going to have." His laughter chases me as I force myself to wake up.

Staring at the ceiling, I tried to remember why the leaves had been falling. I couldn't let whatever had caused it happen. This couldn't be a premonition.

"I can go to Faerie with you." Mavros' voice from across the room startled me. "I wouldn't be welcomed, but like them, I can travel between realms."

I chewed on my lip while I considered the pros and cons of his offer. "I don't know how wise that would be."

"I can't help you." He sauntered over to the side of my bed. "But I can be there for moral support."

I imagined the scarlet leaves scattered over the forest floor. "I don't think you should."

Gnarled branches, bare of leaves, reached into the clearing. Mavros had teleported here with me, then gone back at my request. I wanted to keep up the guise that I couldn't move between realms. I spun around, searching for anywhere safe to stand, but the forest surrounded me. Trees seemed to close in whenever I turned my back on them. I'd always loved the woods, but the ones here were terrifying. There was an unnatural quietness to them. There should have been creatures scurrying through their branches, birds singing, leaves rustling. The trees in this realm seemed to be sentient, and I got the distinct feeling that they didn't like intruders.

Something moved behind me. I turned, expecting to find Kieran there, but I only saw a branch quickly retreating. There was no doubt in my mind that he knew I had arrived and was waiting for him, but if he was here, he wasn't showing himself.

Filling my thoughts with visions of life like I would when healing somebody, I held my hands in front of me and slowly spun in a circle. "I'm not going to hurt any of you." I kept my voice soft and soothing, hoping the trees could understand what I was saying and feeling like an idiot for talking to them in the first place.

Miraculously, they backed away, and the forest felt less sinister. I let out a deep breath and relaxed my muscles.

"Well done." Kieran clapped his hands, but I wasn't sure if he was happy or not. "You will be a welcome addition to Faerie." Apparently, he was.

My fists clenched, and the trees creaked as their branches leaned toward me. I took a deep breath and calmed myself. Keeping my voice soft so the trees wouldn't react, I said, "You haven't won yet."

"Or … I have, and you just don't realize it." He reached into his shirt pocket and pulled out two ragwort stems. Handing one to me, he said, "Today's challenge."

I stared at the fluffy seed head, wondering what he wanted me to do with it. "What?"

"You will use your magic … if you can." A malicious smirk crossed his face, and I realized he thought I was unable to use my powers while I was here. "Turn the plant into a stallion and race through Faerie with me." He waved his hand, and a silvery path illuminated through the forest.

"Rules." I lifted my finger to stop him from talking anymore. "No cheating. No hindering the other contestant. No illusions."

He snickered when I said that one.

"No teleporting to the end. You and your ragwort stallion can only take one form each."

He curled his lip. "Anything else, Princess?"

I stared at the forest, wondering what I was about to get myself into. "The path must be illuminated for me to see at all times."

"Are you sure you're capable of participating in this challenge?" He stepped closer to me. Catching my gaze, he pulled his lips into an imitation of a pout.

Opening my eyes as wide as I could, I shot him my best innocent look. "Of course. Why wouldn't I be able to?"

"Do you really think you can make that into a stallion?" He pointed at the plant and rolled his inhuman eyes. "If you'd like me to do it for you, I can change half of the remaining leaves to red now and turn the other half when you lose."

Tapping my finger against my lips and tilting my head to the side, I pretended to consider his offer. "No … I think I'll take my chances."

"If you're done setting the rules"—he shook his head when he said rules—"then we should begin."

I looked at the stem in my hand and wondered how to turn it into a stallion. Kieran had probably been doing this all of his life. I had seconds remaining to figure it out.

"Having second thoughts?" He twirled his ragwort between his fingers.

I couldn't help it. I snorted. "About taking the acorn? Yes. About beating you today? Nah … I think I've got this."

He narrowed his eyes and turned toward the path through the woods. "Let's go then." As soon as the words were out of his mouth, his seed head transformed into another dapple gray stallion. Before I had a chance to even consider how to make mine change, he was mounted and riding away.

I held my ragwort in front of me. A story that I had seen last night came to mind, and I pictured the stem turning into Enbarr, a steed from Faerie legend. The horse that formed in front of me was white with a mane and tail that seemed to flow even though it was standing perfectly still.

Blowing into his nostrils, I hoped he would accept me and allow me to ride him. Enbarr returned the action. I trailed my hand along his neck and pulled myself onto his back. As soon as I was mounted, he ran, following the path, swifter than the wind.

I held onto his mane as he weaved and dodged through the forest. Never in my life had I moved so quickly. I should have been terrified by the thought of crashing into each obstacle we approached, but by the time I noticed them, they were long gone. Every stride brought us closer to Kieran than should have been possible.

Kieran's steed galloped through the woods in front of us. Seeds blew from the stallion's mane, catching on the wind, searching for the perfect places to grow so they could later be plucked and flown on again.

The horse was giving it his all, but Enbarr raced past like they were statues in a garden. I glanced over my shoulder as we zipped by. Kieran smacked his horse with a crop, but nothing would make his stallion as fast as mine.

Mine was made from the wind, and as long as I sat upon its back, even death couldn't find me.

Enbarr practically flew through the forest, moving so fast that I couldn't even feel his hooves touch the ground. The trees didn't try to stop us. They didn't stretch their branches toward us. They seemed to clear the path, making it easier for Enbarr to gallop past them.

As soon as we crossed the finish line, he stopped. The momentum should have thrown me over the top of his head, but I didn't even lift out of my seat. Once my legs felt sturdy enough to hold me up, I dismounted.

Standing next to him, I rubbed his neck and ears. A normal horse would have been lathered, but Enbarr wasn't even breathing hard. He nickered and lipped at my hair. I petted his nose, the only spot on his body that wasn't pure white, loving the velvety feel of it.

After several minutes of standing there, Kieran finally crossed the finish line. He jumped off his horse, and the poor thing disappeared in a flurry of seeds. "You had no magic!"

"What?" I pinched my eyebrows together and hoped that I was pulling off a confused innocent look.

He stepped back, shifting from foot to foot, and beads of sweat formed along his forehead. "I, uh, I believed your magic was gone." He tugged at the collar of his emerald shirt. "How is it not?"

"Why would it be?" I stepped closer to him, hoping to make him cower a little more. "You weren't breaking the rules, were you?"

His gaze snapped up to mine, and I could see madness, cruelty, and mischief fighting for dominance in his eyes. "The spell was on you before the rules were set." He thrust his misshapen finger toward me. "That is not cheating."

"Cheating or not"—I forced my voice to stay steady—"it didn't work. I won. Thanks to Enbarr."

"Enbarr," he said the stallion's name like a curse, his lip curling up at the end. "I won't forget this."

Pretending like I didn't know what he meant, I said, "Neither will I. It was an honor to ride through the forest on him."

"Two more, Dacia." He lifted two fingers to emphasize his words. "And, they will be mine." He disappeared.

I leaned up against Enbarr. "It looks like he'll know that I can teleport home. I wonder how he'll use that against me."

Chapter 33

Fall Down Seven Times; Stand Up Eight

"*G*ah!" I shouted at the starry sky high above me. I could barely see it through the trees. The constellations were unfamiliar here in the southern hemisphere, but at least, it was still Earth's sky. There would only be one moon when it rose, not three. "I am never going to figure this out!"

I turned toward the tree I had just killed. The once beautiful rosewood was petrified. The stone hadn't taken over fast enough to stop some leaves from falling. They looked like rocks littering the forest floor now.

Mavros strode toward me. "One more, Dacia."

"I can't." The words came out on a frustrated sob.

Cash clapped his hand down on my shoulder and sent his strength flowing into me. "Sometimes, the only difference between can and can't is your frame of mind."

"Right now, my frame of mind says I'm leaving with or without you." I clenched my fists and then loosened my fingers, trying to relax.

Cash tightened his grip on me, ensuring that I didn't leave without him. "I know this is frustrating, but the more things you try, the more ideas you come up with."

"I just keep killing these trees." I turned my face away so he couldn't see me cry. "I know that doesn't seem like much to you, but I can feel their deaths in my soul."

Mavros stood in front of me. The tips of his boots nearly touched the toes of my tennis shoes. He lifted my chin. "None of these trees would have survived the dry season. None of them." He brushed his thumbs over my cheeks, wiping away the tears. "Would you make a cat or dog suffer? Or would you put them out of their misery?"

I lifted the shoulder Cash wasn't holding onto.

"The trees we told you to use your magic on were suffering." Malcolm stood further away from me than the others. His fangs were longer than normal, but he showed no other signs of distress. "They were dying slow deaths."

"Please." I pinched my eyes shut and tried to get my emotions under control. "Please. Can we just go back? I can't do this again tonight. I have no idea what else to try."

Mavros let his hand slide down my shoulder and onto my arm. "Sure, Dacia. We'll go. You can come up with a plan for tomorrow."

I hold the ragwort in my hand, envisioning it as a horse. As soon as I picture it, it transforms into a stallion. He stands next to me. White fur glistening in the afternoon sun.

Enbarr.

I climb onto his back, and he runs. The forest flashes by us in mere seconds. He gallops toward a lake. I clutch his mane tighter, preparing to get soaked, but he sprints across the surface. Mist rises from under his hooves.

He stops on an island far enough from shore that I hadn't seen it, and I slide off his back. As soon as I'm down, he turns into ragwort seeds that float away.

The stem is in my hand again. I look around for some explanation of where it came from, but there's nobody out here, nothing around me at all.

I will the ragwort into a stallion. This time it becomes a dapple gray like Kieran usually rides. He nuzzles against my hand, and I pet his neck and ears. He nudges me until I climb onto his back. Then he gallops across the island. When he stops, I get down, and he bursts into a cloud of seeds. The wind catches them, tossing them into the air, twirling and spinning and playing with them before allowing them to drift to the ground.

Another ragwort stem falls to the rocks beside my feet. I pick it up and wonder if there's anything else that I can turn it into. Is there a reason Kieran always makes it a stallion? Could it be a mare? Could it become a dragon if I chose?

Staring at the plant, I picture it as a pegasus. A golden, winged mare stands in the palm of my hand. When I set her on the ground, she grows, stopping once she's at least fifteen hands tall.

I climb onto her back, and she runs a few steps before launching into the air. Ragwort fluff drifts off her feathers as she flaps her wings, flying across the lake toward the opposite shore. She lowers herself until her hooves skim across the surface of the water.

The wind whips my hair back, and I hold my arms out to the side, feeling free. I whoop with delight.

When she reaches the beach, she drops down, running across the rocks until she slows. She folds her wings back and waits for me to dismount. As soon as I do, she explodes into millions of ragwort seeds.

I'm left holding another stem, tempted to blow the fluff like I did with dandelion heads as a kid. Instead, I wish it into a unicorn.

The animals disappear, one after another, turning into ragwort stems as soon as my ride is over. I speed across the land, fly through the air, and swim through the lake on the backs of horses, unicorns, pegasi, and hippocampi.

Cody shook my shoulder. "Alarm." His voice was thick with sleep.

I rolled over and turned off the incessant beeping. Then I stared up at the ceiling, trying to figure out what my dream meant. Was I supposed to learn something from it? Was there some hidden meaning, or had my mind just wanted to replay riding on a ragwort horse?

Enbarr had been amazing.

Maybe I had just wanted to see him again, but that didn't seem right. No. I was missing something. Some lesson I was supposed to learn. Something to help with future challenges. Something that was eluding me right now.

Cody's finger trailed down my arm. "You okay?"

"Weird dream." I rolled onto my side, facing him. "I think I should write it down. I feel like there's something in it that I'm not seeing right now."

He nodded. "Do that. Then share it with Mavros or Malcolm." He tapped his temple before kissing my forehead. "Maybe they'll see it."

I sat at the table writing down everything I could think of, hoping that I could see whatever I'd missed before, but if it was there, it was still eluding me. As soon as I set the pen down, Mavros and Malcolm joined me. Malcolm's knee brushed against mine under the table. Except for running from the tree in Faerie, this was the closest he'd been to me since the wings had been torn from my shoulder blades.

Smiling at him, I took his hand in mine, then reached for Mavros'. I shared the memory of my dream with them, trying hard not to leave out any details, hoping they could see something that I couldn't.

Once I was done, Malcolm scooted his chair back and walked to the window, opening it, then leaning against the counter. "I believe you're right." He held his hand over his mouth and nose. "There was a reason for this dream, but I don't know what it was." He focused on Mavros. "What about you, demon?"

Mavros still held onto my hand, rubbing his thumb along mine. He stared into my eyes, not even sparing a glance for Malcolm. "I don't know, but if you have this dream again, try to make the ragwort into something that has no equine qualities."

"Okay, why?" I slipped my hand out from underneath his.

He watched me fold my arms over my chest. "Curiosity. It might help us figure out if the dream meant something or if it was just your mind coming to terms with the idea that you turned a plant into an animal." He picked up the salt shaker and spun it in his hands. "Faerie magic is different. Not a lot of humans would have been able to do that."

"I wonder if you can do it here." Malcolm rubbed his hand along his jaw. "Or if you can only do it in Faerie."

I felt my eyebrows pinch together. "Does ragwort even grow here?"

"It does now." Mavros leaned back in his chair. "It's considered a noxious weed in a lot of places. I'm sure we can find some not too far away from here."

"I'll go." Malcolm straightened up, disappearing a few seconds later.

Mavros stood and walked to the refrigerator. "What do you want for breakfast?" He rubbed his hands together and winked at me. "I'm turning into a fantastic cook."

"You ever wanna go to one of the other realms?" Cody asked as he walked out of his room.

Mavros looked from Cody to me. "Not as long as she's here. Besides, there's so much left for me to learn here." He grinned wickedly before pulling strawberries out of the fridge. Then he went to the cabinet and pulled out a box of pancake mix and the syrup.

We were just finishing washing dishes when Malcolm returned with several ragwort plants. Each of them had twenty or more stems that could turn into magical transportation if I could do it here on Earth.

"Ready?" Malcolm held his other hand out to me.

I looked down at my outfit. I was dressed in a t-shirt and shorts. "That depends on where we're going."

"Get your shoes." He let his hand fall to his side and waited while I put socks and shoes on.

Cody put the last of the dishes away, then turned toward me. "Be careful."

"Yeah." I stood up and placed my hand in Malcolm's. As soon as I did, there was a knock on the door, and Cash and Liam strode in. "You too," I said to Cody while Mavros grabbed my other hand.

My body felt weightless, and the darkness seemed unending, but I was comforted by the four presences around me. Their auras brushed against mine as we were transported. When we stopped moving, we were standing in a vast desert. Cacti dotted the open landscape. The sun beat down on us, and I was grateful I hadn't changed into something warmer.

Malcolm handed me one of the ragwort plants. I broke off a single stem and handed the rest back to him. Then I focused on it just like I had in Faerie. The flower transformed into a small stallion. I set him on the ground and stood back with the others while he grew to sixteen hands.

He had a dusky gray coat with dark rings splattered over it. His mane was as black as midnight, and his tail was as white as the new-fallen snow. He was stunning with his ebony stockings and sable eyes.

I felt a pang in my chest as I rubbed his onyx muzzle. He was beautiful and as alive as any of us. He didn't deserve to disappear into a cloud of seeds. Leaning my forehead against his, I closed my eyes and wondered what he wanted. If he wanted. Could a horse created from a ragwort stem want?

"Let him go, Dacia." Malcolm's voice was softened by understanding.

They all knew this was hard on me, creating creatures and having them disappear as if they'd never existed, killing trees that had survived every other hardship before me.

I stepped back and swatted the horse on his haunches. He ran across the desert, kicking up dust behind him. Heatwaves blurred across him, making him look like a mirage, but he never exploded into a cloud of seeds. I watched him until he was a speck in the distance.

"Why?" I turned toward my guards. "Why didn't he disappear? Will he be okay?"

Liam rubbed his hand along his jaw. "Do you think it's because he's here and not in Faerie?"

"Or is it because she didn't ride him?" Cash asked.

Malcolm held the flowers out to me. "Make another. A mare."

I did as he said. This one was a stunning strawberry roan with long stockings and a flowing mane and tail. She stood next to me, waiting for some command.

"Ride her," Malcolm said.

I climbed onto her back and squeezed, clicking my tongue. She trotted around the group. I doubted they wanted me to go too far from them. "Okay." I looked at Malcolm, wondering what he wanted me to do next.

"Let her go." He pointed in the same direction the last horse had run. "She'll find him. Horses want a herd."

I lowered myself to the ground, not wanting to send her away in case she, too, disappeared. I rubbed her ears and petted her neck before smacking her rump. She ran off in the same direction the stallion had, galloping for her freedom. I waited for seeds to fly from her mane, but they didn't.

Looking up at the bright sky, I said a quick prayer that they would find each other and survive in this harsh territory.

"Okay," Liam said. "It must be because she's here. They must only disappear in Faerie." He stared after her until there was nothing to watch.

The day I'd lost the challenge because I forgot to include illusions in the rules, I'd flown on a ragwort horse above Faerie with Kieran. Somehow, I'd rode the stallion back to Earth. He'd burst into ragwort seeds above campus. He'd been created in Faerie, so maybe that had something to do with it. Maybe it was intent, though. I wanted these horses to live, to thrive, and it looked like they might do that.

I watched the mare until she was a speck in the distance. Then I wiped the sweat off of my forehead, grateful that we were here in the morning, not the heat of the day. "So … what now?"

"Now"—Mavros rubbed his hands together—"we see what else you can make it turn into."

Malcolm handed me another flower. I held onto the yellow daisy-like bloom and looked at each of their faces, wondering what exactly they wanted me to do. "Like what?"

"How about a saguaro?" Cash pointed to one.

I stared at the giant cactus. "As long as you aren't planning on asking me to ride it."

Liam was gracious enough to chuckle at my lame joke. Everyone else just waited for me to make the magic happen.

Since I didn't want to hold onto a cactus, I set the stem on the ground. Then I focused on it, imagining the petals turning into thorns as the stalk grew into a towering saguaro.

Seconds later, I backed away from the ragwort when it shot up, growing at least twice as tall as Cash. Arms protruded from its trunk. It stood rooted in the sandy ground.

Cash walked up to it and pricked his finger on one of its longer spines, bringing forth a drop of purple blood. "Well, it's not just an illusion." He sucked on his finger until it stopped bleeding.

After that, they had me turn the ragwort into stone, lizards, snakes, scorpions, and bugs that called the desert home. When the sweat was dripping off the tip of my nose, they finally decided that I had done enough.

Malcolm and Mavros took my hands, and Cash and Liam joined us. We teleported back to their room. I stood in the center of the four guards. "So, what was the point of that?"

"To see what you can do." Malcolm looked at me like I had grown another head.

I lifted my hands in the universal sign of exasperation. "What difference does it make if I can only do it here?"

"You created life today, Dacia." Mavros shook his head at me. "We thought that might make you feel better about the lives you've taken."

Malcolm held the flowers up between us. There were still thirty or more blooms on it. "We thought you could eventually use some of the ragwort to replace those trees."

Without thinking, I hugged him. He patted my back, but the action was stiffer than it had been in the past.

I stepped away, hoping I hadn't broken him, but when I looked up, he disappeared.

Chapter 34

Petrified Forest

$\mathcal{I}$ stand in a forest of dead trees. Some are charred skeletons, some frozen, some turned to stone or crystal. Their carcasses surround me. I feel their ghosts, accusing me.

My chest tightens, and combined with the pain in the back of my throat, I find it harder and harder to breathe.

Kieran appears from behind the enormous trunk of a kapok tree. His hands are tucked in his pockets as he strolls toward me. His hair flops down over his eyes, and the song he whistles calls to my guilt, making the feelings intensify until a sob tears from me.

I clutch my stomach, bending over, trying to stop the remorse from eating me alive.

He places his hand on my shoulder. "Oh, Dacia, if only you would have listened to me." His fingers dig in, not at all reassuring. "All of these trees could have been spared if only you would have understood. No matter what you do, you cannot beat me."

The truth in his words shatters what's left of my soul.

He lets go of me and starts whistling that dreaded tune again. Its notes fill my head, growing until it sounds like a symphony and not just one voice. My guilt morphs into shame, inadequacy, and self-loathing.

I can see that I was wrong. My ego wouldn't let me give up before, but I know now that no matter what I do, Kieran will win in the end. These trees could still be alive if only I would have listened to him from the beginning.

"Stop!" Liam strides toward me, but it's not his aura that I feel. It's darker. "Don't listen to him, Dacia. Tune out his song."

Kieran steps away from me, stalking toward Liam. He looks him over from head to toe, smirking the whole time. "Do you really think you can keep me from beating her?"

"Only time will tell." He shrugs. The cocky attitude he's displaying isn't one I've seen from him before, and when he winks at me, I'm sure he's not Liam. "But you're not going to get her tonight in this dream. This is over, Kieran." He points into the distance. "Leave."

Kieran rolls his eyes. "I don't think so." He starts whistling again, and my guilt gnaws at me.

Holding my hands over my ears, I hum. The sound of my voice cancels out Kieran's tune.

His shoulders shake as if he's laughing. Then his song grows louder. Every tree echoes the haunting melody. The ground reverberates with it. It thickens the air and clings to my skin.

Liam who's not Liam grabs my arm, then smacks me across the face hard enough to wake me up.

Mavros sat on the bed next to me. His hand was still in the air.

My cheek stung, and tears filled my eyes. "Why Liam?"

His grin was malicious. "Because if the faeries are going to go after someone, I'd rather it was the Nephilim."

"Okay then." I thought about Troy and Sebastian, the way they'd treated me. I remembered how Micah had sneered at me. I knew some of them were good. Liam, Vicki, Olivia, and Diana had proven that, but I couldn't bring myself to forgive them as a whole yet. "I can't say I disagree."

His lips pinched together, and his expression turned serious. "It's safe to say he knows what you're doing with the trees." He sprung to his feet.

The sudden movement startled me. I jerked to a sitting position and searched the room for Kieran. Nothing.

Before I had a chance to ask him what was going on. He spun around to face me. "I need to check on the cats. I need to know that they're still guarding your tree."

"So go."

He opened the door. "Cash, tell Malcolm he's needed." Glancing over his shoulder at me, he added, "Don't let her leave, and keep an eye on her dreams. Kieran tried to mesmerize her."

Seconds after Mavros disappeared, Cash sat in the chair at the end of the bed. "Malcolm's here—" he looked at the door "—but he can't be here."

"Anything she can do to fix this?" Cody massaged my neck.

I should have realized he was awake. He'd probably woken up before I had. His fingers were strong and warm, kneading my tense muscles. I relaxed into his touch as much as I could, waiting to hear the answer, hoping there was a way to fix things.

"He's going to need some time away." Cash's lips pinched together before lifting in an imitation of a smile. "I know it's not what you want to hear, and I'm sorry for that."

I tugged my hand through my hair and nodded. "I figured that would be your answer."

"What about you?" Cody slid his fingers down my spine, then up again.

Cash shrugged. "So far, so good."

"The tree's untouched." Mavros' voice was quiet, but it pulled me from my dreams.

I kept my eyes closed, wondering what else he would say and if he would say it if he knew I was awake.

"But for how long?" Malcolm's low growl rumbled through the room. "She's running out of time."

I sat up, pulling the covers with me. A fire seemed to ignite in my stomach, heating my core and fueling my anger. "I know

I am, and I would be happy to hear any suggestions that any of you might have." I glared into Malcolm's eyes, then Mavros', then Cash's. "Anyone?" I waited a few seconds. "No? Then how about you cut me some slack? I'm trying. I'm out of ideas and apparently out of time."

"Calm down, Dacia." Cash's gaze darted toward Malcolm and then back to me.

I clutched the blankets tighter to keep from screaming at him. "I'm angry. He should be fine." I knew I was playing with fire, but I couldn't stop myself. "I'm told that makes me smell rather unappetizing."

"Get ready to go." Malcolm strode past me and out the door. "We're training in five minutes."

Cash patted my shoulder as he walked by with Mavros. "Hold onto that anger. It'll probably help."

"Thanks for the advice." Something told me that training wasn't going to be an enjoyable experience. I swung my feet over the edge of the bed, but Cody grabbed my arm, stopping me.

"Try not to antagonize them." He loosened his grip, letting me know that he'd let me get up if I wanted to.

I dropped my chin to my chest. "I know, but I really am trying. I would love some ideas, but everybody just says I'll come up with it when the time comes, or my favorite, you've got this." I stuck both thumbs up in the air and shot him a cheesy smile in an imitation of support. "I know I have in the past, but what if I don't? What if I can't figure it out?" I peered over my shoulder at him, hoping he would have the answers that nobody else had been able to come up with.

Instead, he just shook his head. "Don't know. Wish I could help. Really do."

"I know." I sighed before standing up and gathering my clothes. "I've gotta get ready. If I don't, they'll come get me."

They took me to the same forest we'd been visiting for the past week and a half. Evidence of my magic surrounded us. I stared at an enormous tree now encased in stone and wondered what people would think when they came upon it. Would they believe someone had erected a statue out here?

The native tribes had believed that these giants contained evil spirits. Would they see this as proof of them?

I held my hand against the trunk. The tree had been petrified in tan stone with sprinkles of other colors throughout it. It was as smooth as polished marble.

"Dacia." Malcolm stood rigidly, holding the remaining ragwort out to me.

I plucked off a stem, walked to an open area, and set it on the ground. As I backed away from it, I heard the first strains of Kieran's song. I spun around, searching for the source of the music.

"What's wrong?" Mavros followed my gaze, but there was nothing.

I shook my head. "Can't you hear it?"

"Hear what?" Cash perked up, pinching his eyebrows together as he listened.

The sound came from behind me now. I turned again, focusing on it, feeling the despair it caused welling up inside of me. "Kieran's song," I muttered.

"There's nothing, Dacia." Mavros grabbed my hand, and in his silken voice, he started singing in a language I couldn't understand. The words cut through Kieran's whistling.

Mavros' song filled me with a sense of peace. I closed my eyes and pictured a butterfly flying across the bright blue sky, looping back and forth. The beauty and hope spread, leaving me to wonder how a demon could inspire these emotions in anybody.

Focusing on the ragwort, I imagined it as a massive kapok tree with sprawling roots. The stem grew, crawling over the ground as it shot up. Mavros' song fueled its growth, lending power to my magic and helping me create the massive tree in record time.

As I stood back and admired my creation, slow clapping drifted through the trees. "Nice trick." Kieran stepped out of a strangler fig's cage.

When my guards didn't acknowledge him, I realized his magic had immobilized them. "Hello, Kieran." I hoped that being nice would prevent him from doing anything drastic.

"I wondered if you were here to kill more trees." He ran his fingers over one of the buttress roots. "Imagine my surprise when you created one." He arched an eyebrow. "And from ragwort, no less."

I pointed to the ragwort in Malcolm's hand. "I have more to plant."

"No, you don't. Not right now." He stared up at the kapok's canopy at least 150 feet above us. "Today, we're going to climb this tree. Whoever makes it the furthest wins."

"Ru—"

His head snapped in my direction. Anger narrowed his eyes. "Don't interrupt. It's not your turn. You will climb it as you." He waved his hand from my feet to my head. "Whatever you are. Not quite human, not quite demon or angel, definitely not dragon. But whatever you are in this form. I will climb it as me. Phouka. Faerie. Neither of us will use magic of any kind. Neither of us will hinder the other, create illusions, teleport to the finish line, or any of your other rules. Neither of us can ask for, expect, or demand help. You on your own, as you stand here before me, will climb this tree. Now … do you have anything to add?"

"You expect me to climb this tree, in this body, without magic?" My gaze shifted between him and the leaves high above me.

He laughed, and the sound was like a thousand spiders crawling over my body. "Of course not. I expect you to fail … epically."

My stomach dropped. The more I studied the tree, the more I realized I had no chance. None. The nearest branches were at least a hundred feet off the ground, maybe more. Unlike the trees at home, these limbs were practically horizontal. There were none below the canopy. There was no point. They wouldn't get the sunlight they craved there.

If I would have known Kieran was going to challenge me to this contest, I could have made the trunk thorny like some other kapoks. I could have made the tree grow unnaturally, but somehow that seemed wrong.

Staring up again, I realized Kieran might not be able to climb this tree as himself either, but if I could get further than him, I could win. Walking around the base of it, I tried to devise a plan to make it as far as I could as quickly as I could. I could climb the roots to get to the trunk, but it was at least ten feet wide, and the bark was smooth. There was no way I would be able to find a handhold.

"We can stand here staring at the tree all day if you would like." I wasn't expecting the overwhelming snark in Kieran's voice. "Or maybe we could get this over with."

There had been one area where the buttress roots had extended at least twenty-five feet in the air. I strode to that point, and then shouted, "Ready."

"No cheating." His voice carried back to me. "Get set. No magic. Go."

I scrambled onto the root. Running bent over with my hands pulling me forward faster than I would normally dare, I scurried up like a monkey. The humidity made my hair cling to my neck. I had never regretted not pulling it into a braid or a ponytail more than now. Sweat dripped off the curls that kinked around my face, but I couldn't stop, not for even one second. I needed to beat Kieran. I needed to make sure that the remaining leaves stayed green until I could figure out how to stop the tree from dropping even one.

Ten feet off the ground quickly turned into fifteen. The root narrowed the higher it rose. My feet slid along the slippery surface. I wobbled. My right leg went out from under me, and

I crashed down hard on my left knee. I clutched the root, trying to keep from sliding to the ground.

Once I caught my balance and my breath, I slowly pulled my foot back onto the root and pushed to my feet. I moved slower, hoping not to slip again.

When I reached the top of the root, I clung to it. The tree rose high above me. I leaned my head back and stared up the massive trunk. There was no way to climb it without using magic. I didn't see any way to continue.

Stretching my hands up as high as I could, I felt for anything that I could grip. I slowly worked them down. My fingers caught in a crack. I pulled myself up and repeated the process, methodically searching for a way up.

One cautious handhold at a time, I made my way up the tree. The progress was slow, but it was progress. Ignoring the trembling in my arms, I reached up, pulling myself higher.

I looked up at the canopy, and a wave of dizziness crashed over me. For a second, I saw multiple trees towering above me. They moved out from the central one before coming back together. They bounced away from each other again, and I pressed my face against the bark and held on, hoping it would pass.

Once my stomach stopped roiling, I stretched my arm up again, but there was nothing for me to latch onto. I slid my hands along the crack, pulling myself to the side, and reached up again. My fingers met with smooth, unblemished bark. There were no more handholds, no way for me to climb higher.

I pulled myself to the other end of the crack, feeling above me for something to grab onto, but there was nothing. This was as high as I could climb without using magic.

Wondering how far I'd made it, I looked down. The ground was at least fifty feet below me. I gulped and pulled my gaze back even with me. I had no idea how long I would have to wait here, and I didn't need any distractions in the meantime.

I pulled my left hand out of the crack and let my arm hang at my side. Shaking it out, I felt the blood flow return to my fingers. After a few minutes, I traded, letting my right arm have a break.

While I clung to the trunk that way, the oak was at eye level. Its leaves rustled. The wind whipped them harder, and my chest tightened. What if a leaf fell? The branches quit moving. I closed my eyes and sucked in a deep breath.

When I looked at the tree again, three-fourths of the leaves were a brilliant red. My grip loosened, and I fell back. The ground rushed up to meet me. I called on my magic, but I continued to plummet.

"Come on," I screamed at my powers.
Strong arms wrapped around me, and I looked up into Liam's face. He hovered a few feet off the ground. "Are you okay?"

Chapter 35

"He beat me." I looked around, wondering where Kieran was and why he hadn't come to gloat. "I really am nothing without my magic."

Liam dropped to the ground and gently set me on my feet, not letting go until he knew I could stand on my own. "You are not nothing." His voice was stern. "You were at a disadvantage."

"There's only one contest left." I lifted my hair off of my neck, letting the breeze kiss my skin. "What if I can't beat him?"

Kieran's tune carried toward me as he sauntered around the jutting roots. "You can't beat me. Haven't I already explained that to you?"

"How did you climb the tree?" I looked Kieran over from head to toe, trying to figure out how he had made it farther than me.

He grinned. It was a smug thing that begged to be wiped off his face. "Why, as a phouka, of course." He transformed into a creature that had a rabbit-like head and ears with a monkey's body. Shaggy, black fur covered him. His hands and feet were thin with long fingers and toes. A prehensile tail waved through the air behind him. "I told you I'd climb as a phouka." It was weird hearing Kieran's voice come from this thing's mouth. "You could have told me I had to stay in human form." He morphed back into Kieran. His hair fell in front of his eyes, and he pushed it back. "I gave you a chance to set your rules."

"He said he was going to climb as a phouka, and you let him get away with it?" Disappointment and anger mixed together in Malcolm's voice.

I thought I was good with wordplay, but Kieran was proving to me that I wasn't. "Yeah." I sighed. "But in my defense, I didn't know that was a phouka. I thought the human-looking Kieran was. I thought he would have to stay in the form he was in when he set the rules."

"He could have chosen any number of forms: phouka, raven, human, goat, horse, dog, rabbit, cat, fox, goblin, wolf. Who knows what else? They're all phouka." Malcolm dragged his hand down his face before he stalked away from me mumbling something under his breath that sounded a little like, "I'll never be able to let her out of my sight."

I looked at Cash, then Liam, then Mavros, hoping one of them might tell me I'd heard wrong, but they didn't. In fact, none of them would even meet my eyes.

"It won't be long now." Kieran shoved his hands in his pockets and began whistling. He turned and strode through the trees. His haunting melody seemed to hang in the air instead of dissipating.

I hummed, hoping to keep the tune from plaguing me. Once the song faded away, I walked to Malcolm and plucked a ragwort flower off the bunch in his hand. Setting it on the ground, I willed it to grow into a rosewood tree. I repeated the process several more times, hoping that by giving life, I could forget about losing to Kieran at least for a while.

I went back to Malcolm to grab another flower, but he pulled them back from me. "You must find a way to change the tree." He nodded toward my arm. "He can make you compete against him again tomorrow if he wants. Your time is up."

"You think I don't know that?" I folded my arms over my body, covering the oak, hiding it from my guardians' eyes. "What do you think I've been doing?" Venom dripped from my words. Heat radiated from my chest, spreading through my body. Hadn't he seen me out here day after day, trying everything in my power to keep the leaves from falling?

Scales lined his cheeks, and he growled low in his throat. "I suggest you start taking this seriously and focus on your well-being instead of worrying about planting trees."

"First—" I stepped up to him, shoving my finger into his chest "—it was your idea for me to plant trees. Second, I'm sorry if I disappointed you in some way, but I am concerned about my well-being. I'm terrified of ending up in Faerie, and I would do anything to stop the leaves from falling, but I have no idea what to do. Everything I have tried here has failed."

Cash nudged Malcolm back, then stood between us, letting me see around his massive form while still keeping us separated. "Maybe everything failed because the trees here were already dying. Maybe one or all of these things would work in Faerie on the oak. Maybe magic works differently there. We've seen that it reacts differently with ragwort."

"But, what do I try?" I tugged my hand through my hair and immediately wished I wouldn't have. The strands were still dampened with sweat. "What if whatever I do reacts the same way that it did here? What if I cause the leaves to fall?"

Mavros walked toward us. He held my gaze with his, letting his obsidian eyes bore into mine. "What if you do nothing and they fall anyway?"

"So … what … when?" I sat on the forest floor, pulling my legs up to my chest.

Cash knelt next to me. "Like Malcolm said, he could take you as soon as tomorrow." He held my hand between his, completely dwarfing it. "You should go tonight or first thing in the morning."

"Tonight?" I jerked my head up and looked directly into his amethyst eyes. "Seriously, tonight?"

"It would be best," Mavros agreed.

I chewed on my lip, looking at each of my guards. "So, this could be my last day on Earth?" I pinched my eyes shut and massaged my forehead. "I need to spend some time with Cody before I go and screw this up."

I paced across the living room from Samantha's door to mine and back again, waiting for Cody to return from class. Since I'd been skipping mine, I hadn't realized what day it was until we'd gotten back. I'd expected him to be here, but it wasn't Saturday or Sunday. It was Thursday. I should've been sitting in Graphic Design, staring at the clock, wondering when Kieran would show up.

"Hey," Cody said when he opened the door. His gaze traveled over me and to Mavros, Malcolm, Cash, and Liam. "What's up?"

Part of me wanted to answer, "The ceiling," but the rest of me knew that now was not the time for that. So instead, I held my arm out, showing Cody the new red leaves. "They think he'll come for me tomorrow."

"So, you're gonna try to beat him to the punch." He set his bag next to the door without looking away from me.

I pulled my lip into my mouth and nodded. "I can't wait around for him to challenge me again."

"Know how to do it?" His voice lowered, and his mask slipped into place, keeping me from seeing the emotions on his face.

I sat on the couch, folding my legs up against me, making myself as small as possible. "No." I dragged my fingers through my hair. "I thought we could spend some time together … just the two of us … before I do this."

"Just in case." Nothing got through the blank expression.

I nodded, wishing I could hide my emotions like he did and wondering how he did it. My insides felt hollow, and my heart ached. Did he feel the same? Did he just cover it?

"Just us?" He shifted his gaze to Mavros and then Malcolm.

Tears prickled in my eyes, but I held them back. "They'll stay out of sight."

"Okay—" Cody walked over to me and held his hand out "—but, not saying goodbye."

I slipped my fingers through his. Letting him pull me to my feet, I tried to figure out where to go. I tugged him over to the door and grabbed my coat. Maybe leaving wasn't the wisest decision, but I need to get away for a bit. I needed to spend some time with Cody alone. Looking over my shoulder, I said, "If Kieran comes for me, can you get Cody back here?"

"Of course." Mavros nodded.

No matter where I went, as long as my magic wasn't blocked, Mavros should be able to sense me. That was one benefit or problem, depending on how you looked at it, of being bound to him.

When I was younger, before Jonathan died, my parents had taken us to a lake in the hills. It had been one of the happiest days of my life. A day that I would never forget. I'd always wanted to go back, but it was a part of life before the fire. Before things had changed.

I focused on it, remembering every detail that I could. Then I teleported us. My body stretched out and pinched in. The world went dark. Then we were standing next to a playground, looking out over the frozen lake.

The surface was almost completely white, but dotted along it, a few spots were blue where the ice had nearly melted through. The lake was in a hilly area surrounded by a deciduous forest that was bare of leaves. Snow would most likely cover the ground for another month or more, and if I wasn't trapped in Faerie, maybe we would come back to visit it then.

I brushed off one of the swings and sat on it, gently moving it forward. The chains protested the action, squeaking loudly as chunks of ice dropped from them.

Cody plopped down next to me. "Start from the beginning."

So I did. Without looking away from the snowy ground, I told him everything that had happened since I crawled out of bed.

"What're you gonna do?"

"What else?" I shrugged. "Try to keep the leaves from falling."

Pulling my swing toward him, he gazed into my eyes. "Not saying goodbye." His thumb skimmed over my cheek, and he leaned in. "Ever." His lips brushed over mine so softly that I wasn't positive I'd felt them.

He eased his hold on my chains, letting my swing go back, but I reached out and grabbed his coat, dragging him closer to me. Then I crushed my mouth against his. I slid off my plastic seat and onto his lap, wrapping my legs around him.

Somehow, he pulled me closer still, sliding his arm inside my coat and splaying his fingers over my spine, while holding the back of my neck with his other hand.

The kiss slowed, and he rested his forehead against mine, breathing heavily. He cupped my face, gently caressing my cheeks. "Come back to me." His sapphire eyes shone in the afternoon light.

"I will do everything I can to make that happen." I kissed the tip of his nose, hoping he knew I meant it, hoping he realized that I would do everything in my power to return to him.

"When?"

I pinched my eyes closed and felt the all too familiar emptiness spreading inside of me, the hopelessness and darkness that threatened to consume me if just given the chance. "I don't know. Tonight or tomorrow morning." I pulled away from him and dragged my hand through my hair. "I'm not ready. I won't be no matter when I go."

"Where are we?" He looked around us, and I was grateful for the change of subject.

"No idea." I stood, and he joined me. Holding hands, we walked toward the lake's edge. "Mom and Dad brought us here before we moved to Bittersweet."

Understanding what that meant, he squeezed my fingers, comforting me. I no longer blamed myself for my brother's death, but for most of my life, I had thought it was my doing. I had believed that I'd killed him the night I burned our house to the ground.

"Hungry?" he asked, and I couldn't help but chuckle.

We sat at a booth in the back corner of The Avalanche. My stomach roiled at the thought of eating anything, but Cody ordered a cast iron skillet cookie for me. As soon as our waiter strode away, Cody stretched his hand across the table. I slid mine over the top of it, expecting a lecture from him about taking care of myself, but he didn't say anything. His blue eyes had a faraway look in them that made me realize he was more worried about the leaves falling than he'd let on.

While we were waiting for our food, the door opened, and an aura that I recognized brushed against mine. It was the first I'd felt of any of my guards since Cody and I left the apartment, and I knew Cash was letting me sense him.

I didn't let Cody know he was there. He needed this time alone with me.

The waiter brought his burger and fries at the same time as my cookie sundae. I grabbed my spoon and said, "You're going to have to eat fast because half of this is yours."

"I'll eat half if you share mine." He picked up his knife and cut his burger down the middle.

My heart swelled. This simple act showed me how much he truly cared for me. It meant more than those three little words ever could. Though, I'd never complain about hearing them. "Thanks." I wanted to say more, but a lump had formed in my throat.

The vanilla ice cream was beginning to pool on the fresh-baked cookie, so I dug into it. When the first bit of melted chocolate hit my tongue, I moaned softly. Before I realized it, I'd eaten the entire thing and was scraping the last traces out of the skillet.

Cody smiled at me and offered up some of his fries. "Want these?"

"No, thanks." I leaned back in my chair and patted my stomach. "I ate way more than I planned on."

While Cody finished his food, I glanced around the restaurant. I could still sense Cash's aura, so he'd either positioned himself out of sight or was invisible.

Other than us, only a handful of tables had people sitting at them. Nobody was waiting on us to leave, so not wanting this day to end, I took my time sipping my drink and even accepted a refill when the server came back.

I studied Cody, memorizing every detail of his face, his eyes, his hair, his mannerisms. If this was the last day I got to spend with him, I didn't want to forget anything.

Despite what Cash had said about my magic working differently in Faerie, I had my doubts. I knew there had to be a way to beat Kieran, but would I find it?

Folding his arms over his chest, Cody leaned back and watched me. He pointed at his lip, and I realized I had been chewing on mine. "Know you don't wanna hear it, but you got this." He picked up his glass and drank half of his pop before setting it back down on the table. He didn't meet my eyes for the whole time, and I wondered what he thought he would see in them.

I folded my napkin into ever-smaller triangles while trying to figure out how to respond to him. All sorts of things ran through my mind, but I clamped my mouth shut. I didn't want to argue with Cody. I didn't want to say the wrong thing and never get to take my harsh words back if I didn't succeed. There were so many things that would lead me down that path. When my napkin was folded as tightly as I could get it, I settled on, "Thanks."

Cody lifted one eyebrow but said nothing else.

We stayed in The Avalanche until they kicked us out. I wasn't ready for this night to be over. I wasn't ready to say goodbye to Cody. Every touch of his fingers, every word from his mouth, every glance that he shot me could be the last, and even though I knew he would probably be safer with me out of his life, I couldn't bear the thought of never seeing him again.

We strolled along the boardwalk hand in hand. The crisp air smelled clean and fresh. It stung my cheeks as I gazed up at a sky filled with billions of stars. We turned down an alley and, after I made sure nobody was watching, teleported back to my bedroom in our apartment.

My new comforter still looked out of place. I missed the bright pink splashes that made the room cheery. The purple by itself was too dark. It made the space seem smaller, and even though I wanted to stay here forever, it felt like the room was closing in on me. I moved toward the door to pull it open, but Cody grabbed hold of my arm.

"Wait." His Adam's apple bobbed in his neck. "I'm not ready for you to go."

I let him pull me against him and wrapped my arms around his waist. "I wasn't going, just opening the door."

"Just a little more time." He looked beyond me.

The voices of our friends carried into my room. Along with my guards, it sounded like Bryce, Cassandra, Dan, and Samantha were also out there. I imagined they all wanted to see me before I left for Faerie, but if I spent time with them, would I still go, or would I lose my nerve?

Nodding, I pulled my coat off and tossed it onto the bed. A shiver tumbled down my spine, and I rubbed my arms to dispel the goosebumps that had risen on them. When the sudden chill was gone, I looked up into Cody's eyes. Fear darkened his irises, making sapphire highlights shoot through a navy sea.

Swallowing over the lump that had formed in my throat, I stood on my tiptoes and pressed my lips to his.

He pulled me closer, sliding his hands over my back, moving his mouth against mine in a rhythmic dance.

I breathed in his scent. The crisp winter's day fragrance sent a pang to my chest. Would I ever smell it again, or would the rest of my days smell like earth and rain? Tears trailed down my cheeks, and Cody took a step back.

One corner of his mouth curled up. "Was my kiss that bad?" He lifted his hands to my face, gently cupping it as he wiped the moisture away with his thumbs.

"What if I lose?" I tried to lower my head, but he held on, staring into my eyes.

He shook his head. "Told you. Not saying goodbye." Then he pulled me against his chest, holding me like he'd never let go. "Not now. Not ever."

Chapter 36

Faerie

A gentle rain fell from the darkened sky. I stood thirty feet from the tree, trying to figure out how to keep the leaves from falling, hoping not to draw attention.

I'd left without saying goodbye to my friends. The thought of facing them with no plan, no idea if I'd come back was too much. Cody had kissed me before dropping my hand and saying, "See you in a few."

Something in the shadows moved, pulling my thoughts from the memory. My eyes transformed into a dragon's. The night brightened, and everything was crisp and clear.

A black cat prowled toward me. Blinking rapidly, I sucked in a deep breath. The beast stood as tall as a German Shepherd with muscles that rippled with every step. I stumbled back, and a branch snapped beneath my foot. The cat's red eyes flicked toward me, and as it turned, I noticed a small white patch of fur on its chest.

I took another step back, moving behind the trunk of a nearby tree, hoping it hadn't seen me. A hand clamped down on my shoulder, and a scream tore from my throat.

"Shh." Mavros chuckled and moved beside me. "Did you really think I would let you come here alone?" He shook his head and with his hand still on my shoulder pulled me out from the shadows of the trees. "This is Kynigós." He waved at the cat. "She's the leader of my faerie cats."

The feline sat down on her haunches and lifted a paw to her mouth, licking it casually. She studied me through slitted eyes. I felt like she could see clear to my soul, like she knew every secret I'd tried to hide, every misstep I'd ever made, and she was weighing the good against the bad.

"Cait Sidhe," Kynigós said in a heavily accented voice, "and beyond the shadow of a doubt, not yours." The cat stood and sauntered away, effectively dismissing Mavros.

"Touchy." Mavros pressed his hand against the small of my back and moved us toward the oak.

As we walked, I caught glimpses of more faerie cats. "What did she call herself?"

"Cait Sidhe." Mavros shot me a lopsided smile. "It means cat faerie, but they're cats. They want to feel important, and to them, it sounds more dignified."

The tree loomed over me. The other ones in this part of the forest grew straight up until their canopies spread out, but the oak's gnarled branches started low, defying nature and not caring that sunlight couldn't reach them.

Something rustled the leaves of a tree behind me, and one of the Cait Sidhe bounded past me, growling low in its throat. Whatever had been approaching the tree scurried off.

The cat glanced at me. Its whiskers were curled forward, and it stood taller.

I stepped toward it. "Th—"

"Don't!" Mavros was instantly between us. Flames danced in his eyes. "Don't ever thank a faerie."

I clamped my mouth shut. I'd heard that rule, but it had never made sense to me. "Why?" Spinning toward him, I stared into his eyes. "It's the dumbest thing I've ever heard. So, tell me why."

"Malcolm's right." He shook his head. "You are never going to be able to be alone." He pulled me closer to the tree. "You've been researching them. Haven't you learned anything?" He held his hand up to keep me from speaking. "Don't answer that. If you thank them, you acknowledge that you owe them a favor. They can ask for anything, and you are obligated to give them what they want."

I looked over my shoulder at the Cait Sidhe. Its head was tilted to the side as it watched us, and if I didn't know better, I would swear it was smiling at me. Remembering what I had read, I said, "Well done. Your help is appreciated."

"She can learn." One side of Mavros' mouth pulled up. "Now, what can you do about the tree?"

I stretched my hand forward, placing it on the rough bark. Unlike on Earth, there were no insects climbing the tree or making homes on it. Nothing was chirping. I couldn't help but wonder if there were bugs in Faerie or if they avoided this tree because it was made from magic and not natural.

A faint pulse pressed against my hand. I jerked away, staring down at my palm, wondering if I had imagined the sensation. "Mavros, tell me if you feel this." I grabbed his hand, but before I set it on the tree, he pulled it out of my grasp and stuffed his fists into his coat pockets.

"I dare not touch it, Dacia." His expression was somewhere between heartbroken and tortured. "I don't know what my essence would do to it. We're too close to the end to risk it."

"I thought it was just my imagination when I'd felt it before."

He stepped closer to me but didn't touch the tree. "What is it?"

Placing both of my hands against the trunk, I waited for a sign that I wasn't crazy. It didn't take long for me to feel the thrum against my hands. It wasn't as consistent as a human heartbeat, but there was no doubt in my mind that that was what I was feeling.

"It's alive," I whispered.

Mavros' eyebrows pinched together. "All trees are."

"No. I mean it has a heartbeat." Hoping I wouldn't cause it to drop a leaf, I focused on life and healing and sent a gentle stream of magic flowing into it. "It's not alive like the other trees. It's alive like I am. Like you are."

The pulse reacted to my magic, thumping against my hands. The new intensity left no doubt as to what I'd felt earlier. I leaned against the trunk. *How do I keep the leaves from falling?* The thought was on repeat, racing through my head.

Free me, a voice that was not mine answered.

Images flashed like memories through my mind, but they didn't belong to me. A girl. I'd seen her before in my dreams. Three moons hung in the sky, watching her dance through a meadow. She was vibrant and brimming with life. Her green dress twirled around her. Dark hair flowed in waves down her back. The wind lifted her tresses, showing me her pointed ears. Her bare feet slapped against the ground faster and faster with each moment that passed.

Kieran stepped out of the trees, making his way to the girl. His yellow eyes glowed in the moonlight.

She spun around, and as soon as she saw him, she stopped moving. She looked over her shoulder as if gauging the distance to the trees. She took a tentative step back, and Kieran took two closer.

Turning, she darted for the trees. The moonbeams chased her, lighting a path for Kieran to follow. He grabbed her arm, then lifted his hand, holding up a glowing acorn.

She was mesmerized. The tension left her body, and she strode toward him. She ran her fingers over the cap, and a smile brightened her face.

Kieran backed away, keeping the acorn just out of reach, luring her into the woods. When trees surrounded them, he stopped moving. This time when the girl grabbed at the acorn, he let her have it.

Roots extended from the seed, wrapping around her. As the acorn sprouted, the girl morphed. Her skin turned brown, then transformed into bark. Her arms lifted to her sides, and branches shot from her fingertips.

"Dacia!" Mavros' voice pulled me from the tree's memories. He snapped his fingers in front of my eyes.

"What?" I swatted his hand away. "The tree was showing me a vision." Wiping the rain off of my face, I tried to focus on what the tree had shown me. The girl had to be alive, trapped inside the tree by some sort of magic. Otherwise, how would I have seen her memories? There had to be a way to save her and keep the leaves from falling.

Water plastered Mavros' hair to his head and ran in rivulets down his face, but he didn't seem to mind. He stood with his hands tucked into his pockets. "What are you going to do, Dacia?"

"I don't know." I closed my eyes and sucked in a deep breath, trying to center myself. "I had planned to encase it in an airtight bubble, kinda like what I put on Argentum's head, and then turn it to stone or crystal or something like that." I flipped my hands up in the air. "I can't do that now, though."

He clenched his jaw and narrowed his eyes. "You can, and you should." He strode toward me. "You need to do whatever you can to keep from being trapped here."

"I can't"—I stabbed my finger at his chest—"and you of all people should know that." I walked back to the tree and pressed my hand against it. "Tell me how to help you and keep the leaves from falling. Please. Help me figure this out so we can both be free."

I don't know how you can help me. The girl trapped in the tree sounded as desperate as I felt. *I will hold onto the leaves as long as I can.*

"Thank you." I leaned my head against the bark. The rain made it feel slimy, but I didn't pull away. I had to figure this out.

Kieran's song broke my concentration. That jaunty tune he whistled sent chills racing down my spine.

"Not now." A giant hole opened up inside of me. I slowly turned, not wanting to face Kieran, but not wanting my back to him either.

Mavros was a statue. His hand was stretched out toward me, and raindrops dripped from his fingertips. I stared at him, pulling on my magic, willing him to be cognizant. Malcolm had told me that I had to be the one to break Kieran's spell. My guardians couldn't do it themselves.

I pushed all my will into releasing Mavros. Just as Kieran stepped through the trees, Mavros' hand grabbed mine, and he squeezed my fingers. Having him with me made facing Kieran a little easier.

"I see you found your tree." The song seemed to swirl around Kieran even though he wasn't whistling it anymore. "It matters not. The leaves will still fall. It is inevitable."

"If that's the case, then there's nothing for you to worry about." I turned my back to him, hoping that I wouldn't end up regretting it.

He laughed, and the sound sent shivers rushing down my spine. "The seventh challenge is to make a leaf fall."

My heart stopped. *No. No. No. No. No.*

"If you don't let one fall, they all will." The smugness in his voice told me he knew he'd won. "Ready?"

"No." I turned toward him. "Rules."

A sly grin tipped up one side of his mouth. "Ah, you and your rules." He flipped his hand up. "Go on then."

"You can't interfere." I prayed the quiver stayed out of my voice and I could hold my resolve. "This is my task and mine alone."

"Very well." He leaned back against another tree, crossing one foot in front of the other and tucking his hands into his pockets.

I chewed on my lip, trying to figure out what he had in mind. "No one, no creature, no force, and nothing other than me can knock a leaf off. Mavros and his friends will protect the tree and me while I do this challenge."

The Cait Sidhe stepped out from the shadows, and Kieran narrowed his eyes at them. "Traitors."

"We are not of your court," Kynigós responded.

Kieran's lip lifted in a snarl. "Neither are you demons."

"Ah—" she lifted her paw to her mouth and casually licked it "—but we are cats."

A black mist spun around Mavros, and he shifted into his panther form. He stood between Kieran and me.

"Very well." Kieran nodded at me. "I agree to your terms because either way, I win."

You can do this, Dacia. I heard Mavros' voice in my head.

I scratched behind his ear, and his wet fur clung to my hand. *I hope you're right.*

"My rule." Kieran held his finger up. "Just one. You have fifteen minutes. If a leaf doesn't drop in that time, you lose."

"Fifteen minutes?" My voice was high-pitched.

He slumped back again. His pose was relaxed, confident. "All you have to do is pluck a leaf from the tree and let it fall. Fifteen minutes is excessive."

"Fine." He was right, and if I pushed him on this, he would lower the time limit. "I accept."

He looked at his wrist even though there wasn't a watch there. "Begin now."

Chapter 37

I've got your back, Mavros said.

Turning away from both of them, I pressed my hands against the tree, closed my eyes, and pictured the girl trapped within. I imagined her long, dark hair twirling around her as she danced out of the tree, her skirt swirling around her legs.

Please don't let any leaves fall, I begged the fairy girl.

Her voice rippled through my head. *I will do everything I can to hold on to them.*

Visualizing the tree, I remembered how it grew on my arm. How the acorn had rooted before growing into a sapling. How it had then developed into a mature tree. Holding these images in my head, I envisioned them reversing. I pictured leaves being sucked back into buds, the buds retreating into the stems, and the branches shrinking until they sunk back into the trunk.

Its growth was retrogressive, diminishing instead of growing taller and stronger.

My magic pulsed inside of me. Then it burst through my fingertips, blasting into the tree trunk. *Please let this work, Lord.* The prayer left me before I had time to consider if God could even hear me from this realm. I decided to have faith that He could and that He would help me beat this curse.

The rain soaked through my clothes, and shivers racked my body. My teeth chattered. I could warm myself, but it would mean pulling energy away from the tree. Instead, I focused on the task at hand, hoping it would be done soon.

It's working. Mavros' words whispered through my head. *Whatever you're doing, don't stop.*

"No!" Kieran's scream pierced through the quiet night.

Footsteps pounded against the ground behind me, but I held onto the tree, hoping Mavros would be able to hold Kieran off.

The wind picked up and leaves rustled. Growls filled the air, followed by the yowls of angry cats.

"Hold on a little longer," I begged the girl inside the tree at the same time that I sent healing energy into her.

Something landed on my shoulder. Sharp claws dug into my skin.

"Mavros!" His name left my lips on a mix between a scream and a sob. I couldn't push the creature off of me. I couldn't let go of the tree. I couldn't give up when I was so close.

Teeth sunk into my collarbone. Something akin to fire raced through my body from where the beast clamped onto me.

I whimpered but held on.

The creature screamed. Its shrill shriek right in my ear was deafening and made me cringe, but I couldn't stop.

My attacker was torn from my shoulder, and I felt Mavros' body press up against mine. His heat infused me. The shivers receded, but there was nothing he could do about the venom racing through my veins. I had to finish before my body gave out.

My heartbeat pounded against my skull. I still couldn't hear anything out of my left ear, and things in my right ear were muted and blurred together. My knees trembled, but Mavros pressed against me, holding my body captive between him and the tree.

The serpent rose in my vision. *Heal yourself, Dacia.*

I can't. My thoughts were disjointed, and I shook my head to regain focus. *I need a few more minutes.*

You are dying. The snake swayed from side to side. Its pearlescent scales were dulled. Its eyes cloudy. *We are dying.*

Just hang on. I clenched my teeth in an attempt to stop the pounding in my head. *We can do this.*

My magic recoiled. *You would die to save her?*

I will die to keep from being trapped in Faerie. In my mind, I reached out caressing the serpent's head. *We have died before, but we won't this time.*

The snake nestled against my fingers. *I will not let you. Save the girl if you must, but I will choose you if it comes to it.*

Wait as long as you can.

I returned my focus to the tree, leaving my powers behind in the darkened room. The dulled noises disappeared. The shock of losing my hearing nearly toppled me, but I held on to the tree, sending my magic streaming into it.

The trunk's girth shrank beneath my hands. I stumbled forward, and Mavros caught me. His hands clutched my arms. Where his skin came into contact with mine, I felt like I was being branded.

He shook me. *Dacia, answer!*

His words tumbled through my mind, making no sense to me. Nobody had asked anything. *Answer what?* As soon as I asked, the fog in my head cleared enough for me to remember that I couldn't hear.

You're ice cold. Fear filled his voice. *Are you okay?*

I didn't mean to laugh. This wasn't funny, but it tumbled out of me anyway, shaking my body, and making me want to clutch my stomach.

His fingers tightened their hold, and I came to my senses.

I'm dying, Mavros. I tightened my grip on the tree as a bout of dizziness washed over me.

His growl ripped through my skull. *Not on my watch.* He started to pull me from the tree.

No. I pleaded. *I have to finish this.*

If he had been any of my other guards, he would have sent healing energy flowing into me, but he was a demon, and the last thing I needed was more of his essence in me. The silver-haired fairies didn't know if they could remove it again, and my eyes already had too many black flecks in them.

Instead of feeding me his strength, he held me up, moving me forward as the trunk diminished. With my eyes shut and my hearing gone, I had no idea what was going on around me, but I trusted Mavros and the Cait Sidhe to keep me safe.

Flesh touched my fingertips. I opened my eyes. My vision was blurred and dark on the edges. Black spots danced through the air as I watched the tree peel back from the girl. She swayed on her feet, stumbling into me as the last of the tree receded into the acorn. Without Mavros holding me up, I would have collapsed beneath her.

The acorn lay on the ground, holding my attention. An eerie green light surrounded it. The magic called to me, but I refused to pick it up or to touch it at all.

Magic coursed through my body, rushing to heal my wounds and counteract the venom. My vision slowly cleared, and sound gradually made its way back to my ears.

I looked around me, trying to figure out what had happened while I freed the fairy girl.

The Cait Sidhe surrounded Kieran. His clothes were shredded where I assumed their claws had torn through the fabric. Blood dripped from brutal scratches. I would have called them off, but the look on his face terrified me.

The girl slumped in my arms. Up close her dark hair wasn't brown or black like I figured it would be. It was emerald. "Thank you for not leaving me trapped inside the oak for eternity." Her voice reminded me of wind rushing through the trees.

"This isn't over!" Kieran shouted.

The Cait Sidhe answered with growls, snarls, and yowls.

The fairy stood up. Her pale skin washed out further as she backed away from me. The temperature seemed to chill further, and the rain hung in the air instead of falling.

I turned slowly, watching Mavros disappear as I did. Icy fingers climbed up my spine, raising the hairs on the back of my neck and settling in the pit of my stomach like a stack of frozen bricks.

I stared into the forest, trying to figure out what had charged the atmosphere. After a few moments, the most beautiful woman I had ever seen strode into view. The trees seemed to part to let her approach. Moonlight broke through the clouds and highlighted her, gleaming off of her golden hair. There was something regal about her gait, her stance, her air.

Her crystal blue eyes locked onto mine and held me mesmerized. "You have bested my phouka." She laughed, and it was like the tinkling of bells.

Her gaze fell on the fairy girl behind me. "And who is this?"

"Kieran trapped her inside the tree." My voice was stronger than I thought it would be.

She turned toward Kieran, pursed her perfect pouty lips, and clicked her tongue. "And still this mere mortal bested you?"

"She cheated," Kieran accused. The phouka who moments ago looked like he would kill me if given the chance now looked like nothing more than a whiny little brat that threw a temper tantrum whenever he didn't get his way.

"Now, now, Kieran," she tutted, "if she had cheated, the magic would have held her accountable." She turned away from him. The movement was more graceful than that of a trained dancer. She smoothed the imaginary wrinkles out of her blood-red gown and glanced back at Kieran. "Well, darling, aren't you going to introduce us."

"Queen Titania—" he bowed as low as the Cait Sidhe would allow him "—this is Dacia Wolf. Dacia, bow before Queen Titania."

She focused on me, and I didn't like what I saw behind her crystalline eyes. I bowed, never pulling my gaze from hers.

"No need for formalities." She waved her hand and smiled a serpent's smile.

I rose up, and the world spun for a moment. When the vertigo was gone, I said, "A pleasure to meet you."

She lifted one slender eyebrow. "Kieran promised to let you go if you won."

"She's mine." His voice was petulant, and I half expected him to stomp his foot.

"We are faeries." She strode toward me, and the moonbeams seemed to follow her every movement. "We must keep our bargains."

"So, I am free to go?" I tried to hide the tremor in my voice, but I doubted that I succeeded.

She laughed, and the tinkling sound sent chills rushing down my spine. "You may leave, but one who outwits a faerie is never free."

Chapter 38

I grabbed the fairy girl's arm and focused on my room. Exhaustion weighed me down, making my limbs heavy. I wanted to sink to the ground and sleep, but I needed to get us out of here. My magic, after being nearly depleted, was slow to respond to my call. I closed my eyes and swayed. The girl latched on, steadying me.

Letting out a deep breath, I hoped I had enough power left for this. My body stretched and squeezed. The world went black, and when my feet touched solid ground again, my stomach lurched. I stumbled to the floor, and the girl knelt next to me. "Are you okay?"

I held one finger up, waiting for my stomach to settle. *Cash?*

Yes, Dacia. Tension lined his voice. *Where are you?*

My arms gave out, and I fell. My face was pressed into the carpet. *My room. I need—*

I woke up on the couch under a heavy blanket. Strong arms were wrapped around me, but they weren't Cody's. He sat on the other end of the sofa with my feet on his lap. His sapphire eyes watched me, his mask hiding his emotions from me.

Mavros sat in one armchair, and the fairy girl perched on the other. The rest of my friends minus Malcolm were scattered about.

"How are you feeling?" Sarah pushed her chair away from the table and strode over to me. "You gave everyone a bit of a scare."

I sat up slowly, not sure how my body would handle it. Cash took ahold of my hand. His energy trickled into me.

"How bad?" I asked him.

He lifted one shoulder. "I've seen worse. Your magic was depleted, and some sort of venom that I've never seen before was wreaking havoc on your body."

Remembering that Sarah had asked me a question, I turned to her. "Better." I rubbed my hand over my forehead, then looked at the fairy. "I'm sorry that I brought you here and then passed out." I tried to smile at her, but my motions felt stiff. "I didn't think you should be left there with Titania and Kieran."

"I think leaving was for the best." She bowed her head. "Your kindness is once again appreciated."

I started to stand, but Cash pulled me back down. "Give it a little more time, Dacia. Your energy is still diminished."

"As soon as I'm strong enough, I will return you to Faerie if you wish." I tilted my head studying the girl. "What should I call you?"

Her lips pinched together for a moment. "You may call me Dahlia."

"Are you part of the Spring Court?" I asked her.

She shook her head. "No. The vision you saw ..." She looked around the room nervously.

"It's okay." I glanced at the people in the room with us. "You can trust them. They're my friends and protectors."

Her emerald eyes shuttered. "I was dancing and didn't realize I had stumbled so close to Spring. Kieran lured me into his territory with the acorn. I tried to resist, but his magic is stronger than I'd ever imagined, and he wanted me for his own." She looked up at me. Fear covered her face. "Dryads are coveted in Spring, but we're not allowed to roam free there. We are used and imprisoned. Neither Kieran nor the queen will forgive you for freeing me."

"That's okay." A laugh escaped me, but it was a humorless imitation. "Neither of them will forgive me for beating Kieran at his own game."

She nodded. "You are right about that." She stood and pointed at the ragwort stems in a vase on the table. "I can get back on my own if I may take one of those."

"You may." I smiled at her. "Be safe."

She grabbed a stem, then strolled into the living room between the couch and TV. She twirled the ragwort between her hands and whispered something I couldn't hear. The dried flower transformed into a dapple gray stallion.

He shook his head, and seeds flew from his mane, dancing through the air and alighting upon my friends.

Dahlia smiled at me, a pure, grateful smile. "You will never be forgotten." She mounted the horse, clicked her tongue, and rode out through the ceiling.

"That was just like magic," Cassandra said with the hint of a laugh.

I settled back against the couch. "It sure was."

Sarah nudged Cody toward me and then sat where he had been. He took the hand that Cash wasn't holding and twined his fingers through mine. "Mavros told us about the tree." He turned my arm and lifted it so I could see.

My skin was smooth and unblemished. The oak was gone. Relief pooled in my stomach, and tears fell from my eyes.

Gone.

The curse was gone.

The queen might have threatened me with retaliation, but for now, I was free from the tethers of Faerie.

Cody wiped the tears from my cheeks, then wrapped his arm around my shoulders. I nestled into his side.

I was safe.

It was over.

The fear of being trapped in Faerie was a thing of the past.

My friends surrounded me, but they didn't push me to tell them what had happened. Their hushed voices comforted me.

I glanced around the room, wondering if I had somehow missed Malcolm when I'd first woken, but there was no sign of him. "Where's Malcolm?"

"Across the hall." Cash nodded at the door. "You were weak, depleted. He didn't know if he could trust himself around you, so in his words, he removed the problem."

"Oh." I swallowed over the lump that had formed in my throat and stared at the doorway, looking through it into the other apartment. Malcolm stared back at me. He nodded and flashed his fangs.

"So, what's next." Dan smacked his hands together and rubbed them vigorously. "Vampires, werewolves, goblins?"

I rolled my eyes. "Peace, harmony, spring break?"

Our feet pound against the snow-covered trail. We've been running for over an hour, but it hasn't lessened Malcolm's anger. His hunger grows stronger by the day, and every time I'm near him, I'm putting my life in his hands.

Maybe it's selfish of me, but I'm not ready for him to go.

Malcolm's cornrows are pulled back into a ponytail, bouncing against his shoulder blades as he runs in front of us, setting the pace. He hasn't slowed since we started up the mountain. My legs feel like rubber, shaking with each step as I continue along the same path we've been running on for most of the winter, but I keep going.

I don't want to give him a reason to think I'm weak.

I can't let him think I'm prey.

"Malcolm," Cash sounds as breathless as I feel, "this is enough."

Malcolm's steps don't falter when he looks over his shoulder at us. His fangs hang over his bottom lip. Scales line his face. "It's enough when I say it's enough." He narrows his slitted eyes at me before focusing on the trail again.

We run until my legs barely hold me up anymore. Finally, Malcolm stops. I bend over with my hands on my knees, sucking in huge gulps of oxygen.

Malcolm pats my shoulder. As I look up at him, his eyes gloss over, and his human-looking features turn dragon-like. His hands lock on my arms.

"Malcolm," I say his name quietly, hoping he won't be able to hear the tremble in my voice.

He cocks his head to the side and stares at my neck where I can feel my pulse pounding. A black, forked tongue slips out of his mouth and slowly traces his top lip.

"Malcolm, please." This time there is no denying the fear in my words.

Talons puncture my skin, and he strikes, sinking his fangs into my throat.

My eyes cracked open, and I looked around. The room was dark, but I was sure this wasn't where I went to sleep. I pushed myself up onto my elbows and let my eyes transform into a dragon's.

The denim and tan comforter from Cody's bed was bunched at my feet. I rubbed my eyes, wondering if I had forgotten. Had I fallen asleep in his room?

My eyes transformed back into my own, and I lay back down, curling onto my side and placing my head on Cody's chest. Something was off. I lifted my hand, feeling the fabric of his t-shirt, but Cody never slept with a shirt on.

"Dacia," Cash said as he grabbed my hand.

I jerked it back. Heat spread up my neck and onto my face. "I'm sorry." I rolled onto my back and pulled the blanket over my head. "I didn't mean to grope you." My voice shook. "Why are you here, anyway?"

"Go back to sleep, Dacia." Marvos' voice startled me, but it shouldn't have. He'd been watching me sleep almost every night since Malcolm had attacked me.

As soon as I had that thought, my dream came back to me. "His eyes weren't his."

"Whose?" Cash rolled me over so that I faced him. His face was just inches from mine.

He was too close. I could feel his breath on my face, caressing it. Lying in bed with him felt too intimate. I scooted back a little, but he didn't let me get too far away. "Malcolm's." I closed my eyes and focused on the end of my dream. "They were his, and then they were glossed over. That's when … when he—" I felt Malcolm's claws tearing into my arms, his hot breath on my face before his teeth sunk into my neck, ripping my jugular out.

"Attacked you?" Mavros asked.

I nodded, and Cash pulled me against his chest. His hands rubbed down my back. The motion was soothing, but I wanted Cody, not him. "Where's Cody?"

"He's sleeping on the couch." The bed slumped down behind me, and Mavros rested his hand on my shoulder.

I tucked my arm under my pillow. If he was out there, things must have been pretty bad.

"I know you'd rather have him with you"—Cash's hand kept moving up and down my back—"but you need my strength tonight."

When I woke up, Cody, Samantha, and Dan had already left for their classes. I should have been going to mine, but judging by the way Cash and Mavros were acting, my wounds had been substantial.

As soon as I walked into the living room, Liam jumped up from the armchair. "You want some breakfast?"

My stomach grumbled in response, and I grinned at him while rubbing my belly. "Healing takes a lot out of me."

"You need protein," Malcolm said as he entered the apartment. He didn't look at me as he strode to the couch and sat down. His muscles were taut. His jaw was clenched tight.

Liam opened the fridge. "Bacon and eggs or an omelet?"

"Bacon and eggs, over medium." I sat down on the opposite end of the couch. "It was a dream, Malcolm."

He leaned forward with his elbows on his knees, staring at his folded hands. "It was a premonition. Every time I smell your blood, it gets closer to becoming a reality."

"I don't think you were in control of yourself." I scooted closer to him. When he didn't move away, I hesitantly lifted my hand and set it on his back.

He jerked but didn't pull away. "Why do you say that?"

"While we were running, your features were dragonesque, but when we stopped, you looked like you do now." I pulled my hand off his back and slid my fingers through his. "Then your eyes glossed over. That's when you attacked me."

His gaze darted from our joined hands to my face. "You're sure?"

"Yeah." I looked at him, and he actually met my gaze. "Your eyes were yours, and then they weren't."

He pulled away from me and stood. "If what you're describing is true, someone was controlling me."

"Who could do that? I mean I know Draconian did, but who else?" I chewed on my bottom lip while I contemplated the consequences.

Bacon sizzling was the only noise in the room while Malcolm thought about what to say. The smell of it made my stomach growl even though I'd lost my appetite.

"Demons, magicians, fae, gods, spirits, undead." He ticked each of his answers off on his fingers. "None of these are creatures you want to face, but if they can control us, that puts you in even more danger."

Chapter 39

If You Love Someone, Set Them Free

$\mathcal{A}$s spring break drew closer, my life went back to normal. I sat at the kitchen table with my laptop open in front of me. I spent every spare minute these days catching up on homework assignments. It would be a miracle if I didn't fail all of my classes.

Malcolm opened the window above the sink, then leaned against the cabinet. Whatever he wanted to say couldn't be good if he was preparing for my emotions to bother him.

I scooted my computer forward and folded my arms on the table, resting my head on them. "What's up?"

"Draconian's the only mage we've been around besides you." Malcolm bowed his head and seemed to shrink in on himself, no longer the imposing man he usually was. "He controlled us. He kept us in our dragon forms. We were ruled by his desires and our instincts. The only time he ever smelled of anything but confidence and cruelty was right before he died."

I pressed my eyes closed, fighting the memory of his death. "Right before I murdered him, you mean."

"We've been over that." He looked at me through slitted eyes. "You didn't murder him. It was self-defense." He breathed in deeply, and I knew my emotions were affecting him. "This is the problem, Dacia. Being around humans should make us more like you." He turned toward the window and inhaled the fresh, evening air. "It must have something to do with your magic, but our dragons creep closer to the surface every day. Even with hunting, it's getting increasingly difficult for us to hold them back."

I slumped in my chair. This felt like goodbye. As irritated as I got being constantly supervised, I couldn't imagine not having them around. "So … what are you saying?"

"We need some time to be dragons." He faced me again, and I could see the depth of his regret in his bronze eyes. "If you need us"—he tapped his forehead—"we will come, but for now, we must leave."

I couldn't hold back the sob that raced up my throat. Covering my mouth, I ducked my head. He didn't need to feel guilty about it. He didn't need to be weighed down by my heartache.

His footsteps were silent as he strode across the room and knelt next to me. He watched me for a minute before wrapping his muscled arms around me. His chin rested on the top of my head. "It is not forever." His hand rubbed my back. "It is only for now. The angel and demon will stay. If we are needed, we will return. Your safety is still our priority."

I nodded against his chest not trusting my voice to be there if called upon.

"We still must ensure that you do not succumb to the call of darkness."

I jerked back, but he held onto me. "Why … why are you worried—" I hiccoughed "—about that?"

His arms tensed around me, forcing my breath from my lungs. "For as long as you live"—his words were spoken so softly that I had to strain to hear them—"if the prophecy is in fact about you, it is a possibility."

"Why?" I swallowed my tears as anger replaced my grief. "Haven't I proven myself? What's it going to take? I transformed into a demon and didn't turn." I pushed away from him, and he eased his grip. "Doesn't that mean anything?"

He held onto my shoulders, keeping me from getting up. "There are things that could happen. Things that would break you beyond repair."

"Like what, Malcolm?" I took a deep breath, trying to ease my frustration. "I had something inside of me, taking over my magic, fighting for control of me. Every time Cody came near me, I risked killing him. That didn't break me. What do you think will?"

He clenched his jaw and stared at me for a long time. Finally, he squeezed his eyes shut. "What if you would have killed him? What if the Nephilim had taken him? What if I would have killed him?" He wouldn't meet my gaze. "I wanted to, Dacia. If Draconian had allowed it, I would have."

Every word he said painted a clear picture of the over-whelming grief I would have faced, of the insurmountable rage that would destroy the good in me.

"Someday, he will die." Malcolm's voice was soft, but his words hit me hard. "What will become of you if you feel you could have stopped it … or worse if you were the cause?"

Cody's lifeless body floated in front of my eyes. I remem-bered flames flying from my fingers, striking him in the chest. Fire danced on the gold chain I'd given him for Christmas. Without it, one of my many premonitions would have come to fruition. "How will you stop me if you're gone?"

"We will never be farther away than a thought." He sat back on the floor, pulling his legs up in front of him. "I vowed to protect you. We all did. We will not forsake you, but right now, our presence may endanger you." He dragged his hand down his face. "Especially mine."

I yanked my hand through my hair. Strands clung to my fingers and snagged on my promise ring. "Why do you all have to go?"

"Cash and I hold the others in line." He looked at the door, seemingly seeing through it. "Without our will, I don't know how long the others could resist tasting your blood, and one taste … one small drop is all it would take for them to lose control. It is like a drug. My craving for it increases every time I scent it. I believed my desire for it would fade with time, but it only grows." He turned back toward me but stared at my feet instead of my face. "I hope that with some time away, its call will lessen."

I should have been terrified by his admission, but I trusted Malcolm more than anyone. He'd been there for me so many times. He would give his life for me. I loved him, not like I loved Cody but unlike I'd loved anybody else. "What about Mom and Dad? Will they be safe?"

"Arianna and Val have seen no sign of the Nephilim. The forest surrounding your house has been free from demons and imps since your return to school." He stood and took hold of my hand. "Khione will stay there for now. Her presence should be enough to deter any trespassers."

I nodded. I had no words. There was nothing I could say to make them stay with me. It was time to let them go, no matter how badly it hurt. Forcing them to remain by my side would make me no better than Draconian, and obviously, this had been in the works for quite some time. I squeezed his fingers. "When?"

"Soon." He smiled at me, but it was filled with sadness. "A few days at most."

"A few days."

Malcolm pulled me to my feet and led me to the couch. He sat next to me and wrapped his arm around my shoulders. "You might get some time to yourself."

"I doubt it." Not too long ago, I would have been grateful for their absence, but now, I was afraid of what would come for me and of what I would become. "Mavros will probably be more vigilant."

"Possibly." He absent-mindedly ran his hand up and down my arm. "I want you to keep training with Liam. Keep using your magic. Even without me here—" his voice caught, and he cleared his throat "—I want you to meet your potential."

Tye steps out of the trees. He looks more haggard than I remembered him. His clothes hang on him, and his cheeks are hollowed out. "Did Malcolm finally tire of babysitting you?"

"Hello, Tye." I don't give him the satisfaction of answering his question. Once upon a time, I had thought he was my friend, but he had just been pretending. He had betrayed the other dragons, acting like Draconian had controlled him and allowing them to continue being used. I wouldn't fall for his deception again.

He steps toward me and lifts his nose, scenting the air. "The demon is still here. I can smell him all over you." His lip curls in disgust. "How can you stand to be near such a hideous creature?"

"I could ask the same of you." *Why did I sneak out without Liam or Mavros? Why today?* "First, you sided with Draconian over your own kind. Then, you betrayed me to Argentum." I take a slow step back, like I would with any wild animal. "You're a traitor, and if they find you, they'll kill you." I stare into his green eyes. The brown flecks in them remind me of the gold and black ones in my own. I wonder if they got there the same way as mine or if they have always been a part of him.

He snaps his head to the side, breaking the connection. "You won't find anything useful there, Dacia. Draconian was never able to glean my true name, and neither will you."

"You can't blame a girl for trying." I take a step back. "What do you want?"

He circles me like a cat stalking its prey. "I want the life you stole from me! I want the luxury and power I had before you came into my life and ruined everything."

"Why now?" I swallow my fear, hoping he can't smell it on me like the others can.

"Because now they're not here to protect you." He bends his knees, sinking into a fighting stance. "Because when the others were here with you, I was free to live my life. Now, they hunt me."

*The best way to help an author or to thank them for writing
a book that captivated you is to leave a review.*

If you enjoyed this book or even if you didn't,
please go online and leave a review.

Reviews sell books.

Without them, authors struggle to gain traction.

Acknowledgments

Writing the acknowledgments is one of the hardest parts of writing a book. What if I leave somebody out? If I do, I'm sorry. Don't hate me.

As always, I need to start by thanking Jeff. He puts up with my long nights of writing and editing and makes sure I get fed on the days when I'm so into my book that I might forget. He is my Cody. The only one for me, and I wouldn't know what to do without him.

Then, of course, I need to thank my kids, Jami and Jesse. You are my pride and joy. The best thing I've ever created. I love you to the moon.

A special thank you goes out to my parents, Jim and Vicki, for always believing in me, for giving me wings, and teaching me to fly.

I also need to thank my brothers, Jason and Zach, for helping me come up with "monsters" that can control people.

I would also like to thank all of the wonderful authors that I've met on this journey. M.H. Woodscourt, Alexis D. Johnson, C.T. Ortega, and Ava Cates, you are all outstanding authors and an exceptional cheering squad.

Of course, I also need to thank my fans. There is nothing quite like finding out that you are somebody's favorite author and having them constantly recommend your books. I hope this book lived up to your expectations!

Thank You!

If you liked this story, you can join my mailing list.
Drop by my website MandiOyster.com
or if you have any comments,
shoot me a note at mandi@mandioyster.com.
I am always happy to hear from people who've read my work.
I try to answer every email I receive.

Facebook – https://www.facebook.com/MandiOysterAuthor
Instagram – https://www.instagram.com/mandioyster/
My web page – MandiOyster.com

About the Author

Mandi Oyster lives in Southwest Iowa in the middle of an enchanted forest where unicorns, fairies, and dragons abound. At least, that's what she assumes when she looks out into the trees. Her husband, two kids (when they're not away at college), four cats, and two chinchillas share the house with her. 

Besides being an author, she also runs her own editing business and works full-time as a digital prepress technician for a local printshop.

You can find her online at:
https://www.MandiOyster.com
https://www.facebook.com/MandiOysterAuthor
https://instagram.com/MandiOyster/

will return